HEAVEN'S SHADOW

HEAVEN'S SHADOW

a novel

JEFF DOWNS

Covenant Communications, Inc.

Cover illustration by David McLellan

Cover design copyrighted 2001 by Covenant Communications, Inc.

Published by Covenant Communications, Inc.
American Fork, Utah

Printed in the United States of America
First Printing: September 2001

08 07 06 05 04 03 02 01   10 9 8 7 6 5 4 3 2 1

ISBN 1-57734-881-8

Library of Congress Cataloging-in-Publication Data

Downs, Jeffery Stephen, 1969-
    Heaven's shadow / Jeffery Stephen Downs.
        p. cm.
    ISBN 1-57734-881-8
    I. Life on other planets--Fiction. 2. Revolutionaries--Fiction. 3. Social control--Fiction I. Title.

PS3604.O69 H43 2001
813'.6--dc21   2001037206
                                                      CIP

ACKNOWLEDGMENTS

This is the kind of page most readers ignore. But since an opportunity like this to thank people rarely happens, forgive me if I take but a moment to thank those individuals who helped make this book possible.

Shauna Nelson for her patience and guidance; the staff of Covenant Communications for believing in my story and making all of this possible; Jim Petruzzelli of Idaho Library Bindery who helped show me the possibilities; JoLynn Davis for listening to my rambling in the first place; Glen Muir for making me feel like a million bucks when at times I felt more like a $1.75—in pennies; Gay Rothwell for encouraging me to send in my manuscript and always being there with words of encouragement along the way; Val Sawicki for cheering me on; Dan Ballard and Sheri Riedelbach for reading my drafts and putting up with my silence in the car pool—thanks, "Captain" Ballard for driving when I needed to type; Ronald Lockley, who kept me writing when I simply wanted to hang it up—I guess those stories we used to make up as kids finally paid off after all; Grandma and Grandpa Downs for their example of hard work and independence (and for Grandpa's unforgettable words of encouragement: "You've got Downs blood in you, boy." Your example gives these words their meaning and power); Grandma and Grandpa Nielsen, who've shown me what true love is all about; my parents, Steve and Janice Downs, for teaching me the value of hard work, education, and giving others your best when it's least expected—you're right, the smile makes it all worth it; Bill and Ila Litz for all of their love and support (and for trusting the blond kid from California in the first place); my children, who are the inspiration behind every story I have ever written—without you, I am nothing; and to my wife, Kara, for saying "Yes" all those years ago, and for putting up with me through good times and bad—you truly are my best friend.

For my children

THE GUY IN THE GLASS

When you get what you want in your struggle for pelf,
And the world makes you King for a day,
Then go to the mirror and look at yourself,
And see what that guy has to say.

For it isn't your Father, or Mother or Wife,
Who judgment upon you must pass.
The feller whose verdict counts most in his life
Is the guy staring back from the glass.

He's the feller to please, never mind all the rest,
For he's with you clear up to the end,
And you've passed your most dangerous, difficult test
If the guy in the glass is your friend.

You may be like Jack Horner and "chisel" a plum,
And think you're a wonderful guy,
But the man in the glass says you're only a bum
If you can't look him straight in the eye.

You can fool the whole world down the pathway of years,
And get pats on the back as you pass,
But your final reward will be heartaches and tears
If you've cheated the guy in the glass.

Dale Wimbrow

This was copied from a small, black book of quotes my grandfather kept in his nightstand, and was the inspiration for my story.

"We are blessed with the knowledge that ours is not the only inhabited *earth*. Rather, Christ acting under the direction of the Father is the Creator of *worlds without number* . . . (Moses 1:27-41; D&C 76:22-24; John 1:1-5; Heb. 1:1-4)" (*Mormon Doctrine,* 212, italics in original).

"The Lord declared to Moses that his great work and glory is 'to bring to pass the immortality and eternal life of man.' For this purpose earths have been and are now being built; and *the Lord's purpose is to provide for his children immortality and eternal life, not only on this earth, but on the countless earths throughout the universe.*

They are numberless to man, yet our Father knows them all and they are numbered unto him" (*Doctrines of Salvation,* vol. 1, 72, italics in original).

* * *

Each earth, when the time is right, receives the gospel with all of its marvelous and eternal blessings.

Of this, I have no doubt.

PART ONE

DUTY CALLS

CHAPTER 1

Matthew Tanner winced in pain as his face slammed into his ship's control panel—splitting his lower lip, bloodying his nose, and overloading the primary life support circuits of his small, battered freighter.

He had blasted from the ore moon of Durin only five minutes earlier, moving into position for a return lightjump to Zerith, when the attack had begun.

Now, finding his body weightless, he awkwardly righted himself and frantically searched for his attacker beyond his scuffed and pitted view port.

Nothing.

His gray-green eyes swept his controls: external sensors down, life support . . . far from critical, but dropping quickl. And then, of course, there was the obvious: tiny, spinning spheres of blood from his battered face, gracefully dancing past his eyes, leaving little doubt that his ship's diagnostic was correct—his gravity rods had also been damaged. If he toggled the jump now, without gravity compensation, he would instantly be reduced to a wet and sticky puddle.

A small speaker at his left suddenly crackled to life. "You will power down your ship and prepare to be boarded!" The voice was deep and raspy.

Matthew couldn't believe what was happening. This was supposed to have been a routine run—his first!

He pulled his weightless body back to his console and hit the response switch. Anger, rather than fear, began to surface. "Luk, I on't . . ." He hesitated. The shift to weightlessness was quickly catching up to him; his face felt puffy, as if all of his blood was rushing to his head. And with his lower lip cut and swelling, he was having trouble enunciating his words clearly. Swiping at the blood with the sleeve of his gray flight suit he began again, only slower. "I don't know who you are, but there must be some mis—"

A burst of light blinded him temporarily as his ship shook with the impact of a second plasma bolt, shifting his craft in space, slamming the side of his chair into his chest.

He hugged the chair with all of his strength as he fought for the air that had just been knocked out of him. He hung on, knowing he'd been fortunate to have collided with his padded flight chair and not some of the more solid surfaces of the cockpit.

The speaker came to life once again. "You alive?"

Matthew was still catching his breath as he gasped, "Yes," into the console.

"Good. We could hack into your computer, but we find that an owner's hand that knows what it's doing sorta speeds up the job. Now, cooperate and we'll find a place to keep your hand, and the rest of you, safe. I'll tell you one more time: power down your ship and prepare to be boarded."

Fear was beginning to surface.

Who are these guys? thought Matthew, his mind spinning. *Does Durin security know I'm under attack? Am I too far out? I could send a distress message, but whoever's out there will be waiting for that.*

As if under an uncontrollable spell, Matthew found himself doing exactly what he had been asked to do. Slowly he began shutting down key power circuits, one at a time, while using his other hand to steady his weightless body.

His hand paused in midmotion, however, when it suddenly dawned on him who they might be. *Pirates?*

But that's ridiculous! He had always believed that space pirates, nowadays, were nothing but a myth, a legend—stories, concocted by more experienced haulers to scare off younger pilots in line for contracts. *But if these guys aren't pirates, who are they?*

Collins had been ribbing him about them for a week now; it was his first flight—it was expected, right?

He shook his head in disbelief, trying, at the same time, to recall everything he had heard about them.

Most pirates had started out as lightpath seekers, determined to find jump routes to more than just the ore moon of Durin.

Durin, with its cleaner reacting ore, had been the only fruit of Zerith's first erratic lightjump nearly one hundred years ago. A fluke, really, which Zerith now depended on for nearly ninety percent of its fuel supply. Many of Zerith's larger corporations were determined, however, to find more: more fuel, more livable land, anything that would put them over the top.

Subsequent jumps had only ended in disaster, with hundreds of contracted ships destroying themselves against the numerous obstacles inherent in long-distance jumps at light speed.

As time wore on, corporate bankruptcy increased while public interest decreased. Soon, Zerith's leaders became convinced that they were simply pushing their luck. Durin's ore was exactly what their small planet needed at the time and was expected to last for thousands of years. Consequently, the government, in the interest of public safety, tightened its grip on the space exploration industry, declaring continued exploration illegal, and forcing driven, non-compliant lightpath seekers into hiding—seekers confident that if they happened to come across anything usable, opportunistic officials would then be more than willing to pay the piper.

Given their banishment from Zerith, raiding supply ships running between their homeworld and the distant adopted ore moon had become these renegades' only means of obtaining fuel and life-sustaining supplies. Hence, the *pirate* was born.

Raids had diminished over time, and many suspected that the infamous bands of pirates had been killed exploring, given up their searching, or were simply dying off. The pirates facing Matthew now, however, didn't fit into any of these categories.

These pirates were real, and obviously desperate to be attacking *his* small ship. After all, he wasn't loaded with any food or medical supplies. He was *leaving* Durin. All of those types of supplies had been unloaded and replaced with unrefined, and therefore unusable, ore.

Fuel? That didn't make any sense. What his small ship carried would only be a drop in the bucket for most ships.

They *had* specifically mentioned his computer, though. Perhaps they were looking to discover when a larger supply shipment to Durin was scheduled.

Did they know this was his first run? If they did, it would be easy to write off his disappearance as simply an accident involving a new pilot.

Now you're being paranoid, Tanner!

Feeling they were desperate and experienced at their job, Matthew clearly felt his only option was to await the boarding party and hope for the best.

Matthew flipped down the last power switch in the long row of switches. The pale wash of emergency lighting revealed a youthful, unassumingly attractive face, wounded and marked with frustration.

His *only* option was to wait.

Or was it?

At twenty, Matthew had very few material possessions. And while his freighter, the *Wanderer*, technically wasn't his, it had taken him nearly two years to convince Warring, the station manager, that he had what it took to be a hauler. On his own time he had studied hundreds of pages of flight manuals, put in hundreds of hours of simulator training, and had even agreed to renovate the older freighter, with Patch and Miller, for the opportunity to try. And though his shuttle couldn't carry as much as the others, his willingness to work on the days that the other haulers had off, combined with how little they would actually pay him, meant extra shipments of ore for less money; Spire had little to lose in hiring him.

Besides, the idea of working in space had always seemed thrilling to Matthew. And it was. But it went deeper than this. His new job meant a small increase in his meager salary; it meant he and his grandfather could eat just a little bit better.

He gazed beyond his view port watching a hulking, cobbled-together craft slowly move into his field of vision, cautiously aligning itself to his starboard hatch.

A cold, icy chill began working its way up Matthew's spine. Chances were, once he allowed them access to his ship's stores and computer, they'd kill him. Wasn't that the ending to most of the stories he had heard?

If I let them walk through that hatch, he thought, *sooner or later, I'm a dead man.*

His brow slowly began to furrow as his confidence began to rise. "They won't take me . . . or my ship," he muttered, forcing back the fear. He clenched both fists. "Not without a fight!"

Quickly, Matthew pulled his body through his ship's long, narrow corridor to the gravity rods located in a small engineering room at the rear of the ship. A quick once-over of the room revealed just how powerful the first hit had been. While the inner hull in Engineering was still intact, the slightly bowed plating let Matthew know that he had been lucky. If the blast had breached the inner hull . . . but it hadn't. It was clear they wanted his ship, and by knocking out only the gravity rods, it had insured them a clean capture.

Matthew pulled himself closer to the rods and examined them. *Not damaged, just not getting any juice. Power cable between the outer hull and inner hull must be damaged.* He ran a hand through ample, sweaty blond hair and shook his head at the hopelessness of the situation. *They knew right where to hit me.*

Placing a hand on either side of the open hatchway, Matthew pulled himself out of Engineering, around the corner, to the nearest porthole. The small, circular window, adjacent to the *Wanderer's* starboard hatch, had already started fogging up with the drop in ship's temperature. Matthew quickly wiped away the thin layer of condensation only to find the massive, gray, pitted hull of the pirate ship commanding the entire view. *It won't take long to attach themselves—five, ten minutes.*

Matthew returned to Engineering and gave the gravity rods an accusing stare. And although he knew it was a futile thing to do, he couldn't help spitting out, "Do you have any idea how long it took me to convince Grandpa he had nothing to worry about?"

Desperate, Matthew pulled himself over to the neighboring aft hold; it was considerably smaller than the other two holds and was the only one he hadn't personally loaded on Durin. As the hatch slid open, he instantly recognized the securely stowed crates; they resembled the ones he had loaded in the *Wanderer's* larger port and starboard holds. Each three foot by two foot crate contained nearly one hundred pounds of Durinian ore—valuable for fuel perhaps, but worthless as a weapon. *There has to be some way . . .*

If there was one word to describe Matthew, it would be *pragmatic.* He had never had much of anything while growing up, so he had learned to adapt and modify—getting by with what little he *did* have. A nervous smile came to his sore lips as he suddenly remembered something his grandfather had always told him whenever his wants overshadowed his needs: "Remember, boy, out of desperation comes brilliance."

I hope you're right.

Matthew bounced awkwardly off the walls of the cramped aft hold, desperately reading the tops and sides of as many of the crates as he could. *Maybe someone loaded a crate of something else by mistake. Anything else!*

All he ended up finding, wedged between a crate and the ship's hull, was the leftover spool of power cable Patch had used on a computer upgrade the week before.

Suddenly, the ship began to shudder. A loud *clang* sounded from the *Wanderer's* starboard hatch.

Frantically, he pulled his weightless body back to the porthole.

A docking tube!

Matthew's mind was reeling. He knew it wouldn't take them long to pressurize the tube and use a lock bypass on his hatch's locking circuit. *Do they have one? Surely they wouldn't blast away the ha . . . that's it! A bypass!*

Without wasting another second, he pushed himself away from the porthole and back to the aft hold.

Pulling the spool of cable free, he uncoiled and cut a large length of it, quickly stripping the ends with his pocketknife.

Returning to Engineering, Matthew pulled the clear outer casing off the gravity rods and searched for a hardwire link—desperately striving to hold back the panic that was so close to swallowing him whole.

Finding it, he hurriedly wrapped three of the four bare strands of wire around each one of the ends of wire going into the coil's primary power supply. *They aren't connections Patch would approve of, but they'll do.*

He then pulled himself out of Engineering and bumped and fumbled his weightless body to a deck access panel, five or so feet from the *Wanderer's* starboard hatch.

Fighting the urge to peer out the porthole again, he pulled the hatch's seals and tossed the piece of flooring aside, sending it bouncing and spinning off the walls of his ship.

As Matthew hurriedly surveyed the deck wiring he could hear the distinct sound of a hatch being opened beyond the *Wanderer's* own.

He grabbed a deck cable and quickly traced its probable path from the floor up to the secondary hatch switch on the wall directly across from him, adjacent the aft hold. Because he might need to load and unload freight by himself on Durin, he and Patch had installed the switch so that he could open and close the starboard hatch without having to stop pushing whatever load he was hauling at the time. It had been a frivolous modification, done more out of fun than anything else. "Not this one," he mumbled as he dropped the cable and pulled up another candidate. His second choice was the one he had been looking for—one of several communication cables.

The *Wanderer's* communication console had four backup power cells scattered throughout the ship, ensuring the pilot, ideally, of being able to send and receive messages no matter where the freighter might be damaged. He had always considered the setup a bit redundant, had avoided studying it, and had even looked forward to using the extra power cells in future modifications. He was now very grateful that he hadn't found the time to tamper with them.

Beyond the *Wanderer's* hatch, Matthew could hear approaching footfalls; several pairs of heavy, obviously magnetic boots pounding against the thin metal floor of a docking tube.

He cut the communication cable in half, pulling on one end of it for slack, and stripped the end of the cable. He quickly began twisting one of the three wires to the cable running to the ship's gravity rods. Deep down he knew this was a gamble. After all, he could very well be using the wrong end of the communication cable, connecting the gravity rods to the communication console rather than to a power cell. Was the power cell he was seeking even charged? The number of disabled or non-functioning circuits he and Patch had worked on had been mind numbing. And even if it was wired to a full cell, would it have enough power to even run the rods?

A *click,* then a *whirring* sound came from outside the *Wanderer's* hatch.

The lock bypass! They have one!

He hovered several feet above the deck; the ship's long, narrow corridor leading to the cockpit was to his left. He had just begun twisting the second wire when the *Wanderer's* hatch abruptly unlocked and shot upward.

It was obvious the pirates had expected some resistance, for not a single one in the motley pack had blindly rushed in. Instead, for a brief instant, the pirates simply stood there, their older plasma and projectile rifles ready, staring at what to them must have been a most curious sight.

Matthew only caught a glimpse of the tattered, scruffy-looking lot as he firmly twisted the third and final wire.

"Alright," began the lead pirate, "drop that and move back!"

The pirates eyed Matthew with suspicion as the young man released the spliced cable and began smiling at the sound of a slight, ever increasing hum coming from Engineering.

He'd guessed right!

He looked deep into the lead pirate's dark, vicious eyes, and, with more confidence than he felt, calmly replied, "You didn't say please."

Suddenly Matthew dropped to the deck, landing feet first, and punched the hatch's secondary switch with his fist. The hatch slammed shut—locking bolts sealing the door into place.

It wouldn't take them long to reactivate the lock bypass—he had only seconds.

He sprinted down the ship's narrow corridor, burst into the cockpit, and with the full length of his left arm activated all power circuits at once while slapping the light-speed toggles with his right hand.

Instantly, his flight plan engaged, sending both him, and his precious ship, thundering into the freedom of lightspace.

CHAPTER 2

Setting the steaming spoon to the side of the stove, Paul Tanner took a moment to breathe in the spicy, satisfying aroma of the stew that had been simmering all day. He was pleased; for not only would he and Matthew have a good, hot meal later that evening, but the aroma had helped to stifle, if only for a day, the all-too-familiar stench of urine and rotting waste that seemed to permeate the air beyond the walls of his tin-built shanty.

Funny, I never thought I'd get used to that smell, he thought, as he slowly, cautiously walked back toward his hide-back chair a short distance from the stove.

At seventy-six years of age, Paul was regarded by most as a walking miracle. Without Arcona's medical care, most people never lived beyond the age of fifty. But then Paul was accustomed to fighting insurmountable odds.

Though slightly stooped in stature, Paul's broad shoulders still conveyed a sense of strength and vigor he deeply wished he felt. For now, every step taken on arthritic knees only reminded him of his age and limitations.

He rubbed his thin, vein-covered hand over his stubbled chin as the shooting pain subsided into a dull, throbbing ache, and wondered if an approaching storm was the cause of the stiffening he was feeling in his joints. He would have given anything to have been able to check the sky for himself, for the pungent odor beyond his doorway's heavy evening curtain stifled everything. Especially the fragile, refreshing smell of moisture prior to a rainstorm.

How long's it been since I've been able to smell the coming of a storm? Eighteen? . . . No, twenty years.

It had to be a storm; it had been quite cool and breezy outside all day—sections of the shanty's tin siding rattling softy against its skeletal wooden frame. Earlier he had considered going outside and asking one of his neighbors how the sky was shaping up, but decided against it. He simply didn't feel ready to face the outside world. Not yet anyway.

Blast! My sight. Of all things to take from a man! Despite an occasional complaint, however, the once-powerful leader of a failed revolution was striving to accept his latest challenge in life. And although it had only been a month, he was already becoming quite adept at fending for himself. He knew that with a little more time he'd have the courage to venture a short distance from his shanty.

From short distances spring long journeys, he reminded himself with a wry smile.

Actually, what he longed most for was the chance to visit with his neighbors. For years, before his blindness had set in, Paul often walked slowly, with his trademark cane, throughout the narrow streets of the impoverished suburb looking for ways to tend to those in need. And while the extra food and clothing he brought were greatly appreciated, often those he visited were simply satisfied with having the chance to talk with another decent, caring human being—someone who tried to leave their meager home a little better than he had found it. Frequently, his conversation would lean toward looking at the brighter side of a situation.

Paul chuckled at his own feelings of frustration. For often, in his visits, he would draw a circle on a neighbor's dirt floor, after having listened patiently to a complaint, and would point out that the circle represented their frustration. He would trace the circle repeatedly with his cane, telling them that often people try to overcome frustrations by using the same failed remedies over and over. "The longer they keep doing this, the longer their frustration remains." After several tracings with his cane he would then add, "If they are still frustrated, it means that they should seek out a new solution; a solution that may come from within themselves or through the aid of others." He would then drag his cane from the circle in a straight line. "Only then can they move on."

Even if a neighbor had already been taught Paul's Principle, they never stopped him from repeating it. Rather, they appreciated the refresher lesson provided by such a legendary man. He didn't *have* to visit them, and they knew it.

I must listen to myself more often, he thought, as he sank into his comfortable chair. *Tomorrow I will take a walk. That will definitely be something I haven't tried. It's been too long already. Who knows, it might even help these tired old knees of mine.*

Images of the sick and afflicted flashed through his mind.

Or at least help me to forget them.

He grabbed his worn footstool from beside the chair, put it in place, leaned back, and put his feet up. Paul closed his eyes and let the verbal collage, coming from the thousands of surrounding shanties, wash over him. The loudest noise, he thought, was coming from the crying Leeland baby, two doors down. Paul made a mental note to have Matthew check on them in the morning. He didn't want the baby going without milk.

As minutes passed, and the baby's crying continued, Paul's eyes began to water. *Poor thing. He shouldn't have to live like this.*

The crying continued.

Nobody should.

Crying.

Paul brought a hand to his strong, yet haggard face, closed his sightless eyes and pinched the bridge of his nose. *What has become of us?*

The second of four planets from the sun, Zerith was the only one capable of sustaining life. Given the fact that its orbital period equaled its rotational period, half the small planet was in constant sunlight while the other half remained a dark and frigid wasteland— frozen water its only usable resource.

Small lakes and streams dappled the light side, sustained by a large ice cap found at Zerith's north pole. Below the cap lay a wide band of forested terrain, teeming with wildlife and beauty. Because of the tilt in Zerith's axis, the northern forests were slightly cooler, and they enjoyed quite a bit of rainfall. Beyond the forest, however, lay nothing but arid wasteland—hot, dry, and uninviting—enjoying only occasionally the cool and refreshing effects of a drifting storm.

For centuries, Zerith's citizens had lived and progressed within the northern, forested region, thriving on its abundant natural resources.

As cities expanded and Zerith's technological revolution exploded, however, greed and the thirst for power expanded within the hearts of Zerith's corporate giants. Little by little, without public knowledge, the planet's government fell under the influence and eventual control of its more powerful industries.

Greed is seldom satisfied, and it wasn't long before they began setting their sights on each other.

Ultimately, it was the Spire Corporation, with the accidental discovery of Durin and its seemingly endless supply of ore, that claimed victory. In the two short years following Durin's settlement, Spire, through clandestine mergers, had stealthily absorbed all of its competition, including the government; and the public was none the wiser.

With Zerith's government under its thumb, and all competition out of the way, Spire immediately turned its attention toward the only remaining resource it had little direct control over—the people.

Based upon fabricated data supposedly compiled by the world's finest scientists and researchers, Zerith's citizens were told that it would not be long before the small planet's basic, natural resources either became unusable or unobtainable. Consequently, in the name of environmental protection, not to mention the preservation of life itself, a new capital city—Arcona—was established within the arid wasteland of the desert. In time it had progressed into a thriving metropolis, while the cities left behind in the forested region were leveled and replaced with Spire's refineries—refineries that nobly managed the collection, care, and distribution of Arcona's much-needed resources; refineries conveniently fueled by Durinian ore.

With their housing provided, jobs secured, and their basic needs amply provided for, the majority of Zerith's citizens had gradually been lulled into believing that their lives couldn't possibly be any better. After all, the uncertainty of their previous, forest past had been supplanted with a more secure and predictable lifestyle—undeniably secure, but unbeknown to them, entirely controlled.

Few were conscious of what their security and peace of mind had truly cost them. Personal freedoms, such as the right to own land, bear arms, raise crops and livestock, pursue an education, and excel in a chosen career, were gradually handed over for a seductive lifestyle that required less effort and little thought.

Those citizens who outwardly opposed the changes fell quickly and mysteriously silent on the matter, while those demonstrating above-average intelligence found themselves whisked away to top research and development centers where they could help in the future growth and development of Arcona. They were often never heard from again. "They are on assignment, dedicating their lives, unwaveringly, for the betterment of the world," was all that their families, and the public, were really ever told. It was an answer that seemed to satisfy many.

But not all, thought Paul.

Anxiously he began tapping his feet together. *Where is that boy?* he wondered. *He's got a lot of explaining to do. Rollyn assured me Matthew was right behind him.*

Matthew was a good boy, he knew, but he was also impetuous, flighty, and, in his opinion, too reckless. *Reminds me of myself at his age,* he thought humorously, stroking his chin once again.

A deep and heavy sigh followed.

He wasn't being fair. Matthew *was* a good boy. After all, how many other boys his age would sacrifice so freely what they worked so hard to gain?

The small income Matthew earned for his work at the Arcona Spaceport had never had a chance to accumulate; Paul could never resist coming to the aid of a crying widow or infant. He still felt an obligation toward the families of those he had once led. "We have each other, Matthew," he often reminded his grandson. "That makes us two of the wealthiest men on the planet. Our spoil we can share. Besides," he would often add with a grin, "when we die it'll be too little to take with us anyway."

Matthew never really put up much of a fuss about that. Of course, now that he's a hauler, he'll be paid a little more . . .

He drummed his fingers on the arm of his chair.

He seemed to really enjoy attending Arcona's Harvest Festival last year. He smiled. *He wanted so much to see the stage plays.* He closed his eyes, remembering the sparkle in the boy's eyes as he excitedly recounted everything he had seen . . .

He'll want his own ship. Is it even possible? With luxury tax as high as it is, it would take a miracle, even for an Arconian. Would Spire even allow it?

His fingers stopped their rhythmic drumming as his thoughts

switched to yet another concern. *The boy is getting older—vulnerable to more of Arcona's enticements. What if he . . . No. He'll be strong. I know he will.*

Just then, Paul heard the unmistakable sound of the wind chime as the front door's heavy curtain brushed against it. Matthew had placed it there before he had left nearly two days ago so that his grandfather would know whenever he had company. He had promised Paul that his first pay voucher would go toward the purchase of a solid door that could be knocked on—luxury tax, or no luxury tax. For now, though, the chime was warning enough; Matthew was home.

"Hey, Papa!" came Matthew's confident, cheerful voice, interrupting his grandfather's thoughts. "Sorry I'm late." Matthew hung his used and tattered flight jacket on a bent nail at the side of the doorway. "Whatever you're cooking sure smells good! Hope it's hot. It looks like we're actually going to get some rain tonight."

Matthew covered the space from the doorway to the stove in only four paces and looked down into the steaming pot, taking a huge whiff. "Hey! Meat! How'd you manage that, Papa?" Matthew flashed him a smile, knowing full well that it was probably another gift.

When his grandfather's blindness had prevented him from making his daily visits, both of them had been astonished at the unexpected outpouring of gifts, usually groceries, that they would occasionally find in their doorway; Paul's lifetime of giving had come full circle. His gifts of charity were now being repaid, with interest.

"You didn't go after the Jansen's dog did you? I know he's a barker, but . . ." Matthew's grin quickly faded when he noticed his grandfather's expression. It was stern and serious—his strong, square jaw locked; sightless, gray-green eyes, similar to his own, staring straight ahead . . . at nothing.

"What is it, Papa?"

Concerned, Matthew walked over and stood directly in front of him. "Are you feeling alright? Honestly, Papa, I hurried home as fast as I could." Which was the truth. That is, just as soon as he'd finished with the station's doctor. Four stitches lined the edge of his bottom lip.

Having lived nearly his entire life with his grandfather, Matthew knew that silence, coupled with this expression, often meant one of two things: he was either angry with him, or a bit depressed over a seemingly hopeless situation he could change with neither mind nor might.

Though their window curtain had been pulled with the evening hour, Zerith's ever present sunlight still managed to find its way past the curled and tattered edges of leather. The small square of a window sat directly behind his grandfather's head, the long slivers of light making portions of the older man's disheveled, white hair appear bright and yellowy.

He's found out something, he thought. *The pirates? Or . . .*

"Lean closer, boy," began his grandfather, softly, his tone of voice revealing nothing. "Lean closer so I can feel your face."

Will he notice the swelling? So far he hadn't noticed a difference in his speech.

Reluctantly, Matthew moved forward and knelt down, helping each of the older man's hands to either side of his face—something the older man insisted on doing lately to make sure Matthew was really listening to him.

"That's it, son."

Slap!

"Hey!" cried Matthew. But before he could pull away the older man pulled him in for one of his bone-crushing hugs.

Confused, Matthew simply held on, waiting for an explanation, running his tongue lightly over his stitches, making certain they hadn't burst.

"Don't you ever do something like that to me again, young man!"

"I take it Rollyn's been by," drawled Matthew into his grandfather's shoulder.

"You're darn right he's been by! If it wasn't for that pesky kid I'd never know *what* you were *really* up to."

He released him. "Told me all about seeing your ship come in this afternoon. Said the back of it looked like it had been punched by some giant beast."

"Papa—"

"He also said *pirates* were to blame. Said they'd stopped you, but you broke away from them. This true, Matthew?"

The young man straightened, touching his lip with a finger, checking for blood—there wasn't any. "Is that *all* he told you?"

"Yes. Why? Is there *more* I should know? What's happened?"

Well, at least Rollyn didn't tell him everything, thought Matthew. *If Grandpa knew just how bad my face looked, not to mention how close he'd really come to losing me . . . Have to give the kid credit there.*

Matthew pulled his own hide-back chair from the wall and placed it in front of his grandfather. "You really oughta stop paying that little spy of yours. The kid isn't even fifteen yet and he's pulling off better surveillance than Special Forces. Look—"

Matthew watched as his grandfather pulled himself to the edge of his chair and put out his hand, reaching for Matthew's face. Finding it, he sternly responded, "No, you listen to me! When they offered you that job, you said they'd be giving you the simple runs."

It pained Matthew to see his grandfather so upset. He made a mental note to have a talk with Rollyn and up his hush money. He didn't mind the younger boy hanging around him, but his grandfather had enough to deal with without having to worry about every run he'd make.

"They're *all* simple runs, Papa. I'm still unloading freight. I'm just taking a bit of a ride before I do it now is all. Simple!"

"Simple doesn't involve pirates, Matthew! What's all that about?" Paul ran a hand through his white head of hair. "I want you to tell them you're through."

"Through?"

"You heard me."

"I can't do that! They're giving me nearly a hundred more dockins a month for this." Paul had raised a hand to interrupt, but Matthew pushed on. "If I hold on for a year they could double that. Double it, Papa! That's more than I'd make on the maintenance line, triple what I'd make in standard freight—"

"If you live long enough!" interrupted Paul.

Matthew ignored him. "I can't throw this opportunity away. It may be the only one I get. And as far as the pirates are concerned, the way I see it, it was a fluke! Most of the pirates out there are probably dead and gone. And I doubt those that attacked me are in good enough shape to try it again anytime soon."

"What's that supposed to mean?" demanded Paul, exasperated.

Matthew knew that if he revealed everything, he'd probably never fly again. He gave Paul's hand a gentle squeeze. "I came home, Papa," he answered calmly. "I handled the problem, and came home."

After nearly a minute of silence, Paul's chin fell to his chest.

Matthew could tell that he was getting through. His grandfather might be stern and stubborn at times, but if you presented your case well enough, and if what you had to say demonstrated thought, he was always willing to meet you halfway.

Matthew, however, was taking little pleasure, this time, with how well his side of the debate was going. He was simply relieved that his grandfather hadn't discovered *everything*.

"Matthew?"

He looked up. "Papa, I'm sorry. I know you worry, but . . . "

Paul waved his hands in the air as if motioning for him to keep silent. "Look, boy. I'm the one who should apologize. You're right. You're becoming a man now; you shouldn't depend on me for everything you need. And . . . as far as this job goes . . . it is an opportunity that may never come around again. It's just . . . I love you so much. It would kill me if anything ever happened to you."

Matthew leaned forward, giving Paul a hug. A hug that Paul freely returned, only more gently this time.

"I promised your parents I'd raise you to adulthood," said Paul, his voice sounding tight. "And it's a promise I intend on keeping."

"I know, Papa. I know."

They held one another for several seconds before Paul leaned back, folded his arms, and scowled. "I do wish I could work, Matthew. You do so much. Too much for someone so young."

It was a comment Matthew was used to hearing.

He couldn't think of a more debilitating punishment that the government could have issued his grandfather, along with all of the other participants of the Rebellion. Descendants of the rebellious were free to acquire jobs in the walled city, but the Rebellion's primary participants had been banished from Arcona—complete outcasts, entitled to nothing.

A moment of silence followed. Paul was obviously struggling with old and new emotions. Emotions, Matthew knew, brought on by *his* actions. And the sight of his troubled grandfather triggered something in him completely unexpected: he suddenly realized he needed to come clean. Not so much concerning the pirates; Matthew was sure that his grandfather knew the gist of what had really happened, and was pretty sure that it was now in the past. What he needed to share with his grandfather concerned the future. *If anything happens to me,* he thought, *he needs to be prepared. I owe it to him. But I have to do it right.*

He reached for his grandfather's face, holding it in his hands, then took a deep breath knowing that he would have to reveal this carefully, clearly. "Papa, I think it's time I told you something." He took another deep breath. "I would never purposefully set out to hurt you, so I think you should be prepared—especially after what happened today."

Clearly startled with this turn in the conversation, Paul straightened in his chair and appeared to be concentrating on the feel of Matthew's hands. "What is it, boy?" he replied softly, concerned.

Matthew looked awkwardly into his grandfather's eyes, wishing they would focus on his face rather than the space beyond his shoulder. "Do you remember all of the stories you used to tell me about the revolution, the Rebellion?"

Paul seemed confused. "What has that got to do with—"

"Papa, please."

"Alright, alright," Paul sighed. "Go on."

"You led a revolt against a corrupt government. 'They had overstepped their bounds,' you used to say. They weren't governing, they were slowly taking control of our lives."

"Corporations, Matthew," interrupted Paul. "The corporations. Our original government was well-founded, meaningful before—"

"Agreed, Papa." Matthew didn't mean to cut him off, but his courage was quickly waning and he wanted to finally be free of the burden he had been carrying for months now. "And money, greed, and power were the driving force behind this change. Right?"

"Of course, Matthew." He patted Matthew's shoulder. "I'm glad to see you've been listening to my babble over the years, boy, but what has that got to do with—"

"In fact, I remember you telling me once that, 'they had chucked truth and justice out the window, leaving only cold emptiness behind.'"

Paul gave a wry smile and folded his arms. "I call it the way I see it, Matthew. You know that."

Matthew's voice softened as he edged closer to the truth. "Years ago, I remember you telling me about the trials—when they quietly eliminated those who opposed them. Including . . . Mom and Dad."

"Yes," was Paul's only reply. His voice was but a whisper and his face clearly began to show anguish at having to discuss such a painful memory.

Despite this, however, Matthew pressed on, speaking just as Paul was about to interrupt. "They were framed for the murder of that official—"

"Framed is right!" interjected Paul. He pointed a rigid finger in Matthew's direction. "And don't let anyone tell you different, son. That *official* just happened to be expendable."

"They were executed."

It had been stated bluntly, and Paul's eyes began to tear under the barrage of memories. He turned his head away from Matthew, breaking free of his hands, and closed his eyes; the images of a more tragic time were obviously very painful, and Matthew knew why.

Spire knew that to permanently silence Paul Tanner, the outspoken and charismatic backbone of the Rebellion, might only validate his cause. Instead of eliminating the source of the problem, they had decided to whittle away at his support structure—one friend and follower at a time. Subsequent accidents and prosecutions had been brilliantly pulled off, with the general public oblivious to any wrongdoing; the media under Spire's control as well.

"Spire controlled everything, Matthew. Still does." Paul brought his hands together in his lap and began massaging his arthritic joints. "My father used to share stories about what it was like growing up in the forest. I've told you," Paul said, his quick smile filling Matthew with some relief. Matthew wanted to talk, not hurt.

"You have."

"He had *always* been suspicious of Arcona. He and others had heard rumors of secret, lavish settlements being constructed in the forest—catering to spoiled big shots. The rumors seemed too farfetched to most. Of course, with Special Forces guarding the borders, *protecting* them, it was impossible to find out if they were true or not."

"But your father wasn't the only one who believed the rumors," said Matthew.

"No, of course not. There were many who wondered; they just didn't wonder out loud. But our fathers and mothers quietly passed their suspicions on to their children and, oddly enough, it was *our* generation that decided to uncover the truth about Arcona—its real purpose."

"Odd?"

"It's odd because we knew no other way of life; the desert was our reality—the forest a dreamlike fantasy. But when we began openly questioning the system itself, people started disappearing, or suddenly changing their minds. We were viewed as extremists by the media."

Paul's hands were still, his voice less animated. "It was shortly after your grandmother's death that things really went out of control." Paul shook his head slowly. "I'm so grateful she didn't have to live through that." Paul sat silent, staring.

Matthew touched his grandfather's knee. "Go on, Papa."

"You know the rest!" Paul spit out.

"I know, but . . . I want to hear it again."

Paul closed his eyes and took a deep breath. He released it slowly. "Many of us felt that we, as a people, had lost control. We were being herded like cattle with no say in where we were headed; our lives and futures were secretly being used to advance a few select families."

"You took action. You fought for freedom."

Paul's eyes opened and his expression was firm, as if he hadn't heard Matthew's comment. "Our assemblies grew, and when it looked like our lives were in danger, we secretly purchased rifles and weapons for protection. When our people started disappearing, we decided that the only way to get the truth out, unfiltered, was to take control of the media, if only for a few hours. We were convinced others felt the same way we did. If they could see that they *could* stand up for what they believed in, that the rumors *were* true . . . But just before the takeover . . ."

"Mom and Dad?"

Paul closed his eyes once more and shook his head, as if trying, Matthew guessed, to throw off the memory. "After what happened to them," he whispered, "I really began to question what we *could* do. The frame-up was too tight, too perfect. Others began to panic. Members of our own organization began selling each other out for protection. The corporations were too powerful, Matthew. And by successfully attacking my family, they'd proved it."

After a few minutes of weighted silence, Paul startled Matthew with an unexpected laugh. He pointed a thin finger in the air. "You've been steering me off the subject, haven't you? You're using my senility against me."

"You're not senile, Papa."

"Well I must be, letting you take that hauling job."

"*That's* settled," Matthew stated firmly.

Paul raised his hands to speak, but then let them drop, limply, into his lap. "I know, I know."

"Papa, I'm asking you these questions for a reason, believe me. I have only one more request."

"What's that?"

"Tell me again why the shanties were built."

"Why go into all of that, Matthew? Haven't we reviewed enough history for one evening? It's getting late. Surely you're hungry."

As Paul began to stand, Matthew gently grasped his shoulder. "Please, Papa? It's important."

Matthew noted the puzzled expression on his grandfather's face and knew he was curious as to where he'd been headed with all of this. Sitting back, Paul patiently cleared his throat. "As I said before, the death of your parents really rattled us. The setup had been too clean and in full view. Many felt that if such an attack was possible on *my* family . . . well, you get the idea.

"When members of our own movement began selling each other out, we simply fell apart. We surrendered and were banished from Arcona—'Outsiders' they started calling us. They said we were a threat to peace and public safety.

"Not wanting to appear completely heartless, they offered us work in exchange for food, clothing, and the scrap to build shelters. Our first and last assignment was the wall."

Though only five years of age at the time, Matthew could vaguely recall images of playing with other kids as tired, ragged adults, including his grandfather, toiled daily on the massive wall that separated their shanty suburb from the enormous city of Arcona.

"People were told that the wall would surround all of Arcona, that it would protect the city from predators, shifting sand, and . . . 'peace-destroying Outsiders.' But only one stretch of the wall was ever finished; the government, Spire, had succeeded in separating us from Arcona. As time went by, the original intent of the wall was *conveniently* forgotten. Of course, with a wall between us and Arcona, the question of how we'd continue to survive was also forgotten. Out of sight, out of mind, I guess.

"At first we accepted our exile as a good thing; if we lived together as a community, our ideals could be passed down to our children. When the wall project was abandoned, though, we soon discovered just how complete our banishment would be.

"Every line of trade had been cut. We were allowed to raise small gardens, but livestock—even wild stock—was forbidden. Special Forces raided us often to keep us in line." Paul ran a finger along the arm of his chair. "Without any supplies, we gave ourselves only a few months."

"But somehow you survived," added Matthew, quietly. "Sharing talents and helping one another has kept us alive."

"The human spirit is powerful, Matthew . . . when it wants to be." Paul pointed toward Arcona. "Deep down, that's what they fear most: the freedom of the human spirit. Our world could become even grander if we were simply free to explore, grow, and develop—on our timetable, not theirs!" He touched his chest, "I feel it in my heart, Matthew. It's true."

He cleared his throat, his voice filling with passion. "Instead, they want you to commit yourself to them. If you do, you are promised that your needs will be taken care of; just do as they ask. We ought to be free to forge a life of our own.

"Now, people have forgotten what it's like to really push themselves. And, through the years, I believe Spire's discovered just how debilitating this can be in a society. All are required to work, but very few have the inner desire to *want* to work. So few jobs offer any real advancement. And believe you me, if they do, you can bet someway, somehow, it's just as controlled as anything else.

"The quality of work is also dying. I can't blame the workers. Why should they go overboard on a project if there's nothing in it for them? There's no dream to work toward; nothing to look forward to. And Spire has to rule carefully, make no mistake about it, or some of what we've been saying over the years just might start making sense."

"Quality work," interrupted Matthew. "That's where we got our break."

"That's right. You children were offered dockins for some of the tougher jobs. You *knew* how to work! All of us knew it would be hard on you, but, ironically, it was teaching you the true value of work— what we had wanted for you in the first place. You worked hard and, little by little, it's paid off." Paul sat up straight and appeared proud. "Our needs are being met. We are alive. We may not *have* everything, but we don't *need* everything, either. And what we do have, we've truly earned on our own."

Paul's shoulders fell slightly. "Truth is, if it hadn't been for you kids, we probably would've died off years ago."

Paul reached out and found Matthew's leg, giving it a squeeze. "It pained me when you took your first job at the spaceport, Matthew."

Matthew remembered very well the first day a transport had taken him to Arcona. He was ten years old at the time. It was the first time in five years he had been beyond the wall, and he remembered being awed at all he had seen that first day.

His grandfather, as well as many of the other parents, had been concerned that Spire was simply trying to lure the children away from their belief system, showing them all that could be theirs if they'd simply leave their families. And over the years, some, it appeared, had taken the bait. Many, though, had not—their small, meager homes, continued to be their base and anchor.

"Patch and Miller have taken good care of me, Papa."

"I know they have, son. I'm grateful for that. I truly am. You've helped prevent many people from starving to death, Matthew. All of you kids have. Feel fortunate you have the strength. We've fared better than most over the years."

Matthew looked fondly into his grandfather's eyes and then to his threadbare, mismatched clothing. *How often did you go hungry while I went to bed full?*

"I often wonder if the youth of today even remember or care why we still live the way we do? It seems like so many have left us."

Matthew reached out to Paul's face, startling him. "And many have stayed. Maybe not physically, but mentally. They want what you once fought for: freedom to grow, excel, develop as individuals."

Paul seemed perplexed. "Just what is it you're getting at, boy?"

Matthew took a deep breath. It was now or never. "Papa," he whispered, suddenly very much aware of the thin walls that surrounded them. "Many of us have not forgotten what you were fighting for. We've listened and . . . are ready."

Paul started, brushing away Matthew's hands. "What?"

"Shhh! Whisper, Papa."

"What are you—"

"Hear me out. For years now, several I'd guess, a new plan has been playing itself out that will break Spire's grip, and restore a true government."

"No! Stop! What are you saying, Matthew?"

"Papa, please keep your voice down!"

Paul gripped Matthew's leg, his voice hushed but stern. "What are you telling me, Matthew?"

Matthew looked directly into Paul's darting, shock-filled eyes. "A new revolution is in the works, Papa. And . . . I volunteered to be a part of it."

CHAPTER 3

It was the fifth and final pickup, and the six-wheeled, lumbering transport stopped with all the grace of an earthquake. Matthew's head bumped against the shoulder of another passenger, arousing both from their naps.

In the past he had often read or talked with Rollyn on his way to work. But when Rollyn had given up his seat for Nadie, a quiet young girl, three stops back, his lack of sleep from the previous night had finally caught up with him.

He watched with disinterested eyes as the last group of employees pushed, shuffled, and mashed themselves into the overcrowded transport. The benches that ran along either side had filled during the first two stops, and now all that Matthew could see in front of him was a forest of torsos, packed tightly into what little space existed between the benches. Many gripped the leather straps bolted to the ceiling in an effort to remain steady during the long and jarring ride.

He felt a pang of guilt as he suddenly noticed Laurie, another young girl nearly his age, standing toward the back of the transport, barely able to reach the worn leather strap above her head. It was too late to offer her his seat now. Not only were those standing pinned against one another, but the feet and legs of those standing around him were pinning him to his spot as well. He made a mental note to look out for her on the return trip that evening.

Matthew, over the years, had grown accustomed to this daily, unnecessarily long, commute and had naturally learned how to tune out the heat, sweat, and body odor of those surrounding him. It was a regular part of his life, and he had learned to accept it.

As the transport slowly continued its crawl toward the entrance of Arcona, Matthew tried to place his elbows on his knees and his head in his hands. Bumping into the thigh of another passenger prevented him from completing the task, however, and so he sat up and forced himself to remain awake.

As usual, Matthew had dropped by Rollyn's shanty that morning to walk with him to the terminal. And, as usual, Rollyn's father grumbled a hello and hollered for Rollyn to hurry, cuffing the back of the boy's head soundly for "lollygagging" before retreating indoors. Nearly twelve years younger than his grandfather, Rollyn's father seemed almost older to Matthew; his eyes appeared more hollow, his appearance more unkempt. He was a bitter man who found little happiness in his situation and often took it out on those nearest him—Rollyn especially.

Normally the two young men shared little in the way of conversation, saving their small talk for the two hour stop-and-go-trip to the spaceport. But upon first seeing Matthew, Rollyn, rubbing the back of his head, couldn't resist blurting out, "You look like garbage!"

Matthew had simply stopped and stared at him. "Do you always greet people like that in the morning, Rolly? No wonder you don't have a lot of friends."

"Sorry, Matt. It's just . . . you look terrible. Didn't you get any sleep?"

Matthew had frowned, walked on, and told Rollyn to get a move on or they'd be late. The only way to get beyond Arcona's wall, legally, was by transport. He had missed it only twice in his life, and he didn't want to risk a third time—considering his new promotion.

Rollyn had run to catch up to him, his feet splashing into a few lingering puddles—remnants of last night's storm. "Hey, I'm sorry. What's eating you anyway? Did your roof leak last night?"

"I don't want to talk about it."

"Come on, Matt. It might make you feel better."

Matthew had stopped and grabbed the boy by the shoulder, turning him so that he could look him in the face. The shorter, towheaded boy's eyes grew wide at the expression on Matthew's face. "What is it?"

"Why'd you have to tell Grandpa about the ship? You had him worried sick!"

Rollyn had smiled. "He pays me more than you do."

Matthew had simply stared at him, trying to digest what seemed to him a ridiculous answer.

"Look, Matt. Come on. He was going to find out one way or another."

"But you didn't have to serve it up on a silver platter!"

Rollyn's head dropped and he kicked at the dirt. "I know, Matt. I'm sorry. Really I am. I saw the dockins and I lost my head. I didn't tell him absolutely *everything*, though." He looked up. "I'm sorry."

His last two words were said with not only words, but two big brown eyes as well. Matthew knew the boy and his father needed the money. Rollyn, an only child, was younger, and therefore ineligible for Arcona's higher-paying jobs; secretly Matthew wondered if this fact only fueled his father's irritability—if it was the reason he seemed to regard Matthew, nearly every morning, with obvious contempt. At that moment he decided that he really couldn't blame the boy for falling for the bribe. And besides, he was right; word *would* have gotten to his grandfather sooner or later. And, looking back on last night's conversation, *it* coming out later would only have made things worse.

He mussed Rollyn's short-cropped hair and let go of his anger. "Runt."

Both had sprinted to the terminal as the transport lumbered into view.

Once seated, Matthew confessed, "To be honest with you, it wasn't *your* fault he got so upset, I guess. It was mine." He hesitated a moment. "I told him about my commitment to . . . you know."

Rollyn's head turned so quickly, Matthew was surprised it didn't snap right off. "You told him?" he whispered.

"I did."

Rollyn let out a whistle.

"I had to. You should've seen his face when I showed up late. He was worried sick! And . . . well, if something, you know, happens to me, I want him to be, I don't know, prepared."

Rollyn seemed to be turning that thought over in his mind. "I guess I can understand that. How'd he take it?"

"Not well."

"Is he going to make you quit?"

"I don't know."

Matthew knew, deep down, that Paul would never force him *not* to be a part of the new Rebellion. But it was now obvious he wasn't about to embrace the idea with open arms, either.

He'd had his grandfather recount their past history in the hopes that it would help to refresh his mind to the feelings and emotions he had once felt so strongly when *he* was younger. Afterward, Matthew had gone on to outline the structure of the Rebellion, as he understood it, pointing out how different its organization and operation was to the uprising his grandfather had commanded so many years before: pockets of Rebels, Arconians and Outsiders, living and working in various sections of Arcona, involved in a variety of career fields, receiving oral direction from regional directors who in turn received their direction from the Rebellion's primary leaders. He had never shared this specific information with anyone, not even Rollyn, and had sincerely hoped that his grandfather would be impressed with how structured and organized the new Rebellion was.

He'd further gone on to explain how he had been approached by their regional director at last year's Harvest Festival, how he had explained to Matthew that liquid funding sources for the resistance had been, in the past, easy to obtain, but now key *collectors* were becoming nervous and insisting a two or three year break was needed to ward off any suspicion that might be directed their way. Feeling that too much time had already elapsed, resistance leaders had developed a new plan for obtaining crucial funding—something the first Rebellion had failed to appreciate the importance of. The messenger then told Matthew there was only one key element missing, keeping them from beginning the second phase of funding. *He* had been chosen to obtain that final element.

Paul, in silent shock, had listened as Matthew explained that he, personally, had no idea what that "piece" was, but felt that this was *his* opportunity to help in the struggle for freedom. In an attempt to further pacify Paul's concerns, he had concluded by telling him how confident the director had been that Matthew wouldn't have any trouble obtaining it. After all, Spire wouldn't expect the Rebels to be foolish enough to involve anyone related to the primary leaders of the first Rebellion, especially after all Spire had given them over the years.

After patiently listening to what Matthew had to say, Paul had become openly frustrated with his grandson's inability to answer any of the more specific questions he threw at him. He was, instead, assured by Matthew that that very ambiguity was in fact the backbone of the new Rebellion: You knew only what you needed to know. Therefore, if one link was broken, it wouldn't necessarily lead to the entire chain falling apart.

When Paul had asked Matthew when his mission would begin, he'd felt a little ridiculous, considering this meeting had taken place nearly a year ago, telling him that he really wasn't sure. All he had been told was that he would be contacted when it was time.

"And you told him everything?" Rollyn was obviously still in shock, and perhaps a little jealous. Neither boy dared say anything specific about Matthew's involvement in the Rebellion on the transport; both fostered paranoid visions of spies scurrying about, listening to everything everybody said. Matthew knew both of them were behaving a bit on the extreme side, but they had agreed, long ago, to always play it safe.

"I had to tell him, Rolly." He rubbed his temples, trying to will his headache away. "Don't ask me to explain why I did. I just felt it was the right thing to do."

Matthew couldn't help smiling inside at the reaction on Rollyn's face; overreacting was his specialty. One afternoon, six months earlier, he had told Rollyn about his decision to join, after Rollyn had shared with Matthew his own concerns about the future of their shanty town and their world as a whole.

Many of Rollyn's thoughts and fears had fallen right in line with what the Rebellion stood for. However, since his father continued to harbor ill feelings toward Matthew's grandfather and the first Rebellion, feeling they were both directly responsible for their present-day hardships—specifically the illness and eventual death of his wife—Rollyn had decided it would be best, for now, to offer the Rebels only moral support—joining when he was older.

And he *had* been a great help. Countless times the two young men had discussed with one another their hopes, fears, and dreams. Sure, Matthew had several friends his own age, but with Rollyn it was different; they both depended on one another, they needed one another. Rollyn needed Matthew for the kindness and companionship the boy lacked at home; Matthew needed Rollyn for his willingness to listen and understand. On final analysis, Rollyn simply made the carrying of such a secret more bearable; he was the little brother Matthew had never had.

The sudden jolt from the front of the transport, followed by another in the middle, and then the rear, let Matthew know that they were now on paved road, ten feet from Arcona's entrance.

The transition from barren wasteland to thriving metropolis was dramatic, and he wondered whether he'd ever live long enough to see the day when the wall would be torn down. Not just the physical wall dividing the two societies, but the social wall that kept the human spirit restrained and submissive.

Closing his eyes, he remembered how his grandfather had thrown up his hands in defeat at the end of their discussion, clearly frustrated with the realization that he wasn't even close to changing his grandson's mind.

Frustrated as well, Matthew had crawled into his bunk and pulled his sheet over his head, refusing to eat the stew that Paul had worked so hard on all day.

Matthew winced as he recalled his stupid remark about Paul not really understanding. And he now found a lump developing in his throat as his grandfather's whispered, final words that had haunted him throughout the night echoed once more: "That's where you're wrong, boy. I do understand. Believe me, I do."

CHAPTER 4

"You're sure that's going to hold?" asked Miller. He was a short, husky man, with a gruff-sounding voice that unintentionally camouflaged his boisterous and otherwise friendly personality.

Patch, lean and whimsical in appearance, ran a greasy hand through his shaggy, light-brown hair and, with a look of hurt on his face, declared, "Have I ever, *ever*, in all the years we've worked together, *ever* attached a piece of equipment that has accidentally come off?" He had tried delivering his question with grave seriousness, but his perennial smile, as always, betrayed him.

Miller thought for a moment. "Well, how about on the Poulson project. I *seem* to remember the—"

"Besides that."

"Okay." Miller ran a thick hand over his dark-stubbled chin. "How about the job we did on the Neeley shuttle. Wasn't there—"

"Oh, sure!" began Patch, securing the access panel and nimbly climbing down from the side of the freighter they had been working on all morning. "Pick a job from my early years, when I was just getting started. Hitting a little low aren't we?"

"That was two weeks ago, you idiot." A satisfied smile spread slowly across Miller's hearty, round face.

Patch reached for a rag on the floor and meticulously began cleaning the grease from each of his long, thin fingers, mock arrogance filling his voice. "Now, now. How do you ever expect to move beyond being my apprentice if you insist on treating me this way?"

The smile that had spread so slowly across Miller's face was gone in a flash. "Why you arrogant, skinny, worthless, good-for-nothing wisp." He began rolling up the sleeves of his grimy, blue coveralls. "For years I've put up with your lip. It's about time I showed you just *who* the apprentice is!"

As Patch dove for cover behind the wing of the freighter, Matthew rounded the corner. "Hey, guys!"

Patch brightened suddenly and called out from behind the stubby wing. "Hey, Matt! Good to see you. How's your lip feeling this morning?"

Any ill feelings harbored by Miller evaporated, as they often did, when Matthew entered the bay. "Hey, kid." He turned and strode to his workbench only a few feet away. "Got something to show you."

Retrieving the item, he tossed it to Matthew who hefted it in his hand as he studied it. "A lock bypass. Is this the one that was on my—"

"The very one."

By this time both Patch and Miller were standing in front of him—Patch consciously maintaining a few extra feet between himself and his bulkier counterpart.

Matthew noticed the gap and grinned. He could think of nobody, aside from his grandfather of course, whom he cared about more. Both men had taken him under their wings and watched out for him over the years. Whenever Matthew had a free moment between loading and unloading freight, Patch would include him in his electrical and computer projects. And Miller, whenever he wasn't busy with Patch, would involve him in his shipbuilding and design work. Both were considered to be the best at what they did, and despite all appearances, were the best of friends.

While Matthew studied the object, Patch folded his long arms and gave Miller a knowing look. Miller returned it and asked Matthew to take a careful look at the controls of the device. "Notice anything strange about it?"

At first, Matthew had no idea what he was supposed to be looking for. But then, in a flash, it registered suddenly. "This thing's digital!"

Patch appeared pleased. "That's right. Now, tell me something. If these guys who attacked you *were* pirates, where in the world did they get one of these?"

Matthew understood where Patch was going with this. After all, pirates, those remaining in business anyway, supposedly roamed space in antiquated equipment. Lock bypasses, legally a Special Forces instrument only, had been around for years. But digital lock bypasses had only been in use for a little over a year now. And the last pirate attack that anyone at the spaceport had remembered hearing about had supposedly occurred over thirty-five years ago; it didn't add up. He looked to Miller. "Where do you suppose they got it from?"

"I have no idea, kid. But it's puzzling, there's no doubt about that." He smiled. "Even Patch is speechless for once."

"That's where you're wrong, my portly partner," proclaimed Patch theatrically.

Miller flinched. "Just who you calling portly, wisp?" Miller began rolling his sleeves even higher. "I think it's about time I . . ."

"Spire?"

Both Patch and Miller looked over at Matthew, Miller suddenly appearing a bit uneasy. "Look, kid. Let's not start jumping to conclusions here, alright? Besides, it's really not our place to make that call."

"Coward," crowed Patch, ducking a punch and running for cover. Miller didn't pursue the chase, but turned to Matthew instead. "Really, Matt, we've got to be careful here. We don't really know why they attacked you, and we have to watch what we say. There has to be some kind of a connection, but we don't know all the facts. I just thought it was interesting is all."

Matthew wasn't too surprised with how serious Miller had instantly become. After all, the man often steered away from conversations involving Spire and politics—most people did.

Matthew hadn't given the matter any *real* thought, so he simply shrugged his shoulders. "Okay. Sure, Miller." He handed the bypass back to him.

From behind the wing of the freighter, Patch called out, "Warring said that he needed to talk to you later this afternoon . . . take down your official statement on the attack."

Their station manager was a decent enough guy, but Matthew dreaded talking to the man, feeling he had the uncanny ability to see right through him. "Alright. Thanks."

Turning, he began walking toward his pad with Miller. "Say, how much longer till I fly again?"

Patch had scurried from behind the wing and caught up with the other two, just in time to hear Miller's answer. "We'll have it ready to go in four, maybe five days I'd guess. Your ship's been grounded for a few days, though, until the investigation's been completed. You'll probably be flying by the end of the month."

"End of the month!"

Miller cleared his throat. "Kid, contrary to popular belief, you aren't the only freighter using this spaceport. I've got two with bad thrusters, one with a leaky fuel drive, one needing a complete hull replacement, and then there's a rumor Governor Adams's wife wants to host another party soon; you *know* what that will involve."

Patch slipped a skinny arm around Matthew's shoulder. "Besides, we've done a marvelous job of teaching you over the years. There's no reason *you* can't get started on it. And you know what we say about that."

Matthew smiled as all three repeated the familiar phrase: "You'll get it as soon as *you* really want it."

As they broke up and headed toward their respective projects, Matthew warmly reflected on how many times these two friends had worked their magic in his life. He didn't think they purposely set out to make him feel better—it just happened. And he loved them for it.

* * *

When the heavy leather curtain was pulled aside, sounding the wind chime, Paul rolled over on his side, his wooden cot creaking and cracking under his weight. "That you, boy?"

"Yes, Papa. It's me." Matthew seemed to hesitate for a moment, then kneeled at his grandfather's side. "I'm sorry I'm late."

"I was worried."

"I know. I . . . I dropped some milk by the Leeland's, and we got to talking." He placed his hand on Paul's arm. "I'm sorry about some of the things I said last night. I want to talk about it some more, but it's late. I work the noon shift tomorrow. We'll talk about it in the morning when we're both fresh."

Paul nodded. "That's fine, son. We'll talk." His hand fumbled on his cot until he found the boy's other hand. He patted it. "Goodnight."

As Paul laid back and listened to Matthew getting ready for bed, his heart swelled with pride. *He's a good boy. He really is. And he's right. Tomorrow would be better to discuss such a serious topic; fatigue only seems to make tough situations tougher.*

As he listened to Matthew settle onto his own cot on the other side of the room, Paul wondered how Matthew would react knowing what he had come to grips with only hours before he had arrived. Throughout the day, Matthew's words had haunted the old man; he saw in the boy's words images of himself many years earlier.

And those images had begun to stir Paul Tanner's blood . . . again.

CHAPTER 5

"Who in blazes is hammering this early in the morning?" shouted Paul as he jammed his pillow over his head.

More hammering followed.

Clearly frustrated, Paul threw the pillow aside. "Matthew? Matthew!"

The hammering stopped.

"Yes, Papa?"

"Would you go out there and tell whoever's hammering to knock it off. It's too early!" Then, under his breath, "Of all the inconsiderate, selfi—"

Matthew walked over to his grandfather. "It's nine o'clock, Papa. I waited as long as I could. I just wanted to get this done before I had to leave in an hour."

"An hour? Nine . . . what are you talking about, boy?"

"You've been sleeping like a baby all morning."

"I've what?"

"You slept in, Papa. I could hardly believe it myself. But when you slept through breakfast and were still asleep after I fetched today's water . . ."

"I don't believe it. I've never slept in past six!"

Matthew started to laugh. "Don't worry, Papa. Your secret's safe with me."

Paul swung his legs over the side of his cot and, out of habit, rubbed his eyes with the heels of his hands. "I don't believe it." Suddenly, his head rose up. "So it's *you* that's making all the racket?"

"Like I said, I just wanted to get this in before heading off to work. The transport leaves in less than an hour."

"Get what in?"

Matthew was grinning from ear to ear. He took hold of Paul's hand. "Come with me. I want to show you something."

"Boy, I'm not decent to go anywhere. Now what's with all the mystery?"

"You'll solve this mystery in six steps if you'll trust me."

Paul hesitated for a moment before allowing Matthew to help him to his feet. "Alright, let's get this foolishness over with." He held out his right arm. "Lead the way."

"We're walking to the doorway curtain."

"I told you I'm not decent to . . ."

"I know, Papa. Trust me."

After several small steps they came to a stop. Each step had only increased Matthew's amusement and excitement. "Okay, Papa. Pull back the curtain."

Paul's face clouded over with confusion. After giving a small sigh, he reached out. But instead of touching the familiar, stiff leather, his hand met up with a hard, solid object. "What in blazes?" His fingertips ran along the smooth surface before him. As they moved down the barrier, they collided with something he hadn't used in over twenty years: a doorknob. "What is this, Matthew?"

"It's a wooden door, Papa. I told you I'd get you one."

"I know it's a door, boy! But . . . how . . ."

"After I gave my statement to Mr. Warring, about the pirate attack, he paid me for my first week as a hauler. I got permission to leave a little early and bought this from one of the shops near the transport station. I've had my eye on it for weeks. I left it outside last night, before I came in."

"But we can't afford this! You have to take it back, Matthew."

Matthew laughed. "I don't think the people on the transport would really appreciate that. They were patient and understanding enough when I brought it back with me, but I wouldn't want to push my luck with a return trip."

"But, Matthew"

Matthew placed a hand on Paul's shoulder. "It's okay, Papa. We'll be fine. I still have enough to see us through until next week, and that includes some extra milk for the Leelands *and* the Smiths." Paul started to interrupt, but Matthew beat him to it. "I can't remember the last time we spent money on ourselves. Can't we just enjoy it this once? Please?"

Paul turned and faced the door once more. He reached out, found the doorknob, and turned it, opening the door—the sound of the chime noticeably absent. When he closed it, he shook his head, tears filling his eyes. "It's very nice, Matthew. It really is. Thank you."

Matthew was pleased. "It wasn't the fanciest, Papa. In fact it's rather . . ."

"No! Say no more." Paul opened and closed the door again, marveling at its smooth, graceful motion. "You hung it well. It's perfect. It's just perfect."

"Well, now that it's in I'd better be getting ready for work."

Paul reached out and found the youth's arm. "Matthew, I'm sorry I slept in. I guess I was making up for the sleepless night I had the night before last."

"I can understand that."

"Listen to me, Matthew. I'm your grandfather. I worry about you. That's the way it is, the way it should be. I don't want to see anything bad happen to you, but I . . . I know and understand how you feel about needing to do *something*. Our people have survived for many years, but I know we can't last too much longer under these conditions. And neither can the Arconians, whether they see it or not."

Paul placed his hands on either side of Matthew's face. "Don't let me, or anyone else, dictate to you what you should or shouldn't do. You're the one who has to face the man in the mirror every morning, and nobody else. You do what you feel is right in your heart. As long as you promise to do that, I will support you one hundred percent."

"Thank you, Papa. It means a lot to hear you say that."

The two embraced.

"Alright. That's enough, boy. I'm sorry we don't have more time to talk, but I don't want you to be late. I do want to talk some more about this later tonight, though. That is, I can understand why I wouldn't be asked to help directly with the Rebellion, but I'm sure I could be helpful in *some* way."

Matthew smiled and clapped him lightly on the shoulder. "I have no doubt about that."

As Matthew packed his lunch and got ready to leave, he noticed his grandfather quietly shaving and getting dressed. In fact, it was

Paul who opened the door ahead of Matthew just as he was about to leave. "Papa? You feeling alright?"

"Of course I'm feeling alright! Haven't you ever seen a man go for a walk before?" His voice didn't come out as confident as he appeared, and Matthew could see perspiration already beading his grandfather's forehead. "Now, if you'll excuse me, I have some visits to make that are long overdue." And then, under his breath, "It's time to look beyond the pit and see what the field has to offer."

As Matthew watched his grandfather slowly let go of the doorway, and inch his way beyond it with the use of his cane, he was convinced that he was witnessing one of the bravest feats he'd ever seen.

CHAPTER 6

Removing his leather gloves and welding goggles, Matthew stood up and stretched his aching back and arms. He had spent the entire morning on the scaffold, cutting away the last of the *Wanderer's* damaged hull, and he was tired.

Squinting his eyes, he took a moment to take in more than the glowing lines of melting metal he'd been staring at for hours. As his tired eyes drifted around the massive spaceport, he suddenly realized just how far he had come. To his left, beyond the Durin freighter bays, he could see the warehouse and shipping bay that had been his life for so many years, and he marveled over the fact that he was now piloting a ship of his own (in a manner of speaking). Granted, the *Wanderer* was nothing to get excited about by most pilots' standards, but to him it meant the chance for something more, something better.

To his right, he could see other pilots and crews preparing their ships for departure; and loading crews, scurrying like insects, determined to meet their respective deadlines.

Beyond Durin's freighters, several shuttles were docked, and beyond them stood the massive hanger doors. He never really understood the purpose of the doors, for they had remained open for as long as he could remember—shuttles and freighters coming and going around the clock. Whether they were touring shuttles, mining freighters retrieving water from the polar and frozen regions of Zerith, or shuttles filled with goods from the many refineries scattered throughout the forested region, the doors had always remained open. He fancied the huge, enclosed spaceport as being Zerith's living heart. A heart through which coursed a steady stream of life-sustaining elements. Shut the massive doors and . . .

Matthew shook his head in an attempt to clear it. *Enough already, Tanner. If you want to get back into action then you'd better get a move on.*

Slipping on his work gloves he reached down and pulled the freshly cut chunk of plating loose, letting it drop to the hanger floor with a crash. His eyes spied the crushed conduit housing the damaged power line that fed into the gravity rods. A shiver ran up his spine as he reflected on how close he had come to *not* surviving his first run.

He collected his tools and climbed down the scaffold. Miller had been kind enough to offer Matthew any tool he had needed. Not wanting to risk losing any of them, though, Matthew took only what he needed for whatever stage of the repair he was working on.

After visiting with Miller, and collecting the tools he would need to remove and replace the damaged conduit, Matthew was surprised to find a man he had never seen before checking—or at least appearing to be checking—the stability of the scaffold. When Matthew approached him, he was caught off guard by the forward-ness of the stranger's approach. "Ah, you have the tools. Great! Let's get started." He then proceeded to climb the scaffold toward the *Wanderer's* gaping wound. Seeing Matthew's hesitation, he quickly called out, "Hey, mountains don't move themselves you know."

Matthew felt as if he had been slapped in the face; he had just been given the code phrase he'd been told to expect from his contact, when he was needed by the Rebellion.

He said it! He actually said it! Often Matthew, and later Rollyn as well, had tried to imagine just where he'd be when the call to serve actually came. He never imagined it would happen during a ship repair.

Forcing back the shock, he started climbing, stiffly calling back his countersign. "No . . . they . . . It takes many hands . . . I guess." He winced. *Boy, did that sound weak.* Sheepishly he resumed his climb until reaching the stranger at the top.

Matthew looked into the other's eyes with a sense of wonder. "Look, relax, Matthew, okay?" the man said softly, patiently. "Try to act natural. Now, hand me that *whatzit* and let's get started."

The whatzit? Swallowing, Matthew fumbled for the tool he would have started with and passed it to the stranger, nearly dropping it in the process.

Reaching into the large hole, the man whispered, "Lean in closer. Pretend you're really getting a good look at what I'm doing."

Matthew did as he was told, but couldn't help taking a moment to study the man before him. He looked nothing like who he had always imagined would contact him. He was shorter than Matthew, and far too skinny. His blue coveralls were greasy alright, but his hands were thin and unscarred—definitely not the hands of a mechanic. He had a thin, bird-like face with dark hair, short and receding. His small, dark eyes and kindly smile didn't fit the warrior image at all.

"Listen, we don't have much time. Was anything given to you on Durin?"

Matthew was suddenly very confused. He was about to check over his shoulder for onlookers, but caught himself before doing so. "What are you talking about?" he whispered. "I wasn't told to bring back anything."

The stranger gave a patient smile. "That was intentional."

"What do you mean?"

"One of our agents slipped you the final key we've been waiting for. We wanted to be sure you acted naturally, so you weren't told what to expect."

Matthew felt his face flush with embarrassment. Given his recent, poor performance, he could only imagine how badly he would have botched up his assignment *had* he known. The pirate attack immediately sprang into his mind. He gestured toward their handiwork. "Someone knew."

"The pirates you mean? We feel it was a coincidence. There simply wasn't any way for anybody, other than a few of our most trusted agents, to have known about the transfer."

Matthew was still confused. "Well, if I wasn't told *what* to pick up, how am I supposed to know *what* to give you?"

The agent's patient smile reappeared. "Think back. Did anyone give you something, aside from cargo, that you didn't have when you arrived there?" Having posed his question, the stranger went back to fumbling the tool around the conduit.

After several minutes of reviewing everything he could remember, Matthew came up empty. He just couldn't think of anything *given* to him. "I'm sorry, but . . ."

"Think hard, Matthew. I don't need to tell you how important this is." Which was true. And that very fact only frustrated Matthew even more.

After another minute of thought, Matthew exclaimed, "Food! I was given food!"

"You mean to take with you?"

"No, I was given a dinner in the Mess before leaving."

The stranger chuckled. "I doubt they'd pass the information on to you that way."

Matthew caught the humor in the thought. "I would hope not," he said, chuckling as well.

"Alright, how about any new clothing?"

"No."

"Trinkets? Souvenirs?"

"No, I can't afford stuff like that."

"Did you take your shoes off at any time?"

"No. I helped unload the ship, grabbed a quick bite to eat, helped with the reloading, rested a few hours, and headed back home."

"What about when you registered in or out of the launch bay. Anything unusual happen there?"

And suddenly it dawned on Matthew. He *had* been given something. "My log book!"

"What do you mean?"

"Don't you see? When I checked in and out of the Security Office, I received an ink stamp each time in my log book. It's the port seal—Security's way of making sure you made it to and from your destination. Every freight station gives them."

The stranger looked Matthew in the eye and smiled. "Well done, Matthew. Well done indeed. That *has* to be it. Where's your log book now?"

"Follow me."

Both emerged from the opening as casually as they could and climbed down the scaffold and in through the *Wanderer's* starboard hatch. Once in the cockpit, Matthew reached under the pilot's chair and withdrew the small, worn log book. He thumbed through its pages.

Each page of a log book was divided with a thick black line. The left-hand column logged arrivals, and the right-hand column logged departures from whatever port, refinery, or outpost a pilot visited. He found both of the seals he had received and showed them to the stranger.

Glancing at them, they looked like any other seal in the book, though of course they were distinctive in their design, pattern, and color—separating them from the rest of the seals.

After only a few seconds, the stranger began laughing out loud. "Why that sly dog."

"Is that it then?" The suspense was killing Matthew.

The stranger immediately began sketching what was in the log book into a notepad he had removed from his breast pocket. "This *has* to be it, Matthew. I'm copying the seals so I can have them analyzed."

"You mean you don't know what they mean?"

"No, of course not."

"Then how do you know this is it?"

"Because I was told that our agent on Durin went to school with me—a childhood friend. I was also told I would recognize the information as soon as I saw it." He paused, obviously concentrating on his sketch. "He's put initials we used in a clubhouse we once built into one of the seals. It's in the scroll design, at the top. See? He's altered the stamps. This *has* to be it."

As the stranger continued to sketch, something caught Matthew's eye beyond the port side view port: three people running toward his ship. Matthew flinched. "Someone's coming."

The stranger glanced upward for only a second, then continued his sketching. "I'm almost finished. I must capture every detail. I don't know what's important and what's not important."

Matthew anxiously glanced at the stranger's notepad. It was a remarkable copy—nearly photographic. "You're an artist."

"All of us have different talents, Matthew. We're chosen to help where we can do the most good."

Matthew glanced out the view port again and was shocked to discover that he actually recognized those running toward him. It was Rollyn, with Patch and Miller running after him from behind. *That's impossible. Rollyn has the day off.*

It *was* Rollyn, though. And from the look on his face something was horribly wrong.

"I'll be back. I know them."

Leaving the stranger to complete his work, Matthew hurried down the Wanderer's narrow passageway and out through the port side hatch. By this time, all three of them had reached the Wanderer and were out of breath—Rollyn teary and hysterical.

"Matt! Matt!" Rollyn was gasping for air, trying to catch his breath. His face, neck, and arms were sunburned, his entire body dripping with sweat. *He's run the entire way. How'd he make it past the wall?*

"It's your grandfather." He bent over, gasping for air. Patch and Miller, on either side of him now, kept him from falling flat on his face. "He's . . ." Pain and anguish filled the boy's face. "Something's happened. Oh, Matt . . . he's hurt bad."

Matthew's eyes turned to Miller and then to Patch.

At that moment the stranger exited the Wanderer, and Matthew's eyes went directly to his breast pocket. *Notebook . . . The seals! . . . I'm involved now . . . I'm involved!*

He felt the blood drain from his face as an icy fist gripped his heart.

Fear erupted into panic as he grabbed Rollyn's shoulders. "What's happened, Rolly?" he shouted. "Tell me!" But Rollyn crumpled out of pure exhaustion.

Matthew released him, letting him fall to the floor, and started sprinting toward the nearest exit.

After only a few steps, Miller's powerful hand found the boy's coveralls sleeve, spinning him around and bringing him to a stop. "Kid! I've got my motorbike out front. We'll take that."

Matthew, wide-eyed and in shock, merely nodded his head and then continued his sprint to the door.

Just as Miller started to follow, Patch grabbed Miller by the arm. "What about the guards at the wall? They won't let you pass!"

Miller glared hard into his friend's eyes. "Let 'em try and stop me." He broke free from Patch's grip and followed after Matthew.

* * *

Returning the schedule clipboard to its hook, Corporal Pierson leaned back in his weather-beaten chair and eyed his new trainee through the arched window of the small sentry station nestled to the side of the wall's only entrance.

His former partner of three years had been transferred to another post two days ago, and though the new recruit, Saunders, seemed an adequate replacement, their difference in ages gave the two little in common.

Pierson knew he couldn't complain; he had a good job that paid well. But after seven years of training new recruits for the same post, he was beginning to feel restless. From a genetic viewpoint, he knew this was precisely where he was meant to be and, until he was told otherwise, had no reason to long for anything else. He would never voice his complaint, but on days like these he found his assigned role in life a bit monotonous to say the least.

Absentmindedly he ran his index finger over the top of his desk, leaving behind a clean trail in the thin layer of dust that constantly covered it. *Seven years. Seven years . . .*

It was the sound of an approaching motorbike that shook him out of his stupor. Lazily he turned his head in time to see Officer Saunders move to the center of the wall's large entrance, his rifle coming to bear in preparation for the stop. He couldn't help rolling his eyes at the crispness of his movements, chastening himself at the same time, realizing that he would do well to follow the young recruit's example; he'd simply grown lazy over the years. *Lazy, or disinterested?*

Losing interest, his eyes then turned to his right to study, beyond a second arched window, the barren landscape that stretched far beyond the wall's boundaries, and wondered for the hundredth time if his old partner had made it to a forest post. *Now* that *would be something!*

It was a shout that brought Pierson's head around just in time to see a man on a motorbike yank Saunders's rifle out of his hand and grab the front of his uniform—nearly lifting the rookie off the ground.

Pierson leaped out of his chair and grabbed his own rifle that had been leaning against the wall, his mind welcoming the diversion. Stepping from the sentry station he leveled his rifle. "Alright, let him go, nice and easy."

The stranger hesitated a moment and then tossed Saunders against the edge of the wall. He turned to eye Pierson.

"Miller? Miller, what in the world do you think you're doing?" Pierson didn't recognize the young man sitting behind Miller, but he appeared anxious and upset.

"Lou, this kid's grandfather's hurt, and I need to get him home. Now!"

Saunders was getting up, eyeing the rifle in Miller's hand though hesitant to reach for it.

Pierson noticed Miller was keeping a careful eye on both of them. "Miller, you know as well as I do that Outsiders must use the transport. It's the law. Now, why don't you hand Saunders there his rifle and we'll see about getting your friend on the afternoon transport. It'll be here in a few hours."

Miller glanced coldly at Pierson, his eyes cutting back to Saunders. "Lou, cut me some slack!"

"No can do." His rifle swung back to Miller, and Pierson knew his meaning had been clearly received.

"A young boy came through here not more than ten minutes ago," growled Miller. "You let *him* pass."

"He was coming in. You're going out."

Miller's eyes narrowed. "How much does he have to bring you tomorrow, Lou?"

Pierson bristled, not over the accusation of extortion, per se, but the fact that it had been said out loud—in the open. He smiled. "Twenty dockins, Miller. A fair and reasonable alternative to a month in prison I'd say."

The young man on the motorbike then whispered something in Miller's ear. Miller looked up, obviously displeased at the situation, but clearly realizing his hands were tied. "How much, Lou?" he asked.

Pierson straightened, pleased. "For you? Five dockins. For him," he indicated Matthew, "one hundred."

Miller glared at Pierson, causing him to flinch—in spite of himself. After several uncomfortable seconds Miller suddenly tossed the rifle to Pierson's feet and throttled the motorbike. Turning around sharply, Miller retreated in the direction he had come.

Pierson simply smiled. "Too much, I guess," he commented to no one in particular.

Saunders continued dusting himself off and began walking toward his commanding officer. "He caught me by surprise, sir. I didn't see that coming. He moves fast for a man his size."

Pierson's eyes narrowed at the young officer. "Then it appears we have more training to do after all, don't we?"

"Yes, sir," replied Saunders, his eyes averted.

As Pierson leaned over to pick up the weapon, he vaguely noticed the sound of Miller's retreating motorbike suddenly growing louder. Before he had straightened, Miller and Matthew shot past both guards, nearly clipping them in the process. Saunders spun and snatched his rifle from Pierson's hand just as the motorbike left the pavement, hitting the desert ground and sending a cloud of dust in its wake.

Pierson pushed the rifle aside as Saunders fired, the plasma bolt missing Miller by several feet. "Did I say fire?" he yelled.

Saunders looked confused. "But I—"

"Do you have any idea who that was?"

"No, sir."

Pierson shook his head at the rookie's ignorance and disappeared into his office, returning seconds later with the keys to his patrol skimmer. "Call for a backup team while I warm up the skimmer *that man* built! We'll follow him."

Pierson didn't wait for the "Yes, sir" but continued around the wall to the parked skimmer. "This had better be good, Miller," he mumbled. "This had better be good!"

* * *

Miller wheeled his motorbike through the narrow, shanty-lined streets, weaving and dodging any and all obstacles in his path. As the distance to Matthew's shanty decreased, they noticed the number of people they were dodging gradually increasing. Eventually, Miller could go no further.

Matthew leaped from the motorbike and ran toward home, bumping into and fumbling past neighbors either coming from or going toward his shanty. He paid little attention to the expressions on their faces, hardly noticing their surprise, and then sorrow, at his approach.

His shanty now in view, Matthew began shouting, "Papa! I'm coming, Papa!"

Slowly the words began registering in the minds of those obstructing his progress and they began parting, allowing him to go by.

When he reached his doorway, his heart stopped at the sight of the new wooden door, wide open, splintered from gun fire, hanging awkwardly from only its bottom hinge. He walked slowly through the doorway, squeezing his way past neighbors and friends—their eyes filled with tears and pain.

Finally, at the end of their grief, lay his grandfather. He was lying on his back, Mrs. Leeland crying as she cradled his head in her lap—blood from an obvious head wound matting his hair and staining her faded day dress. "I'm sorry, Matthew." Her face was streaked with tears. "I'm so very sorry." Her large eyes closed as she renewed her sobbing.

Matthew fell to his knees, tears falling freely from his eyes. He reached for his grandfather's limp hand and tenderly held it against his cheek. "Papa, please," he whimpered. "Don't leave me. Please don't leave me."

But there was no response; his eyes remained closed.

Paul Tanner, the former leader of a failed revolution, was dead.

* * *

As the patrol skimmer approached the shanty town, Pierson immediately felt hundreds of eyes boring into him. He was used to that, though he had to admit that they seemed more intense today; the number of people out and about was also greater.

They happened upon Miller's motorbike, lying on the ground, just short of the bustling crowd. Several children stood around it, as if protecting it, scattering the moment Pierson stepped out of the skimmer. And while the motorbike, one of the targets of his search, lay at his feet, it was the milling crowd that was holding his attention; several adults seemed to be avoiding eye contact, while many others simply stared.

Knowing he'd probably waste a lot of time getting a straight answer from the adults, he called to one of the children staring at him from the distance. "Boy! Yes, you! What's going on here?"

The young boy appeared nervous but gave Pierson the straight answer he'd wanted. "Paul Tanner's been shot. He's dead."

Pierson's eyes returned to the milling crowd, his mind absorbing the news, his skin suddenly very uncomfortable at the mass of people before him. He noticed more adults stealing glances in his direction as memories of all the rumors he'd been told regarding the infamous Paul Tanner swiftly returned.

Quickly, Pierson walked back to the skimmer—Saunders curious as to where they were going next. "Get us out of here."

"What are you talking about? Let's find . . ."

Pierson switched the controls of the skimmer to his side. "I said we're getting out of here!"

Pierson imagined more people suddenly staring in his direction. He reached for the acceleration bar. "Paul Tanner's been killed."

The young rookie was obviously puzzled. "Paul Tanner? Who's he?"

Ignoring the question, Pierson's eyes locked with several adults who were clearly distraught, undoubtedly curious as to the officers' presence at a time like this.

"Who's Paul Tanner?" repeated Saunders.

Pierson pulled back on the accelerator. "Rookie, you've got a lot to learn."

CHAPTER 7

". . . he was a man of character. And many of us here today have been the recipients of his generosity and goodwill. We will all remember with fondness the small visits he made to each of our homes. For Paul Tanner, they were more than simply social visits, they were untiring attempts at rebuilding, at healing our collective soul.

"I can recall one visit, in particular, that he made to my home only a month and a half ago . . ."

The words of Mr. Jacobs, for Matthew anyway, were simply words. He had no idea what the aging pedagogue, dressed in his simple black robe, had spent the last ten minutes talking about, and had no desire, really, to piece together what he had missed. Rather, Matthew's weary eyes continued to focus on the body of his grandfather, wrapped in a coarse, broadcloth blanket, bound with cords, lying adjacent a dark and abysmal grave.

The graveyard, a mile beyond their shanty town, had grown considerably during Matthew's lifetime. Simple hand-carved grave markers dotted the wasteland; and a cloudy, steel-gray sky only heightened his feelings of loss and sorrow.

For Matthew, it seemed wrong to bury Paul without a coffin or a more lasting headstone. But he knew his grandfather wouldn't have wanted it any other way. "I have suffered as the rest have," he often said. "And I will go the way *they* have gone. Remember that, Matthew."

Reluctantly, he had.

Jarred into the present by a firm grip on his shoulder, Matthew began to shake hands with the hundreds of well-wishers who were now preparing to leave. He accepted their predictable words of sympathy with an occasional nod or empty thank-you—nobody took offense; they all appreciated the magnitude of the young man's loss.

Deep down, Matthew really *had* appreciated their coming. Even those, who at times in the past had resented his grandfather, including Rollyn's father, had recognized the significance of Paul's passing and had come to pay, if only from a distance, their final respects.

After several well-wishers had passed by, it was Miller's voice that snapped him back into reality for a second time. "Kid, I want you to know I respected him. I truly did. My father never understood his convictions—too old and stubborn I guess." He then leaned in closer, his voice falling to a whisper. "But, believe me, kid, even though I was only a few years younger than you at the time, they made sense to *me*. They really did."

Each of Miller's words seemed to chip away at Matthew's emotional reserve. And when he had finished his final sentence, Matthew fell into the man's open arms.

Tears flowed freely as Miller held him tight, his own eyes shining. "It'll be okay, kid. You've still got *us*. Remember that!"

After a minute or two, Miller pulled away and looked deep into Matthew's eyes—his voice low, yet stern. "Now, listen to me, Matt. There are hundreds of people here that knew and loved your grandfather. His passing means a lot to them too. Let them have the chance to *share* your grief. Shake their hands, kid. Look deep into their eyes when they speak to you. Let them share their love with you. *You* need it, and *they* need it. Your grandfather would have appreciated that. You know that."

Matthew knew Miller was right, but to give at a time like this simply seemed impossible. "I hope I haven't gotten you into too much trouble."

"Who, me? Nah, don't worry about it, kid. I'll just remind Lou on my way back about all those patrol skimmers we've got in the shop. Not to mention that new shuttle they've got me designing. Besides, if they want to throw me in the clink for a while, let 'em. I could use a rest. Take care, kid."

The man clapped the youth on the shoulder and left. Matthew stared at Miller's back for several seconds as he worked his way through the milling crowd. *He's a true friend*, he thought.

And then it dawned on him—so were many of the others who were approaching him now. He recognized *all* of their faces, and knew nearly all of them by name. Suddenly, he felt embarrassed at not having realized this sooner. He now understood what Miller had been trying to say: "Stop taking them for granted."

As the minutes rolled by, Matthew found himself paying more attention to each person, holding and shaking their hands. He took the time to listen to their anecdotes and condolences, and began feeling some comfort and solace in exchange for his effort.

But once the cemetery had cleared, Matthew found himself staring at the fresh mound of dirt that covered his grandfather, and he began sliding backward to the easier, more natural state of hopelessness and despair.

He ignored the small pockets of admirers who remained in the distance, and knelt on the ground.

He wanted to offer a final good-bye . . . but the words simply wouldn't come.

Burying his face in his hands, Matthew wept.

* * *

Several hours had passed before Matthew finally found the strength to go home. By the time he had returned to the shanty town it was well into the evening hour—the majority of the door and window curtains were drawn, and the streets were now empty and desolate.

At first he'd been fearful of coming home, not wanting to see the spilt blood and damaged door again. As it turned out, his fear had been for nothing; thankfully a few neighbors had scraped the dirt floor clean, and had moved the wooden door to the side of his shanty. He would chop it up and use it for cooking fuel in the days ahead; he had no use for it now.

It took Matthew several minutes to re-hang the old door leather. He then drew the window curtain, plunging the room into its familiar, shadowy solitude.

Dropping into his own hide-back chair, Matthew numbly studied his surroundings. All of the frightful images had been carefully removed, and yet it was now the common articles, scattered throughout his humble home, that inundated his mind with the memories he'd wanted to avoid.

His head leaned back, overwhelmed by it all, his face wooden.

This morning, he thought, *everything was so* good *this morning*.

Turning his head to the side, his eyes happened upon Paul's cane, leaning, as it often had, against his larger, hide-back chair. And at that moment the one emotion he had been trying so hard to keep at bay surfaced as fear.

He folded his arms and pulled them tight against his body as tears resurfaced and flowed unchecked. Suddenly, for the first time in his life, Matthew was truly alone.

* * *

Morning found Matthew just as evening had left him—in his chair, bleary-eyed and in shock. He'd caught only snatches of rest, and it wasn't until he heard the familiar sounds of a new day beginning that he found the strength to stand. His back and neck ached, but he hardly noticed. He considered washing up, even collecting fuel for the stove, but as he reached for the two large buckets with which to fetch the day's water, he realized these actions were merely a result of habit. Chores, his job, the community, even his role in the Rebellion, meant very little to him now. His world seemed empty and, deep within, he felt lost. Spying his cot, he went to it and collapsed with fatigue. Matthew shut his eyes and willed the world away, then mercifully fell asleep.

Matthew found himself not ten feet from his shanty, staring at the closed wooden door before him. His feeling of pride returned, knowing how happy he'd made his grandfather. The door had been a small gift, really, but had been greatly appreciated to say the least.

Slowly, it dawned on Matthew that his grandfather's death must have been a dream.

His body and soul filled with relief.

He ran toward the door, throwing it back, longing to hug his grandfather and tell him all about the horrible nightmare he'd been experiencing.

Once inside, however, he found himself smothered by an intense feeling of fear, pain, and guilt; on the floor lay his grandfather—dead.

Matthew sat up gasping for air, his body covered in sweat. He called out, "Papa!" But when no answer came, and the reality of his situation began to develop in his mind, tears came yet again with the realization that his *nightmare* was very much a reality.

Judging by the sounds outside he knew he had only slept for a few hours at best, but he returned to his chair and wiped his eyes, determined not to revisit his dream.

He spent the afternoon listening to the muffled sounds surrounding him, ignoring the calls of occasional well-wishers from without, and forcing himself to stay awake.

By evening, Matthew began tentatively addressing his feelings of guilt and anger over Paul's death.

He couldn't shake just *how* his grandfather had died. To die from poor health, or from an accident was one thing, but murder . . .

Inwardly Matthew struggled with the guilt of knowing that somehow *he* had to have been the one responsible for his grandfather's death. He'd overheard several people outside his shanty talk about two guards who had arrived shortly after he and Miller. Then, upon hearing of Paul's death, they had immediately turned and left. After what had happened at the wall he had little doubt as to why the two had pursued them, but why leave? Did they fear retribution? But if Spire *had* been responsible for his grandfather's death, surely they would have informed the guards at the wall to keep an eye out for any signs of retaliation and to avoid the area altogether.

Perhaps this was a message addressed only to him, warning him not to become involved in the Rebellion—the same kind of message sent years earlier to his grandfather . . . with the death of his parents. If this was the case, Matthew wondered if resistance was even possible? Perhaps Spire *was* too powerful.

And then there were the pirates. After all, it had been an older, projectile weapon that killed his grandfather. Maybe this was simply an act of revenge for Matthew outsmarting them at Durin. His grandfather was an easy target, and this was an act that Spire would applaud rather than avenge if the pirates happened to get caught.

The digital lock bypass sprang to Matthew's mind next. Maybe Spire and the pirates were working together.

Spire, pirates, or both—it seemed each had the motive and the equipment necessary to carry out such an act. But why hadn't anybody noticed any strangers? Why hadn't they heard anything?

Hundreds of other shanties surrounded his own, making it nearly impossible for any stranger to wander around unnoticed. Yet, based on what Matthew had overheard outside, that's exactly what had happened. It just didn't make any sense. None of it made any sense!

Late into the evening Matthew knew he couldn't remain in his chair any longer. The pain in his back and neck were simply too much. Slowly, he made his way to his cot. Though fearful of revisiting his nightmare, deep down he knew that he had to get some sleep.

Pulling his worn sheet over him, Matthew forced his eyes shut immediately, not wanting to see his grandfather's cot, or the floor beneath his bunk—the spot where his dead body had once been.

Several minutes passed by in virtual silence and, try as he might, images of that frightful afternoon continued flashing through his mind. He tossed and turned, then finally curled up in a tight ball, determined to ward off the intense cloud of terror and despair that seemed intent on enveloping him.

"Help me, Papa," he whispered out of desperation. "Please. Help me!"

A few minutes later Matthew drifted peacefully to sleep . . . and back outside.

Matthew stood looking at his shanty, noticing this time that the wooden door was missing. In its place was the heavy leather curtain that had always been there. Matthew also noticed an increasingly bright light coming from within, its rays escaping from every crack and opening. The light seemed brighter than sunshine, and the longer he stared at it, the greater the peace he felt growing within his heart.

He walked slowly toward the shanty until he found himself standing directly in front of the doorway, his hand gripping the edge of the curtain.

He somehow knew he needed to go inside, but hesitated, fearing what he might find beyond the heavy leather curtain. And yet as quickly as this doubt had entered his mind, the peace, coming from within, seemed to extinguish it; a pleasant contrast to the feelings he'd experienced earlier.

He pulled aside the curtain, and stepped inside.

Beyond the doorway there was only light. There appeared to be no floor, though he was sure he was walking on solid ground.

Suddenly, he noticed a man walking toward him, the light being too bright to make out any specific facial features. He noted, however, that the man seemed to be dressed in normal clothing, though mismatched, tattered, and worn.

As the distance between them lessened, the man's facial features became clearer. "Papa?" exclaimed Matthew.

Realizing it was his grandfather, Matthew ran toward him, meeting him in a hug.

"Papa! It is you!" He could actually feel him!

The two embraced, his grandfather remaining silent.

When Matthew stepped back, he was shocked to see that his grandfather's eyes were looking directly into his!

"Easy, son. Easy. Don't be afraid."

"But, I can't believe you're—"

"Listen to me, Matthew. Listen." And with his words came tears of his own. "I promised you we'd talk. And I intend on keeping that promise. Now, please. Listen to me . . ."

CHAPTER 8

Matthew awoke with a start and took a moment to gather his senses. He remembered desperately trying to get to sleep the night before, but . . . then what?

Shaking his head, he realized it didn't matter. The fact was he felt much better this morning—human again—and chalked it up to having gotten a good night's rest.

Sitting on the edge of his cot he suddenly realized how hungry he was, which surprised him. For the past two days he hadn't cared about eating at all, hadn't cared about anything, and now . . .

Work. I need to get to work! The darkened room felt stifling, and Matthew knew, deep down, that if he did sit around all day again, he would do nothing but continue to wallow in self-pity and paranoia. He didn't want to be alone. He knew he had to keep moving. He couldn't let the grief overtake him.

He reached for the small windup clock he kept on a crate that served as his nightstand. *Nine forty-six! The transport!* He knew if he hurried, he just might be able to catch it at ten o'clock.

Untangling the sheet from his legs, he bounded for the earthen washbasin and filled it with what little water remained in the water barrel. He lathered his face up with soap, and with his razor quickly swiped at the stubble he'd neglected over the last few days, carefully shaving the whiskers around his healing lip.

Pulling the towel from the nail, he dried his face and inspected it for a minute in the piece of mirror hanging above the basin. He felt alive this morning; there was no doubt about it. He was still suffering inside, he could feel it, but life seemed more bearable than it had the night before. His eyes locked onto his own reflection. *I need to carry on. I have to! If I don't I'll . . . I'll be letting* myself *down!*

His doubts and fears from the night before began nibbling at his heart, but he kept moving, refusing to give them a chance. *No time for this now, Tanner.*

Grabbing a grain biscuit from the pantry, he changed into a cleaner pair of coveralls and hurried to the terminal, boarding with only seconds to spare.

The first several minutes of the trip felt painfully awkward. All of the passengers were well aware of Matthew's loss, but neither they nor Matthew knew just what to say. His own, "Good morning," however, broke the thick ice, and soon he was lost in a welcome barrage of small talk.

* * *

Matthew's arrival at the spaceport created quite a stir with those who knew him personally. Patch and Miller were shocked he had even come at all, figuring he'd be gone for at least a week. Once he had explained his preference for keeping busy, however, they seemed to understand his reasoning and supported him wholeheartedly.

What he hadn't expected, catching him completely off guard, was a visit from Warring himself—on the work floor no less. Having learned of Paul's death from Miller, he too was surprised to see the young man back so soon after such a tragic loss. "Son, why don't you take two or three more days off? The Harvest Festival started today. Go. Gather your thoughts." And then, as if to cover up his softer side, he added gruffly, "You're no good to me unless your head's on right."

Matthew had never seen this side of his boss before. He was always so stiff and demanding. He was stunned, yet appreciative. "Thank you, sir. I just feel I'd be better off working on the *Wanderer*—moving forward, if that's alright with you."

The thin, bald, leather-skinned man studied Matthew's eyes for several seconds. "Alright, I guess I can understand that." Then, before leaving, he mumbled, "Glad to have you back," glancing about quickly—making sure nobody else had seen or heard what he'd said.

After laying out his tools, Matthew prepared the slab of metal sheeting for cutting. He laid the large, thin sheet onto two supports and ducked underneath it, making sure the supports would remain clear of his cutting torch. Satisfied, he stood and was surprised to find a young man, about his own age, standing near the stubby wing of his ship.

The boy was carrying a large box and wore the orange coveralls of a shipping bay worker, the kind of coveralls *he* had worn, until recently.

"Can I help you?"

"You ordered a ten-foot length of conduit and cable?"

"Oh, yes. Thank you." As Matthew reached for the box, however, he was again caught off guard by what the messenger said next. "Thanks for the hand! Mountains don't move themselves you know."

Matthew froze.

This was it. All he need to do was return the countersign. If he wanted out, he need only accept the box in silence.

The fear and doubt that had begun nibbling their way toward his heart earlier returned. If he remained involved with the Rebellion, would Spire continue eliminating his closest friends one by one until he quit? And if they could do that, did the Rebels even stand a chance? And if *pirates* really were to blame for his grandfather's death, was it fair to the Rebels for him to continue, not knowing when or if they'd attack again?

All these thoughts flashed through his mind while his hands rested on the box, his heart pounding with each passing second. "I . . ." Hesitating, he searched deep within his soul. *What should I do?*

At that moment the feeling of peace he'd felt earlier slowly began to build, the image of his face in his basin mirror flashed through his mind. He knew what he needed to do.

Matthew cleared his throat as his confidence began to build. "No, it takes many hands."

Setting the box on the floor, he looked up to find the messenger smiling. "Glad to hear it." He pulled a receipt book from a leg pocket and asked for Matthew's signature in confirming the delivery of the package.

On seeing the receipt book, and not a message, Matthew was at first confused. However, not wanting anything to appear out of the ordinary, he accepted the book and signed his name on the required line.

As Matthew wrote, the messenger whispered what he had been waiting for: "Harvest Festival. Second day. Rock Hill Cave. Two-thirty P.M."

He had completed his signature just as the messenger had finished giving him the time. Matthew casually returned the receipt book. "Thanks."

"Thank *you*." The messenger turned and had taken only a few steps when he stopped and turned around. "Matthew?" he began hesitantly.

Matthew looked up from the box.

"Sorry about your grandfather."

From the look on his face, Matthew could tell that he genuinely meant it. "Thanks."

The messenger nodded and headed back toward the warehouse, leaving Matthew to ponder over what he'd just agreed to.

Second day of the festival, huh? His eyes drifted toward Mr. Warring's office window, high above. *I guess I'll be taking you up on those days off after all.*

CHAPTER 9

Closing his ledger, the aging Chief Executive Officer of Spire leaned back in his chair, stretched his bony arms toward the ceiling, and brought his head back to rest within the interlocked fingers of his hands.

The numbers were great. In fact, they were outstanding. Each district of Arcona, as well as all outlying refineries and treatment plants were, for the most part, in the black—production costs remained low, profits high. It was a pattern that had more or less remained steady over the past several decades, but he still found pleasure in recording the overall monthly totals in his personal ledger.

The final briefing on the pirate attack, involving one of their smaller freighters, had proven disappointing earlier that morning. He had demanded a thorough investigation the moment he had received Warring's report, but now he had learned that by the time Durin security had been alerted, the pirates had long since vanished. Frankly, the fact that any pirates existed at all had surprised him. Many years ago he'd had the pleasure of personally executing what had been thought to have been the last remnants of that miserable strain.

Damage to the freighter had been minimal and nothing had been lost, but the thought that they'd somehow gotten hold of a digital lock bypass was troubling. He had Governor Adams's word that he would beef up Durin's patrol runs and check on just who might have supplied the pirates with the bypass—outside of this, there was little else the CEO could do this many light years away. Distance often made dealing with *some* problems difficult.

But the Tanner murder—that should be different.

He checked his wall clock. *Harris should be here any minute now.*

Swiveling his chair away from the desk, he absorbed the view from the window that was the east wall of his plush, high-rise office suite. He stared absentmindedly at the thousands of citizens who were out and about far below, and at the varying assortment of buildings that made Arcona what it was today—a thriving metropolis. Though outwardly unremarkable, each edifice contained hundreds of thousands of Arcona's citizens. *Satisfied citizens*, he thought. *Content citizens.*

He smirked. *Puppets. Nothing more than puppets. But oh, how I love the show!*

And he did, as had his great grandfather nearly one hundred and sixty-five years earlier, when Spire had been officially organized. It had taken his family decades to obtain the power, each predecessor having his share of obstacles to overcome or destroy. But nothing, absolutely nothing, was going to take it away from him.

He turned to his desk and hefted his large, worn, leather ledger. It was his great grandfather's, and had been passed down from father to son as the family dynasty had grown and expanded.

Eight inches thick, pages yellow and brittle with age, the book had helped organize the corporation's acquisitions and assets for years. And though secure computers had been handling all aspects of Spire's record keeping for decades now, he had chosen to maintain the archaic record out of respect for his ancestors, as had his father before him. Many of his advisors had recommended destroying the book when he assumed his position nearly thirty years ago, especially after several prominent government officials had been added to the extortion roster. He told them at the time that he would "consider" their suggestion, and simply left it at that. No one dared bring it up again.

And though he had opted to hold on to the heirloom, in spite of the potential danger such information would spawn if made public, he *had*, in a way, taken their concern to heart. He'd had his team of craftsmen construct for him a desk of solid steel—each drawer a miniature vault. Now he could honor the past, he believed, without compromising his future.

After voicing a series of numbers, the locking bolts within his top drawer clicked, and the drawer slid open. He replaced the ledger, careful not to bump the brittle, fragile spine of the book against the side of the drawer, and then watched as the drawer withdrew into the desk, its locking bolts sealing it in place. He then sat back to continue his wait for his First Assistant.

Sure, for *now* he was alone. But soon he wouldn't be. He closed his eyes as he tried to decide just what he was going to do first on his retreat to his favorite forest resort. Outwardly it looked like any other refinery that had been constructed over the years. Within, however, was a palace. It had been elaborately decorated and supplied, and secretly staffed, with anything and everything to satisfy his, and his council members' physical pleasures.

The soft chime of his desk intercom pulled him, reluctantly, from his wicked thoughts. "Harris would like to see you, sir."

"Thank you, Lori. Please send him in, will you? And see that we're not disturbed."

"Of course, sir."

The two large and intricately carved wooden doors slowly and simultaneously opened inward. And as his nephew entered, the CEO couldn't help admiring the young man's confident gait. At twenty, he had everything going for him—good looks, high intelligence, and the imminent promise of having the entire world placed in the palm of his hand

Physically, Spire's CEO had been incapable of having children of his own. And so to maintain the family dynasty, he had selected his younger brother's only son to be his successor. At sixteen, the boy had come on board with great enthusiasm, having already enjoyed the fruits of a "select life"—and driven, it seemed, to want more. Often the CEO fancied seeing himself in the younger man. Even though his own once dark and wavy hair had disappeared some time ago, he had the same strong chin.

By the time Harris had reached the older man's desk, the office doors had closed.

"I'm glad to see you, Harris. What have you discovered?" the CEO asked, remaining seated.

"I've checked with all our key resources. They have no idea who murdered Paul Tanner."

Don't know, or are simply not telling? he wondered, leaning back in his chair, motioning for his nephew to take a seat.

The youth sat on the edge of the plush couch that was in front and to the right of the polished-steel desk, rested his forearms on his knees, and brought his hands together; the fingertips of his left hand touched those on his right. "I do, however, have the names of the guards who chased his grandson: Corporal Lou Pierson and Officer Jacob Saunders."

"Excellent!" Spire's CEO leaned forward, an ever patient, chilling smile parting his lips. "Had they simply caught up with this Johannes Miller and the boy and verified their excuse for leaving them at the gate, we could have dismissed the incident out of compassion. But you saw our informant's report. They turned and ran, Harris. They appeared weak and incapable. The investigation into Tanner's death should have begun then and there. I don't want those homeless maggots thinking they can intimidate us with their ragged numbers. Pierson and Saunders must pay for their cowardice."

Harris's response was immediate. "Do you remember Gerald's report on Northern Outpost G6?"

"Vaguely, why?" Actually he remembered the outpost supervisor's recommendation all too clearly, and knew immediately where his nephew was going with it. But he chose to hold his tongue and allow his nephew the opportunity to stretch. *How else will he learn to lead?*

"He mentioned that the cold in that region has really taken its toll on the plant's equipment. It's old and inefficient, hardly worth fixing."

"So?" He was enjoying this immensely.

"So, why can't we take care of both problems at once?"

"An accident?"

"An accident! Two deaths would only bolster our decision to close the plant. We could impress the public with our concern for the safety and welfare of our employees."

"Compassionate."

"Exactly. Good public relations, and the elimination of a few *weak links*."

He was proud of the boy. He was everything he would have wanted in his own son. He was learning fast. And soon, when he retired, Spire would be in good hands. "Alright. See that it's taken care of immediately, will you?"

Harris grinned. "I'll enjoy that."

"I have no doubt you will. Oh, by the way, I also want you to make sure that our *dear* president has made arrangements to have two agents sent out to the Tanner place."

"What for?"

"I want them to do a little looking around. If we can't figure out who's responsible for this murder, then perhaps we can at least stop the overly suspicious from jumping to any rash conclusions about the government . . . or Spire." He winked. "Good for public relations."

The youth grinned and stood. "Consider it done." He turned to leave.

"And, Harris. I'll be gone for about a week inspecting one of our *forest-based refineries.*"

Harris flashed his uncle a knowing look—a look the CEO readily returned.

"If anything, and I mean anything, new on this matter comes up, contact me immediately. You know how to reach me."

"Of course."

And with that, Harris departed.

The large doors closed as Spire's CEO swiveled his chair once again to take in the majesty of Arcona.

There had always been rumors of a second revolution being planned, but he and his council had never been able to dig up anything solid to justify their suspicions. And while it may not have been related to these rumors, he was sure that Paul's murder meant *something*. Just what that something *was*, he wanted to know.

CHAPTER 10

"Tomorrow's the big day, Papa. They're going to let me know what I'll be doing next."

"You don't sound too excited, Matthew. What's wrong?"

"It's just . . . "

"The agents rattled you didn't they?"

"No. They were gone by the time I got home from work. Mrs. Leeland said they simply asked people questions about what they'd seen and heard and looked our place over. They didn't stay long. Probably just going through the motions."

"But you don't know that for sure, do you?"

"No, I don't." That's another thing, *he thought*. Why isn't he allowed to tell me who's responsible!

Paul scooted his hide-back chair closer to Matthew's and leaned forward. "Then what has you rattled, boy?"

"I'm just not sure about all this. What if . . . What if we fail, like . . . " Matthew winced, wishing he could pull the words back.

"Like me?"

"I'm sorry. I didn't mean it the way it sounded. I—"

"Relax, Matthew. Relax. I know what you meant." Paul sat back and folded his arms across his chest. "But we've had this discussion before, haven't we?"

"Yes." Matthew was looking down at his feet.

"And I seem to recall you telling me that this was something you knew *you* had *to do.*"

"But that was before you—"

"No, Matthew. In your heart you knew *this was something you* had to do. Hold on to that! Don't doubt it! Believe in yourself! There's a reason you were called for this."

Silence followed, and Paul's words seemed to hang in the air.

"It would help if I could remember our conversations during the day."

"I told you that wasn't permitted."

"I know," And he did know. He just didn't quite understand why.

Paul could see the frustration in Matthew's face . . . as well as the fear. He straightened, his voice taking on a more reflective tone. "You know, I remember a wise man once said, 'I would rather fail miserably doing something, than remain with the cowards who forever live with the knowledge that they'd never even tried.'"

Matthew looked up from his hands. "I like that. Who was the wise man?"

Paul smiled smugly. "Me."

Both burst out in laughter, each enjoying the sound of the other.

Matthew wiped the tears that had come to his eyes, his face quickly becoming somber. "I miss you, Papa."

Paul's face rapidly followed suit. "I miss you too, boy. Believe me. I miss you, too."

* * *

The sheer spectacle of the event was enough to bowl anyone over. Hundreds of colorful booths lined the edges and borders of Arcona's largest outdoor arena. Food, crafts, and wares were all being peddled, all proceeds going to the city, while thousands of citizens from all over, including youth from beyond the wall, enjoyed the open-air festivities.

Loud street bands, balloons, and banners from ground level, along with an occasional confetti shower from above, served to remind all in attendance that the new year's Harvest Celebration was in full swing.

For many, it was an opportunity to enjoy being with other people—to perhaps see something unique and original, like a play or variety show. And though Arcona's government had long since taken from farmers the responsibility of food production and distribution, it had seemed reluctant to remove a tradition so much a part of

Zerith's culture. Besides, it kept Arconians content, pacified. And as far as Spire was concerned, it was money well spent.

As Matthew and Rollyn applauded the actors at the close of the play, Rollyn leaned over, shouting above the clamorous applause. "I liked last year's better!"

Matthew nodded, feeling the same way.

Actually, had he been able to give the actors his *full* attention, he probably would have enjoyed this year's play as well. But in less than half an hour he would be receiving his next official assignment, and he was finding it difficult to even sit still.

As they made their way out of the theater with the rest of the crowd, and into the open air of the park, Matthew turned to Rollyn and gave him the agreed-upon signal. "You're sure you're not hungry?"

Without hesitating, Rollyn replied, "Nah. I'm not hungry. You go ahead. I'll meet you over there by the ring toss when you're through."

Matthew gave the boy a wink and a wave, turned, and began walking toward Rock Hill, a small rise nestled behind a long row of food booths on the far side of the park.

As he walked, he reflected on how relieved he had been to run into Rollyn earlier that afternoon. The boy had worked the early-morning shift and had decided to walk through the arena on his way to the transport station. Matthew hadn't seen the boy since that fateful day when he had barreled into the spaceport, sweating and out of breath. At first Rollyn had seemed shy and awkward, like most people lately, not knowing how to really talk to a person in mourning. But as the afternoon wore on, he'd slowly begun acting like his old, annoying self. Matthew had talked him into taking the later transport and was now very much enjoying the company.

Over lunch he had told Rollyn about his appointment, omitting the information regarding the hill of course, and had enjoyed watching the shock and thrill play across the boy's face. Then they carefully choreographed their time of separation. It was overkill, they knew, but they had had fun imagining all of the possible dangers. And, in a way, it had helped Matthew to relax—feel like his old self again.

Now, as he neared the food booths, he concentrated on walking as casually as he could.

Under the shade of the large trees that ran along the edge of the small hill, booths of all sizes and shapes seemed to silently beckon the hungry, their menus offering everything from the plain to the exotic.

A cold-dessert booth sat directly in front of the small hill that was Matthew's target. Ordering a snow cone, he asked for the time.

"Two-fifteen," replied the attendant, pouring the blue syrup over the ball of crushed ice, and handing it to Matthew.

Matthew paid the man, took a seat at one of the many picnic tables in front of the booth, and did his best to look casual while observing others attending the festival. But even as he conscientiously tried to enjoy his snow cone, his stomach churned at the thought of what was coming.

After a while, he knew that it had to be close to two-thirty. Not having a watch of his own, and not wanting to ask another person for the time, he crumpled his paper cup and proceeded to look for a trash can—the ruse he had settled upon late last night.

Acting as if he hadn't noticed the can at the far edge of the dessert booth, he walked between two of the booths and emerged behind them. At that moment, he realized that though the booths were different this year, the hill was the same hill he had visited a year ago.

At that time one of the stage actors had been assigned to ask him if he would be at all interested in becoming part of a second revolution. Out of pure curiosity, he had agreed. He wondered how different his response might have been had he known then what he knew now.

The small rise behind the booths formed not only Rock Hill but the western edge of the park as well, drawing very few visitors. And the shade trees, planted along the border, hid any movement from prying eyes that may have been watching from buildings high above.

Locating the correct tree was easy, because it had the widest trunk. Nervously, he waited for the signal.

The whistling of a man rounding the corner of the dessert booth nearly sent Matthew into a panic. But he held steady, turning his back to the stranger, while anxiously continuing his pursuit of a trashcan.

He could tell by the whistle's volume that the man was coming straight toward him, and he decided at that moment to try the straightforward approach. After all, if it *was* indeed one of the many Special Forces Officers peacekeeping the event, he *had* a viable excuse for being where he was—at least he hoped it was viable.

When he turned, however, he was surprised to find that the

whistle belonged to a white-uniformed groundskeeper sweeping up litter into a scoop and working his way toward Matthew.

The middle-aged groundskeeper stopped in front of Matthew and gave him a friendly, even smile. "Toss it on the ground. I'll take care of it for you."

"Thanks."

"Don't mention it . . . Matthew."

Their eyes locked.

After exchanging code phrases, Matthew followed behind the man, anxiously awaiting his cue.

As they neared the large tree, the groundskeeper began talking, motioning all around him with his arms, broom, and scoop. "Don't you just love the festival? The chance to visit, laugh, and sing? There's so little of that these days. It's a shame we have to schedule a holiday to feel this way."

As they rounded the tree's massive trunk he turned, his voice hardly skipping a beat. "I can't seem to get enough of it." Matthew's attention was immediately drawn to the stranger's smiling eyes as they darted back and forth, seeming to take in everything around him.

Then, suddenly he said softly, "You're clear. Jump!"

It was just what Matthew had been waiting for. He jumped feet first into the tall grasses behind the trunk of the tree, disappearing instantly into the ground.

His first jump, a year ago, had been terrifying. Knowing what to expect this year made the experience a bit more bearable, even fun.

Matthew slid downward nearly ten feet in the four-foot-wide shaft, lined with grasses, landing in a huge pile of straw.

The straw mound took up most of the northern wall of an underground cave.

A solitary man, wearing the brightly colored costume of a game booth operator, held a burning torch at the base of the straw and smiled wide as Matthew righted himself, brushing bits of straw from his hair and clothing while keeping a keen eye on the torch the man was holding, certain that a simple toss of the torch into the dry straw would have been more than enough to *detain* any unwelcome guest.

But Matthew *was* welcome and was greeted warmly by the same older man he had spoken with a year ago—the Regional Director. Matthew didn't know his name. But, as was the case with all of the other Rebels he'd met, he had no reason to.

"It's good to see you again, Matthew."

The two shook hands as they walked toward a small wooden bench that sat along the eastern wall of the cave, the man wedging the end of the torch in a crack in the wall.

The cave itself seemed cool and dry, with the biting smell of smoke in the air. Again, Matthew found himself fighting the inner desire he'd had the year before to explore the cave; its true dimensions were in the pale torch light a mystery to him.

Once seated, the older man, who shared many of the same physical characteristics of Matthew's grandfather, though slightly bulkier in the waist, expressed his sorrow over Matthew's loss and then surprised him by asking if he was still willing to be a part of the movement. Matthew's answer, in the affirmative caused the man to nod approvingly. He gripped the young man's shoulder. "Your grandfather would have been proud."

Somehow, deep down, Matthew knew the man was right.

The older gentleman then picked up a stick that had been resting on the side of the bench and proceeded to draw a circle in the dirt. "Matthew, this is our world, Zerith. As you know we have been preparing secretly to regain control of our world and bring freedom to its people. The key to our entire operation has been patience. And, patiently, for many years, we have been clandestinely diverting funds within some of Spire's key corporations to acquire the money needed for fuel, weapons, and travel. In time it will be returned, but for now this tactic has been necessary. I believe I alluded to this last year."

"You did. But you also mentioned some people were getting nervous about getting caught—requesting a break."

"That's right. You *were* listening." He paused a moment, giving his next sentence even greater weight. "*You* are going to help relieve them."

Matthew hadn't expected this. "How?"

"We feel we have sufficiently stockpiled the equipment and supplies we'll need for a temporary takeover. What we're lacking, now, is *raw* collateral."

"I'm not sure I understand."

"You know as well as anybody how much Arcona has come to depend on Durinian ore. Well, we're told that we probably won't be able to successfully overpower Durin at the time Arcona is scheduled to fall. The number of Spire supporters appears too great for the number of people we have working for us; it's too risky. Consequently, when we do make our move, there is a good chance we'll be cut off from Durin until the terms and conditions of a surrender have been agreed to.

"If the governor of Durin wanted to, he could withhold ore shipments from the moon, possibly moving many of Arcona's more spoiled citizens into an uprising. A few inconvenienced citizens are manageable—several thousand might be unstoppable. We have to be ready to supply Arcona with what it needs until law and order can be reestablished."

"And if you *are* capable of sustaining yourselves, then it will be *Durin* that will eventually be forced to comply once their supplies are used up," Matthew replied thoughtfully.

"Exactly."

"So you want to stockpile ore?"

"Yes."

Matthew's head spun at the thought. Embezzling liquid assets and storing away a few guns and rifles was one thing; smuggling thousands of tons of ore was something else! "But how am I—"

"Take a look."

The man drew a smaller circle about five feet above the circle he had made earlier. "This is Durin—none of this is to scale of course." He then drew a line between the two. The line wasn't straight, but had two, ever so slight bends in it.

Matthew immediately recognized it for what it represented. "The flight path to Durin."

"The *charted* flight path," corrected the man. He then placed his stick at the Durin end of the path and drew a straight line back to Zerith. The line naturally created two slight, yet distinct, gaps between the straight line and the curved line. "When you make your ore runs each week, you will leave Durin along the standard flight path. At some point you will then follow a new path." His stick then followed the straight line that ran adjacent to the well-traveled curved path. The stick slowed near the center of the first arc. "Here you will reduce your speed and jettison part of your load into space." Noticing Matthew's widening eyes, the man paused a moment. "Remember, Matthew," he calmly reassured, "we wouldn't be asking you to do this if we didn't think you could handle it."

Matthew felt his face turning red. *He has more faith in me than I have in myself!* "I'm sorry. I know that. It's just . . . "

"Please, let me finish. The amount you'll be dumping won't be large and shouldn't be missed. Dewy, your contact on Durin, will fill you in on all the technical information. To be honest with you, it's way above my head."

Dewy? Durin's port master? I never would have suspected him *of being a Rebel!*

The older man cleared his throat and brought the stick down to where he had left off. "You will continue dropping off the ore, three times a week, in the same spot. You *will* average three runs a week, won't you?"

"I should, as long as I keep up on my prep schedule."

"Very good. Now, the ore will be dropped at a speed that should place its eventual arrival right about here at the time of our attack." His stick pointed at the second gap that had been created with the straight line, the gap nearest Zerith.

"How can you be so certain?"

"Matthew, I don't pretend to understand completely the mechanics of what I'm showing you. My task is simply to give you the basics. Perhaps Dewy can explain it better when you visit with him. Now where was I? Oh yes, the ore should end up here at the time of our attack." Again he pointed at the second gap.

"And you'll be free to harvest it three times a week, assuming you have control of at least one freighter," said Matthew.

"Precisely."

"But the ore will be passing through the charted flight path three times a week as well."

The man smiled. "Actually, the coordinates you'll be using place its incoming path at a slightly higher altitude, relative to the charted path—a safe distance from any passing traffic—that much I do know."

"That amount of ore certainly won't be enough to keep all of Arcona running," Matthew countered.

"No, but it *will* insure the continual operation of at least some of Arcona's primary utilities."

"And if you can't gain control of a freighter?"

The man grinned matter-of-factly. "Then I am told Durin will have the most incredible meteor shower it's ever seen, three times a week, for as long as you've kept this up."

Matthew tried to laugh with him.

"We'll have the freighter, Matthew," he reassured. "We have to, and so we will."

Matthew gazed at the sketch near his feet.

"Matthew, I've told you this much because I want you to understand the magnitude of your assignment. But please, don't trouble yourself with all of the other details. They have been assigned to others. The man responsible for discovering these gaps, developing this theory, has fulfilled *his* assignment. The man who then passed that information on to you has fulfilled *his*. The artist, his. We each do what we can with what we're given. And, if we all do it well, everyone benefits."

Matthew began to feel doubt creeping into his heart. "But if I fail,"

"You won't." The man slowly began erasing the sketch with his foot. When he had finished, he looked deeply into Matthew's eyes. "And as long as you give this your best effort, no one, and I mean no one, Matthew, will hold you responsible if you do. That's all any of us have been able to do. Now, when will the *Wanderer* be ready to fly?"

Matthew, still trying to absorb everything, replied numbly, "Three or four days at the most."

"Can you make it six? We didn't think we'd be able to contact you as soon as we did, after your grandfather's death and all. We should have everything in place by then."

"Of course." Matthew was still wrestling with doubt as his mind began itemizing and prioritizing the last of the repair work that needed doing. The older man's voice startled him.

"Give us your best, Matthew. That's all we're asking."

As the two stood and Matthew prepared to walk with him toward the exit shaft beyond the darkness, he turned to face the man who had just placed on his shoulders the largest responsibility he had ever had in his life. A glimmer of confidence found its way past his doubt as he extended his hand and stood straight, a sense of pride beginning to fill his chest. "I *will* do my best, sir." He smiled. "And if my grandfather were here, I know what *he'd* want me to say."

"And what's that?"

"I'm a Tanner, sir. And giving others our best is what we do."

The man put his arm around Matthew, pulling him close. "I knew your grandfather, son. And that is *exactly* what he would have said."

CHAPTER 11

"Papa?"

"Yes."

"You say Dad and Mom are with you?"

"They are."

"Why can't I talk to them?"

"I'm afraid that's not permitted. Not yet anyway."

"Oh."

"But I can tell you they're awfully proud of you, Matthew—how you've grown."

"Tell them I love them, will you?"

"Of course, boy. Of course."

* * *

As it turned out, stretching his repairs out to six days hadn't been difficult at all. The rumor Miller had alluded to the week before had become a reality, and both Patch and Miller had their hands full prepping three of Spire's more elegant shuttles for a special dinner to be hosted on Durin later that week. This left Matthew responsible for the bulk of his ship's repair work. And though he had often found the work challenging, and at times downright frustrating, he had loved every moment of it. Now, having helped in the loading and unloading of those shuttles numerous times in the past, he was excited that he would actually be joining them at their final destination.

A trip to Durin lasted approximately twelve hours. And aside from monitoring the three course corrections that took place during the flight, there was very little to do. After putting the freighter on autopilot,

Matthew studied a few more of the *Wanderer's* wiring schematics, then had finally resorted to catching up on some badly needed rest.

Awakened a few hours later by his ship's chronometer, he eased himself into the pilot's chair and disengaged his lightspace accelerator, watching lightspace gradually refocus into realspace as the *Wanderer* began decelerating.

He stretched, stifled a shiver, and then ran a finger over the new, tender pink skin of his bottom lip, now free of stitches; the last time he had come out of lightspace he had been huddled within his emergency heating blanket, manually bleeding his oxygen tanks for air.

With the stars in focus, and Durin rapidly beginning to fill his forward view port, Matthew powered up his ship's transmitter. "Durin security, this is *Wanderer*, Flight Nine-One-Seven, requesting permission to land."

Out of the corner of his eye he thought he saw one of the Durin's four orbiting observation ships disappear around the moon's eastern horizon, but wasn't sure. The small ships' black finish made them nearly invisible against the darkened moon and the velvety backdrop of space.

"Copy that, Nine-One-Seven. You are clear to land. Proceed to Landing Pad Eight."

As the moon's surface neared and rolled beneath his freighter, Matthew easily spotted the work lights from the various ore digs that dotted the moon's surface . . . and then, finally, the moon's primary base. Its sparkling exterior with its hundreds of outdoor lamps gave it the appearance of a lonely jewel set against the background of an otherwise dark and sterile moon.

The base looked like a "T" from above, lying on Durin's barren, rock-and-crater-strewn surface. It appeared odd and out of place—several deep, tread-flattened trails testifying of its necessity for the continued existence of human life.

A long, two-story building made up the body of the "T." Along the ground floor ran a series of tall rectangular windows, a third of them making up the governor's living area—large and spacious enough for several families, Matthew felt, yet set aside for only Governor Adams, his wife, and daughter. The station's galley took up the middle portion of the wing, with administrative offices filling out the remainder of the building. On the second floor, above the governor's quarters, was the station's ballroom created especially for the governor's wife. The walls and ceiling of the huge room were constructed of massive glass panels, and, though darkened now, the room was renowned for the banquets and parties it hosted. Adjacent to the ballroom and taking up the remaining two thirds of the top floor, was the recreation hall, filled with game rooms, a pool, a gym, and a sick bay.

Lying next to the massive complex, and forming the top of the "T," was an enormous building, divided into two unequal parts. Half of the smaller portion was set aside for the base's guard housing, an upper floor housing the base's miners and administrative staff. The other half of the smaller portion was the haulers' barracks, with a private recreation room and mess of their own located directly overhead. The larger half of the building made up one of the most spacious hanger bays Matthew had ever seen.

Passing through the bay's protective energy shielding, Matthew watched and manually followed the directions of a lone guide man flagging him in from below, dreading what he had to do next. The old man in the cave had assured him it was Dewy's idea, but still Matthew found himself swallowing hard, bracing himself as his ship now hovered lazily above the hanger bay floor.

* * *

"That's right. Easy now. That's it." The guide man, tired and in need of a break, crossed the glowing guide rods over his head giving the incoming pilot the signal to bring his freighter down and cut his engines. Satisfied his job was complete, he switched off the rods and turned, calling out to his assistant on duty. "Pete! He's in. I'm going to go grab me a bite to eat."

The sound of twisting metal startled him, spinning the guide man around just as the *Wanderer's* port side aft landing strut folded in on itself after slamming into the hanger bay floor. The hard, solid surface of the bay, as far as the guide man could tell, hadn't suffered any damage. But the crumpled skid underneath the awkwardly resting *Wanderer* had. He winced—not in response for the damage the small freighter had suffered, but in genuine sympathy at what he knew would happen next.

* * *

Shaking his head, Matthew let out a low whistle. *If that looks anything like it felt . . .*

He quickly shut down the *Wanderer's* flight systems, fished his log book from beneath his seat, and nervously headed for the starboard hatch.

The moment the seal was broken, Matthew knew from the distant cursing and yelling, that Dewy was on his way. "Just what is it you're trying to do?" growled Dewy, rapidly making his way toward Matthew from the opposite end of the hanger.

Matthew walked to the end of the loading ramp and anxiously shifted his log book from one hand to the other.

He had met Dewy only once before, when he had first landed on Durin nearly a month ago. Dewy, all muscle, and standing nearly a foot taller than Matthew, had merely sneered at the sight of the smaller craft. Matthew remembered him grumbling, to the delight of one of his deck officers, "Pretty soon we'll be loading the ore in *wagons*, and sending it home with the kiddies."

His long black hair swung wickedly from side to side as he walked, reminding Matthew of the blynabeast he'd seen at the Harvest Festival only a week earlier.

Stopping within a few feet of Matthew's face, Dewy's small dark eyes bore into him, his broad, angular face nearly double Matthew's in size. "Well?" he yelled. "Give me an answer!"

A small group of mechanics, loaders, and guards had begun to gather, becoming more and more interested in the show beginning to unfold.

One guard stepped forward, ahead of everyone else. In his mid-twenties he had a clean-cut appearance—his sturdy frame and short black hair giving one the sense he'd been born to wear the Special Forces uniform—his patronizing smile the only feature defiling an otherwise amiable face. "Need any help, Dewy?"

Dewy turned to address the officer, returning his smirk. "That's quite alright, Dirk. As I've said before, my pilots must answer to *me* first." He swung around and faced Matthew once more. "You can have what's left of him when I'm done."

From the way Dirk was laughing, Matthew sensed he'd heard the line before.

"Matthew Tanner, am I correct?"

The hanger was uncomfortably silent—Matthew's mouth dry as he looked deep into the man's anger-filled eyes. "Th-That's correct."

A humorous smile spread over Dewy's face. "Now we're getting somewhere." His voice rose in volume. "Tell us, son, why did you just crash your freighter in *my* hanger bay?"

Matthew swallowed, completely caught off guard by this twisted turn of events. "My . . . My hand . . . slipped."

Silence.

A deep and rumbling laugh worked its way up and out of the bigger man's throat. He turned to face Dirk and the crowd, pointing at Matthew as he shouted, "Did you hear him? His *hand* slipped!"

The crowd burst into laughter while Matthew offered a faint smile in return—feeling humiliated.

And when Dewy turned back from the crowd, he unexpectedly slapped Matthew's face sharply with the back of his massive right hand, sending him sprawling to the floor. This brought an even louder response from the crowd.

Sitting up, feeling warmth from the blood rushing toward the left side of his face, Matthew couldn't help wondering if anyone had bothered letting *Dewy* know that he was part of the Rebellion.

He remained on the ground as the larger man walked past him, and around to the other side of the *Wanderer* to inspect the damage as the crowd began to disperse.

After a long string of curses, the man returned and pointed a large index finger accusingly at Matthew. "It's bad enough I've got to take the time to load this puny ship of yours, but now I've got to wipe your nose as well!"

Reaching down, he grabbed Matthew's shirt and yanked him roughly to his feet.

His breath stunk as he hollered, "Let's get in this *wagon* of yours and see how bad the frame is! It has removable deck plating I hope?"

Matthew nodded and was then twisted and shoved toward the *Wanderer's* open hatch.

Dewy turned to face what remained of the crowd. "Alright! Everyone back to work! Can't you see I have enough to deal with around here?" He gave Dirk a mock salute. "Everything's under control, *Officer*. Carry on."

Dirk returned the salute, then he and what remained of the onlookers dispersed, laughing and joking, obviously having enjoyed the momentary diversion.

Once inside the *Wanderer*, and out of the crowd's view, Matthew spun around after being shoved forward and stood his ground. "Look! I don't know what's going on here but I thought I did just what you wanted me to do!" As soon as he'd said this it suddenly dawned on Matthew: *What if Dewy wasn't a Rebel after all! What if—*

"Relax, Matt. Relax. I *had* to do what I did. They would have gotten suspicious had I done anything less. Really, Matt. I'm sorry. Let's start over." He extended his meaty hand.

Matthew reached for the side of his face before offering his own. "That's easy for you to say."

Dewy's deep and hearty laugh began to stir once more but was immediately cut short; he apparently didn't want to jeopardize their cover.

After the routine exchange of code phrases, Dewy was all business. "Alright. We don't have much time, so follow me and listen closely."

Matthew followed Dewy toward the cockpit. "I've studied your ship's schematics but I need to check one thing before we really get into this."

Startled, Matthew was about to ask Dewy how he'd gotten a copy of his schematics when the larger man began again.

"Perfect!" Dewy was staring at Matthew's flight console. "Alright. We'll start here. Three hours and sixteen minutes into your flight you're going to monitor your ship's first course correction. As soon as you see the computer's registered it, you're going to manually return to the path you were on when you left Durin. Hold that course for two hours, twelve minutes. Then, drop out of lightspace, reduce your speed to 477.3, increase your relative altitude to about here—" he was pointing at a number on a glass covered dial "and push this button." The button he was referring to belonged to one of three that had at one time controlled a set of landing lights, broken and in need of repair.

"You know about the extra power cells don't you."

"Of course," said Matthew.

"You haven't messed with them have you?"

Matthew thought for a minute. "I used a cell to power the gravity rods in an emergency a while back."

"Oh yeah, the pirates." Dewy nodded. "Pilots are still buzzing about that. I think we'd all written them off years ago—probably all cannibalistic nut baskets by now. We still haven't figured out who they got the bypass from. I've grilled everyone, personally, and no one's talking."

Matthew suppressed a smile. *Do you blame them?*

"From what I heard happened to you, though," continued, Dewy, "I doubt they'll be bothering anyone for quite some time—if at all. You were lucky."

"I know," said Matthew. "I reconnected the cell, though. It's just as it was before."

"Good." Dewy turned and walked to the aft hold. He opened it and stabbed a finger inside. The moment you push that button it's going to trigger the outer door of the hold."

"*Outer* door?" Matthew was puzzled.

"Yours is one of the few remaining ships that can still be accessed from the outside," said Dewy. "It's great for unloading light cargo, but impractical for hauling ore. We use a freighter's existing ramps now. That way we don't have to clutter up the hanger bays with external ones. It's cheaper, it's faster, it's Spire." Dewy paused a moment, snickering at the wittiness of his jab. "I'll run four poles, two at the top of the hold and two at the bottom. Each pair will have a strip of steel running from top pole to bottom pole. They'll hydraulically push whatever cargo's inside gently out of the hold, and then retract. They'll have to extend into Engineering, but I figure if anyone questions you about them you can make up a story about some modification you've been working on." He jerked a thumb toward the secondary hatch switch Matthew and Patch had installed. "Wouldn't be too much of a stretch."

"You'll make sure the freight straps are loose before I leave?"

Dewy smiled. "Of course." He then returned his gaze to the aft hold, filled at the moment with food supplies. "The hold's outer door circuit should still be intact. I'll just use one of your power cells to give it the juice it needs. When the poles have extended, count to five and hit the button again. They should retract and the bay should seal itself up again.

"As soon as the drop's made you will manually change course and gradually arc back to the standard flight path." Dewy gave Matthew the coordinates, altitude, and speed he would need to maintain.

"Accelerate slowly and enter lightspace only when you're back on course. Any course deviations, as well as your changes in speed, and the lightjump, recorded between the first two course corrections, will be erased later—I'll get to that in a minute. Are we clear so far?"

"What about my fuel and distance indicators?" Matthew asked. "Aren't they going to register different values?"

"That's the beauty of the new path; it's shorter. As long as you increase your speed as you gradually get back to the charted path, nobody should notice any significant difference in the readings. The differences in time, distance, and fuel consumption should nearly balance out."

Matthew was impressed.

Dewy continued. "Once you're back on the original flight path, return to lightspace. You'll then have a little under seven hours, after the second course correction, and before the third and final one, to skim ore from the port and starboard holds to make the aft hold appear full again."

"What about the weight and volume scan? Nobody escapes that," Matthew added.

A wicked grin parted the man's thick lips. "Yes. I know."

Dewy walked toward the pilot's chamber, sandwiched between the cockpit and the starboard hold. The room had just enough space for a bunk, a small sink and toilet, and a small closet for personal storage. The large man, nearly filling the room, pointed toward Matthew's bunk. "Underneath your bunk, in the corner, I'll install a small button. You have to manually push it after the second course correction, but before the third one. Just hit it after the second one and then you won't have to worry about it."

"What's it going to do?"

"The switch will activate what I call a 'scrambler' that I'll hide within the casing of another one of your unused power cells. I'll feed it the weight and volume of the ore we've loaded in your aft hold each time you leave here. When you activate it, it will then adjust your ship's sealed onboard computer record. I'll adjust the computer logs here as well. It will also erase your course deviations and the lightjump you've made between the first two course corrections. I'm having you activate it manually in case something should go wrong with the drop. If I had it activate itself, and you weren't able to make the drop, your weight and volume record wouldn't jibe with a scan—we'd be dead in the water at that point. This way, if you can't make the drop, any course deviations could be explained away with a little creativity, while your weight and volume record remained the same."

Matthew still had some concerns. "What if they run a ship's diagnostic? Wouldn't that detect your 'scrambler'?"

"It's been programmed to crash your entire computer system in the event of a diagnostic," Dewy replied. "We're dead in the water if that happens, too, but given the age of your ship, I doubt they'd really suspect us of anything. What *would* die, however, would be the completion of our part of the Rebel plan.

"Really, the only concern I have is that you're able to smoothly cross between the old and new flight paths. Leave the rest of it up to me."

"And you're sure the ore will continue on to Zerith?" asked Matthew.

"Unless something disturbs it, it should continue in a straight line all the way home. It's one of the basic laws of motion."

"Then," said Matthew "why do we plot course corrections in the first place? Why don't we simply plot a direct course to Durin if the ore—?"

"Whoa, Matt." Dewey cut him off. "That's not for us to question." Sensitive to the pressure Matthew was undoubtedly feeling, Dewy gripped the boy's shoulder. "Look, I don't have all of the answers, Matt. We can only deal with what *we've* been given. You'll do your job, and I'll do mine." He gave Matthew's shoulder a squeeze. "You can handle this, Matt. We're in this together."

After reviewing with Matthew one more time the key numbers he would need to remember, Dewy turned. "Now, let's get moving; you've got supplies to unload, and I've got repairs *and* some modifications to make. Stay clear of me. Let *me* handle all the repairs. I'll also need to prepare an accident report for Warring back home. Don't worry, I'm pretty creative when it comes to reports."

It finally dawned on Matthew why Dewy had wanted him to damage the *Wanderer* in the first place; it provided him both the time and the cover he needed to complete the modifications.

Dewy took only a few steps, then turned suddenly. "Say. I anticipate this job will take at least two or three days. The governor's wife's holding a dinner and a dance the day after tomorrow. All of us have been invited—a morale booster. Pick up some decent clothes from upstairs and join us." And then in a sly voice he added, "Six families from Arcona have been invited. Bound to be a few babes your age there to dance with. Besides, staying in the open's the easiest way to avoid suspicion, not to mention boredom."

"Me? At a dance?" Matthew sounded skeptical.

Dewy roared with laughter at the sight of Matthew practically speechless and appearing more than a little embarrassed. His expression had finally given Dewy's loud and obnoxious laugh precisely the excuse it had been waiting for.

CHAPTER 12

Maybe this wasn't *such a great idea.*

It was obvious to Matthew that he had missed the dinner. Beyond the opened doors of the ballroom he noticed several attendants quietly removing flatware, while many of those who had been eating were now dancing to the rich, lilting melody coming from the orchestra playing in the far corner of the ballroom.

For the past few days Matthew had tried to relax, but had found it nearly impossible.

Bored of table games, and having had his fill of swimming, Matthew reluctantly decided to take Dewy's advice and attend the dance that evening. Besides, with the arrival of the governor's invited guests the day before, the more open spaces of the base had filled rapidly, forcing Matthew, who never felt comfortable amidst a crowd of strangers, into retreating to the more peaceful surroundings of the pilots' barracks, where few pilots ever stayed over more than one night. Within this virtual solitude, however, he soon found his thoughts returning again to the loss of his grandfather, and then to the overwhelming demands of his mission for the Rebellion. And so, to keep his mind busy, he had decided that perhaps the dance might not be such a bad idea after all.

Aside from the time it took to finally work up the courage to go, he had wasted nearly an hour trying to figure out how to tie his black bow tie. Had it not been for another pilot's early return to the barracks, he might never have figured it out.

Before entering the ballroom, Matthew straightened his stiff, black jacket once again and self-consciously ran a hand through his thick blond hair—naturally falling into a part—wishing he could have afforded a haircut from the station's barber. The suit rental had claimed the last of what dockins he had.

"May I help you?"

A bit startled, Matthew gave a nod to the stout greeter who'd approached him. He too was dressed in a formal dinner suit, though he sported a white apron around his large middle. "I see I'm too late for the dinner. I was just wondering if it would be alright if I attended the dance?"

"Of course! Please, enter. You have missed the welcome and formal introductions by the governor and his family, but other than that a meal's a meal." His bright, round face beamed, his smile contagious. "Enter and enjoy!"

"Thank you. Thank you very much."

Passing through the entrance, Matthew was astounded by the ballroom itself. The walls and ceiling, made almost entirely of glass, afforded Matthew an incredible view of the moon and the dark sky above. The faint glow of Zerith's sun intermingled with the even fainter stars that dotted the blackened sky—a stark contrast to the environment Matthew was used to back home.

He had, of course, admired the view before from the many windows that surrounded the station, as well as from the *Wanderer's* cockpit. But to actually stand in a room where the blackness of space seemed to encompass him was breathtaking.

Light from the elegant, crystal chandeliers overhead was dim, and the melodious richness of the orchestra only added to the awe and splendor of the atmosphere surrounding him.

Matthew immediately noticed an ornamented table that ran along the wall to his left, supplying light dessert and drink for the nearly one hundred or so in attendance. Drawn to the far end of the table, he quickly picked up a drink to give himself something to do as he took a moment to adjust to the unfamiliar surroundings.

Several potted trees, with vines running randomly from one wall to the next, lined the edges of the great glass walls, giving a touch of life to the barren landscape beyond the thick glass.

Comfortable with the layout of the room, Matthew began studying the faces of the many smiling, well-dressed guests, searching hopefully for a familiar face.

It didn't take long to realize that Dewy had been right; there *were* several young ladies present, no doubt friends of the daughters of the visiting families. The gowns were incredible in both their color and extravagance. As elegant and refined as *they* appeared, however, Matthew had little trouble distinguishing the visiting guests from the station's more permanent employees. Hardened from years of mine work, the men and women of the mines appeared a bit rougher around the edges—enjoying the evening's festivities in spite of the formalities.

Matthew presumed morale was everything within such an isolated and potentially claustrophobic existence, and admired the governor for respecting his employees enough to include them in his activities, giving them the chance to cut loose with him every once in a while. Then again, maybe he had little choice in the matter—a recent reminder concerning the potential of inconvenienced citizens quickly coming to mind.

He recognized some of the faces from the few days he'd spent at the station, but none with any real familiarity.

He spied Dewy laughing, towering above the young lady he was dancing with, but knew to keep his distance. The man had continued to rail on Matthew whenever the opportunity presented itself, complaining of how much extra work the young man was causing him. But knowing just where the man stood made the confrontations bearable. And Matthew felt he was doing a good job at playing the part of the Intimidated Pilot. *Of course, with Dewy,* he thought, *who wouldn't?*

He quickly brought the drink to his lips in an effort to suppress a laugh. *I'm amazed they actually have a suit that fits him!* He took a sip of his punch, and found his thoughts suddenly turning to Rollyn.

The boy had always made new experiences, such as this, easier, giving Matthew the extra nudge he had always needed. He would have loved the chance to bounce his mission off of the boy beforehand, but one of the last things the man from the cave had warned Matthew about was the need for complete secrecy. He felt bad having to leave Rollyn completely in the dark, but was grateful that he seemed to understand. Almost pleading, Rollyn made Matthew promise that the moment his work was no longer a secret, he would come clean on everything.

Rollyn was also gutsier, socially, and found it easy to mingle with girls his own age. He'd tried convincing Matthew that girls *often* took an interest in him, and if he'd simply look up every once in a while he'd notice their glances too. But Matthew found the suggestion ridiculous, chalking all of it up to Rollyn's gift of exaggeration.

This year Rollyn *had* succeeded in persuading Matthew to go with him to the outdoor dance of the Harvest Festival, but only after significant begging and pleading. He'd had fun, he had to admit, and had even danced a little, but as he studied the elegant ballroom before him now, he realized that dance had been considerably more relaxed than this one; and it was precisely *this* thought that made Matthew realize just how out of place he was.

I don't belong here.

Placing his empty glass on a passing silver cart, he headed for the door.

As he politely made his way around clusters of people busily socializing, he happened to glance across the room . . . and unexpectedly found himself looking directly into the most beautiful pair of eyes he had ever seen. Their eyes had locked for only a split second, but for Matthew it had been as if she'd physically touched him.

An instant later she turned and, with a friend, proceeded to walk toward the orchestra.

"Excuse me. Can I get by?" Without realizing it, Matthew had blocked the entrance, and quickly moved aside to let an attendant pushing a small catering cart go by—losing sight of the young woman in the process.

Intrigued by this new and startling sensation, and forgetting all about his earlier feelings of self-doubt, Matthew slowly made his way through the crowd in an effort to see her again, to see if in fact he'd really felt what he thought he'd felt—whatever *that* was.

A minute later he found her talking and laughing with her friend near one of the potted trees. What caught Matthew's eye first was the gown she was wearing. Her friend, along with most of the women, wore what he considered brightly colored works of art—elaborate and, in some cases, Matthew felt, ridiculously extravagant. This girl, however, was wearing a more simple, white gown—close fitting and trimmed in delicate lace that seemed to draw his gaze to her face . . . and those eyes.

Another glance triggered the same unexplainable feeling Matthew had felt earlier.

She was beautiful; the red highlights in her auburn hair reflected the dim light from above.

A dancing couple brushing up against him seemed to push him slightly closer, placing him only a few feet from her, reminding him of why everyone, including himself, was there in the first place. "Excuse me. Would you like to dance?"

At first her light brown eyes had appeared startled at his question, making Matthew want to dart for the door out of pure embarrassment. But when her eyes brightened, and she smiled, accepting his hand, Matthew knew he could hold off on his retreat—for now, anyway.

His heart pounding, Matthew placed his right hand at the small of her back, and extended his left hand with hers. Awkwardly he struggled to concentrate on the rhythm of the music, consciously focusing on the movement of his feet. "I'm sorry. I'm not that great of a dancer. I haven't had much practice."

The young girl smiled. "You're doing fine. Just relax a bit. That's it. See, nothing to it." He smiled at the compliment, knowing she was simply being polite.

"It's a beautiful ball, don't you think?" She was trying hard to put him at ease.

"Yes, I can—" As he spoke, he lost his concentration, inadvertently catching her foot under his own. "I—I'm sorry. Are you alright?"

The young girl simply laughed as Matthew stopped moving, standing rigid with concern. "Trust me, you're not the first one to step on my foot tonight. I'm fine. Really." She held up her hands and waited for his. "We'll dance for a bit before I ask you another question. Fair enough?"

Blushing from embarrassment, Matthew gratefully took her hand.

Seconds passed as the two danced, Matthew looking straight ahead—concentrating. Soon, however, he relaxed, finding his rhythm. When he finally did look down, she was looking up—smiling. "See, nothing to it. You're a natural," she said.

Matthew laughed. "Careful. By talking with me you run the risk of serious personal injury."

She laughed and then assumed a more serious expression. "I do so appreciate the warning. However, I think you should know that you're looking at a girl who doesn't flinch easily."

"Is that so?"

"That's so," she teased, looking him directly in the eye. "Go ahead, talk to me, I dare you!"

Matthew grinned at her theatrics, causing her to break up laughing in the process.

Just then the music ended. He let go of her hand and joined the rest of those on the floor in lightly applauding the orchestra. Turning, Matthew leaned over. "I appreciated your willingness to dance with disaster. Perhaps a little later—"

When she took his left hand and raised it, her right hand going around his waist, he was startled. "One more dance, alright? I don't think you're safe out there just yet. It's not just me I'm worried about; I owe it to all of the other girls out there."

Matthew laughed. "What a martyr."

The two continued dancing, gradually working their way to the center of the dance floor, and from a distance Matthew caught a quick wink from Dewy who also happened to be dancing; thankfully he was keeping his distance.

"So, If I may be so bold, what part of Arcona are you from?" she asked.

Matthew looked down, suddenly feeling awkward all over again. He stammered, not really knowing how to answer her—afraid of how she might feel about Outsiders. "Oh, well, it's one of . . . the more obscure districts. You've probably never heard of it." And, in an attempt to change the subject, asked, "So, were you able to attend this year's festival?"

At this, her face brightened. "I did! Wasn't it fantastic?"

"It was."

"I just loved this year's play."

"Play? You enjoy the theater, too?"

"I look forward to it every year!"

"I can't get enough of it, either."

Suddenly Matthew noticed her expression change. "Tell me," she began with noticeable caution, what did you think of the final scene between Lyll and Tobia?"

Matthew appeared puzzled. "Well, I'm sure it would have been a great scene . . . had they been in it. But Lyll and Tobia were the primary characters in last year's play, not this year's."

The young girl was beaming. "Quite true. You're absolutely right."

"Why do I get the feeling I'm being tested?"

She flushed, obviously embarrassed. "I'm sorry. It's just sometimes people agree with me when . . . never mind. Tell me, what did you think was the best part of this year's play?"

Matthew grinned. "Tell you what, why don't you tell me what your favorite part was first, that way *I'll* know we've seen the same play?"

"Touché. I'd have to say the final scene—when Judith and Camille reveal their love for the same man . . . I don't think I've ever seen that much emotion on stage—why are you laughing?"

"Oh, please. It was that scene that blew the whole thing. You can't tell me that you would let—"

"It could happen!"

"Sure."

"Are you disagreeing with me?" she asked, cocking her eyebrow.

Matthew smiled at her apparent shock. "Yes I am. Why? Don't I have the right to?" And for several seconds Matthew held her gaze. Then, feeling a bit nonplussed, he quickly began offering his opinions on this year's actors, which eventually led to a discussion on the subtler nuances of some of the more memorable dialogue each had remembered. As they talked, Matthew was taken aback with how bright and witty she was, enjoying how closely many of her opinions and observations mirrored his own. She had a sparkle in her eye and a zest for life that Matthew found refreshing, and appealing. And though the music had changed, taking on a peppier beat, the two remained lost in their conversation, oblivious to their surroundings.

It was several minutes before either of them caught on to how ridiculous they looked dancing slowly to an entirely different tempo. And both blushed at the snickers aimed in their direction. Matthew grinned in embarrassment. "Sorry. I'll start paying more attention."

The two parted, dancing with energy and smiling throughout the next number.

When the tempo slowed once again, Matthew chuckled. "You know, I haven't even told you my name."

She accepted his hand without hesitation, and fell into step naturally. "You're right, Mr. Dangerous, you haven't." She dropped her eyes. "But you know mine?"

"How could I?" He waited until she looked up again. "I'm Matthew."

When she spoke it was with a shyness Matthew guessed rarely displayed itself. "My name is Rebecca. My friends call me Becca."

"Well, it's truly a pleasure to meet you, Becca. You're a brave woman." Both smiled. "I must apologize, though. I asked you for one dance and I seem to have lost count of the number of selections that have gone by. I hope I haven't embarrassed or hurt you too much."

Rebecca moved in closer. "Not at all, Matthew. Believe me, it's been refreshing." Rebecca placed her head against his shoulder, the music seeming to sway them both with little effort on their part.

His heart pounded, and Matthew closed his eyes, basking in a moment he'd never thought possible. He was an Outsider—a nobody. And yet here he was at a ball, dancing with a girl that had stolen his heart with merely a glance. *I don't think I've ever felt happier*, thought Matthew. All doubt, insecurity, and worldly stress melted away as their bodies kept time to the soft romantic sounds coming from the orchestra.

"Excuse me!"

Startled, Matthew and Rebecca both turned to find the young, Special Forces Officer Matthew had seen two days earlier standing before them. "Well, well. If it isn't Matthew Tanner."

Rebecca rolled her eyes. "Back off, Dirk."

Dirk gave her a patronizing stare. "Miss Rebecca, my job at these functions is to ensure your safety."

From his tone of voice, and the way Dirk glanced at him, Matthew thought he detected a hint of jealousy in the officer; he was sure his concern went much deeper than mere protection. "If you don't mind, I'll be cutting in." He then placed a hand on Matthew's chest and slowly, forcefully, pushed him aside.

Rebecca was furious. "Dirk, you have no right—"

"Oh but I do. I promised your father and mother, who left an hour ago, that I'd keep you safe from any riffraff tonight, as I always do." He tossed Matthew a disdainful look. "And I consider *him* riffraff. I let it go for a while tonight, but the sight of him holding you was making me sick. Perhaps you'd like to wash your hands?"

Matthew was seething. But before he could speak, Dirk moved in for the kill. "Don't you know what this guy is?"

Rebecca forcefully pulled her hands free of Dirk's, a move that caused many to stop dancing to watch. "He's an ore hauler. And not a very good one at that. Isn't that right, Matthew?" Rebecca, about to protest, was suddenly cut short. "Hey, you don't have to take my word for it. He busted up his little freighter landing just the other day." And then, over his shoulder, "Isn't that right, Dewy?"

Several eyes turned as Dewy, who'd been watching the tiff with interest, snarled, "That's right!" Matthew saw the disdain in Dewy's face, but caught the painful apology in his eyes.

Dirk glowered at Matthew. "Now, being a hauler isn't necessarily a horrible thing, but he's an Outsider as well. Hardly suitable for you, my dear."

All the anger that had filled Matthew's heart was suddenly replaced with shame. He quickly looked into Rebecca's eyes; they were full of surprise. "But, Matthew, I thought you said—"

Matthew cut in, embarrassed. "I'm sorry, Rebecca. I . . . I guess I should have been more clear." He looked around at the crowd surrounding them. By now the band had stopped playing and the rumbling of curious voices began working its way through the crowd.

"Thank you for the dance, Becca. I guess it's time for me to be leaving." Matthew turned, humiliated, and worked his way through the crowd.

The conductor of the orchestra rapped his baton against his music stand and rapidly gave the signal for the next number as Matthew made his way to the door. *What was I thinking? An Outsider with an Arconian?*

Passing through the doorway, Matthew painfully left behind the distant, jazzy sounds of the orchestra, the wry grin of a cocky officer, and the hurt-filled eyes of a young woman who, only minutes earlier, had found herself falling in love.

* * *

"That was some girl you danced with tonight." His grandfather flashed him a quick wink and a smile.

"She was pretty incredible."

"You don't sound too excited, Matthew. What's wrong?"

Matthew's arms and hands opened wide. "What's the point in getting my hopes up, Papa? I don't have a prayer with someone like her!"

Paul's brow furrowed in confusion. "What do you mean, boy?"

"Oh, come on. Isn't it obvious? She may have found me a little interesting, but we both know that's as far as it's ever going to go. Dirk's right! She's from Arcona; I'm the garbage thrown over the wall—an Outsider. What does a guy like me have to offer a girl like that?"

Paul gave the boy a minute to calm down and cleared his throat before beginning. "Matthew. Listen to me."

Matthew inhaled, his mouth opening.

"Tut! I said listen to me."

The boy's mouth clamped shut as he looked down at his folded arms, frustrated.

"Matthew, you have more than the Tanner charm. You have the Tanner will." He extended a hand, keeping Matthew from responding. "You say you have little to offer. Just what is it you think you really need?"

Matthew let out a laugh. "I'd at least like to be able to provide a roof and food for her—"

"Whoa! Hold on now. You talk as if you intend on marrying her tomorrow."

"No. That's not . . . I don't know what I mean!" His eyes seemed to be focusing on something distant. "Her eyes, Papa. When she looked at me . . . I felt . . . I felt as if she was looking right into my heart. My stomach . . ."

"Matthew, you've had girlfriends before. Didn't they make you feel the same way?"

"No, Papa. That's just it. When our eyes met for the first time, it was as if my heart was saying, 'Oh, there you are.'" Matthew let his body flop against the back of his chair. "I don't know how to explain it."

As Paul sat back and studied the boy's face, a knowing expression began to form. "Oh, Matthew. I know what you're saying. I felt the same way when I met your grandmother."

Matthew immediately sat up. "Then you should understand me when I tell you that it's hopeless."

"Hopeless?" Paul chuckled. "Few things are ever hopeless, Matthew."

"But how would I ever be able to provide for someone like her?"

"Just what is it you feel you have to provide?"

"Well, like I was saying before, at least decent food and shelter!"

"And that's good. I agree with you."

Matthew spread his arms in a hopeless gesture. "But all I've got is this!"

"And just what will it take to obtain something better? 'More suitable,' if that's what you feel you need."

"Papa, don't you see? I'm an Ousider. I'm not permitted to have anything better than what I've got."

"What about this revolution you're fighting for. Won't it—"

"But it could be years before I'm able to earn what she deserves! And that's if we succeed! If we don't . . ." Matthew's face fell into his hands at the futility of even imagining a life with such a woman.

Paul scooted his chair closer and placed a hand on his knee. "Matthew, I've always taught you that with hard work, patience, and determination, any dream is possible. I still believe that."

Matthew didn't bother looking up. "But this revolution . . . when it's over, it might take forever for the dust to settle."

"Huh! Boy, where I am, I see forever. Let me tell you something: three, five, ten years is nothing compared to an eternity."

"If I became an Arconian citizen, I'd have everything I needed in a week." It was stated under his breath, he hadn't really intended for his grandfather to hear it.

It was Paul's turn to straighten in his chair. "And if you did that, I'd want nothing to do with you!"

He realized his words had come out a little more harsh than he had intended, and he quickly added, "Son, you've got a strong mind and an able body. The only thing you're lacking is perspective. You're not taking a moment to consider what might lie ahead of what you can see.

"If being able to provide for a girl, and eventually a family, is what you want, then buckle down and work for it.

"Yes, Arcona, Spire, could hand it all to you next week if you accepted their handouts and terms. But what have I always said about that? What do they rob people of in the process?"

Matthew remained silent.

"Character, Matthew. That's what they're robbing their citizens of. It's through struggle and hardship that character is molded and shaped. And if people are deprived of that opportunity, and it is an opportunity, Matthew, then how can they possibly be expected to grow? They can't. They'll never really

progress. They'll remain weak and dependent, unable to take care of themselves."

"I know, Papa. I know."

"You could have it all next week, if that's what you want, Matthew. But it will mean so much more to you if you can earn it for yourself."

Matthew mumbled something under his breath.

"What was that?"

Matthew looked up and began to laugh. "I just remembered something you told me a long time ago."

"What's that?"

"Remember when I was repairing the roof? I think I was twelve at the time."

Paul nodded.

"It was hot and I was sweating something fierce. I started to whine about it, trying to earn a little sympathy. Just when I thought I had you convinced the work was too hard, you looked right up at me and said, 'Sweating flushes out the evil, boy; purifies the heart.' Then you walked off to fetch the day's water."

"And the roof's held up well, hasn't it?"

"It has."

Paul patted Matthew's knee. "So have you."

Tears came to Matthew's eyes. "Thanks, Papa. It means a lot to me . . . to hear you say that."

The two sat in silence, each lost in their own thoughts.

"Papa, I know I've mentioned this before, but . . . I sure wish I could remember our talks when I'm awake. It would make things a lot easier."

"Boy, you've got a sensitive spirit. It'll remember everything we've discussed. The essence of our discussions will always be there. You just keep doing what's right, no matter how hard it might seem, and you'll have what you need when you need it. I promise."

CHAPTER 13

With only four minutes remaining until the *Wanderer's* computer initiated the first of three course corrections, Matthew again wiped the sweat from his hands on the legs of his gray flight suit.

Spire's pilots had been trained to monitor each and every course correction in the event of computer failure. However, given the fact that there had only been two recorded accidents, and those nearly thirty years earlier, it was rare for veteran pilots to give the course grid even a glance during flight. For Matthew, it was the only object he was focusing on.

A small green dot represented his ship and was moving ever so slowly along a permanently etched background, making the last few minutes feel like a lifetime. The numbers to the left of the graphic were counting down the seconds to the engagement of the computer's first corrective subroutine.

Throughout the past several minutes, after clearing Durin's hangar bay, entering lightspace, and initiating his autopilot, Matthew had spent his time examining Dewy's work—getting to know the modifications that were now putting his young life in jeopardy. It had helped to pass the time and get his mind off of pirates, his grandfather, and . . . Rebecca.

Now, with only seconds remaining, Matthew was anxiously preparing to break away from what had always been regarded as the only safe route between Zerith and Durin.

Twenty seconds.

His hands gripped the controls; his eyes locked on the course grid.

The Rebels know what they're doing.

Doubt began tickling his heart.

They chose me. I can do this!

At that instant, the program engaged.

Locking onto new coordinates.

Shifting . . . shifting . . . locked!

Matthew gently turned the nose of his ship, which disengaged the *Wanderer's* autopilot—standard protocol in the event of an emergency. He watched closely as the locator coordinates scrolled to their previous value.

Unaware he had been holding his breath, he released it, simultaneously relaxing the wince tightening his face.

With the first course correction logged into his flight computer, he engaged the autopilot and sat back in his chair, the blurred and distorted images of lightspace masking his forward view port.

"Well, that's that."

A few more deep breaths found him in a more reflective mood, and as he stared at the familiar, unfocused collage of light ahead, his mind went immediately to Rebecca.

It had taken him quite some time to fall asleep the night before and he rubbed his burning eyes with the heels of his hands. *I . . . I can't shake her. I just can't shake her.* He *had* arisen this morning feeling better than he had expected to; the messenger who had let him know he was clear to leave gave him little time to shake off the morning stupor. "Dewy wants you ready to fly in ten minutes!" he'd called out. And then, over his shoulder added, "Says he's sick of looking at you."

Matthew now smiled at the flippant remark. Though many had stared and snickered at him the night before, he knew that in Dewy he had at least *one* friend on Durin—whether anyone else knew it or not. Outwardly, this giant of a man appeared to be a beast, but inwardly, Matthew believed Dewy to be a kindhearted man.

Kindhearted . . . like . . . And for the next two and a half hours his thoughts returned to Rebecca—her eyes, her laugh, her beautiful face, the look of interest she had shown toward his thoughts and opinions, the haunting echoes of the music, the feel of her hand . . . and the look of shock in her face.

When his eyes glanced at the course grid, his head shot upward, his back ramrod straight. *Three minutes! I nearly missed it!*

"Focus, Tanner. Focus!" *You have to concentrate! There's too much at stake!*

He continued berating himself, both verbally and mentally, as his fingers hovered over the lightspace toggles.

A moment later, he flipped the switches—lightspace gradually coalescing into real space.

Reducing his speed to the assigned level, and adjusting his altitude in relation to the standard flight path, he hesitated pressing the button Dewy had assigned him.

He swallowed. *Here it goes.*

Jabbing the button, he listened as a heavy rattle, lasting only a second, let him know the aft hold's outer door had opened, the sudden shift in air pressure jostling the loose crates of ore.

The grumble and hiss of a hydraulic unit reassured Matthew that Dewy's contraption was at work.

After several minutes the hissing stopped. Matthew counted to five and jabbed the button a second time.

That click had to have been the outer door.

For the next half hour he focused intently on his coordinates, altitude, and speed, manually guiding the *Wanderer* back to the charted flight path.

Once there, he reentered lightspace, engaged his autopilot, and leaped out of the pilot's chair, racing to the door of the aft hold.

Standing to the side of the door, with his body pressed against the wall, he triggered its release.

Air was immediately sucked into the depressurized hold. Matthew, ears popping with the change in air pressure, stared at the empty space in triumph. *It worked!* His head spun with euphoria. "I did it!"

Granted, he would spend the next several hours moving ore, and he still needed to activate Dewy's scrambler. But both of those actions would be performed within the safety of the charted flight path. The real *physical* danger was over.

Letting out a *"Whoop!"* Matthew started to retrieve his freight dolly, only to find himself stopping to gaze soberly once more at the empty hold.

Before, his involvement in the Rebellion had been minor, if not an unconscious effort. If he had ever been confronted with what he'd done, he could always have feigned ignorance. And, for the most part, he'd have been telling the truth. But this—this was different; for what he'd now done went far beyond that.

With the dumping of a small load of ore, Matthew Tanner was now, undeniably, part of the Rebellion.

CHAPTER 14

No alarms. No rushing troops.

A weight and volume scan was made the moment a freighter was on the ground. It took only seconds. The fact that his landing had been completely uneventful was a good sign he'd passed.

With his log book in hand he slowly made his way to the starboard hatch, his body aching from the ore he'd finished skimming only a few hours earlier. He was greeted by a very familiar face. "Saw your name on the incoming list. How'd it go?"

"It's good to see you, Rolly. I was beginning to forget what a *friendly* face looked like." He mussed the boy's hair as he passed him.

"Wow!" he shouted theatrically. "That's the first time anyone's said they were glad to see *me*!"

Matthew turned with a grin. "Don't let it go to your head, Rolly. I'm not *that* happy."

Rollyn's face fell at the teasing remark but just as quickly recovered as he rushed to catch up with him.

As they strode to the Security Office, Rollyn asked excitedly, "Well?"

"Well, what?"

"So have you finished your mission?"

Matthew froze in place and quickly shushed his friend. "Are you crazy? Keep your voice down, Rolly!" He looked around, making sure they hadn't drawn any attention. "This isn't something you discuss idly. You know better than that."

"Sorry, Matt. I . . . I guess I just lost my head. Sorry."

There were those big brown eyes again.

"Ah, forget it. Look, I thought I told you before I left I'd tell you all about it when I was through."

"But aren't you thr—"

"No. It's going to be quite a while I'm afraid. It's . . . *ongoing*. Really, Rolly, don't ask me again, alright? It's taking everything I have to keep my nerves from snapping as it is. I don't want to have to worry about the questions you'll ask every time we're together. Alright?"

Rollyn nodded and tried to look mature, but Matthew knew he'd have a hard time of it. He understood. *How long* was *it going to last anyway?* Even *he* wasn't sure.

He considered bringing up the dance as a way of changing the subject, but wasn't quite ready to delve into that just yet, either. He decided to keep walking instead.

To Matthew's relief, the security officer stamped his log book with hardly a glance.

I'm clear then. Dewy's scrambler's going to work!

Rollyn interrupted Matthew's private celebration, asking him if he would be riding home with him after work on the evening transport. He said he would and watched as the boy sprinted back to his department, grateful the boy was looking and acting like his old self again. He'd never forget the day Rollyn had delivered the news about his grandfather; he was a good friend.

Reluctantly, he glanced toward his freighter. A team of workers were already making their way to the *Wanderer* with portable ore lifts and dollies. He stretched his sore and tired muscles. *Well, there's one thing I do know for sure about this mission: I'm going to be in great shape when I'm through.*

Matthew's face was dripping with sweat when Miller approached him from behind. "Well, well, well. So, how's our *Mover* and *Shaker?*"

Matthew was just beginning to wheel his dolly up the *Wanderer's* starboard ramp to secure it. He turned, curious as to why his friend was so happy. "Hey, Miller. I guess you heard why I was late."

"Oh, you bet I did. But it's been a few days. Warring's had a chance to cool off a bit. He wants a word with you when you're finished unloading."

"I'll bet he does." Matthew continued up the ramp with the dolly.

"Well, these things happen." Miller's voice then took on a more playful tone. "And such a shame for you, having to just sit around, eat . . . go to dances . . ."

Matthew had just about reached the hatch, but stopped, feeling a bit uncomfortable. He tried changing the subject. "So, where's Patch?"

"Locked him in the men's room this morning," he answered matter-of-factly.

"Locked him in?"

"The twerp was bragging about how well he could crack any lock on the planet. Electronic ones, mind you."

"And?"

"So when he paid the room a visit I scrambled the lock." He glanced at his watch. "Been about three hours now."

"He's going to be furious!"

"Patch? Naw, he loves challenges like this." He laughed. "But, hey, you're changing the subject on me."

"I don't know what you're talking about."

"Is that so?" He took out a small envelope from the arm pocket of his grease-stained coveralls. Holding it at arm's length he squinted at the writing. "So, I guess the name *Rebecca* doesn't mean anything to you."

Matthew dropped the dolly he'd been leaning on, leaped off the ramp, and snatched the envelope from Miller's hand. "Where'd you get this?"

Miller was obviously enjoying himself. "From Collins. Came in ten minutes ago. Said she'd begged him to make sure you got this. He gave it to me when I mentioned I was coming over here to see how you were doing."

The words, "Matthew Tanner," were written on the outside of the envelope.

Even her writing's unique.

"Kid, you must have what it takes. It isn't everyone that can sweep the governor's daughter off her feet."

Matthew's heart stopped.

He looked at Miller. "What are you talking about?"

"Rebecca. *Rebecca Adams*—daughter of Durin's governor, Mitchell Adams." Miller's face lost some of its cheer. "Don't tell me you didn't know!"

"I . . ."

At this Miller laughed out loud. "Well, go easy, kid. She's one of the *Elite*." He laughed some more. "I've got to go tell Patch. He'll kill me for letting him out early, but this is too good."

As his friend departed, laughing and shaking his head, Matthew was still standing in shock as he stared at the envelope in his hand. *How could I have been so stupid?*

He opened the envelope, taking care not to damage it too much. He unfolded the sheet of paper and cautiously read:

Dear Matthew,

I want you to know how sorry I am for what happened at the dance tonight. Dirk is an idiot! He's been after me for the last two years—about as long as he's been here I guess. I made the mistake of going out with him a few times, and ever since then he can't seem to let go. He shows a different side to my parents that I think they've bought into—Dad more than Mom and I'm really quite sick of it.

I also want to apologize for not being very honest with you myself—about my father being Governor. At first, I thought you knew. And then, when I saw that you didn't, I didn't want you to. That may sound crazy to you, Matthew, but, trust me, it's not easy living under my father's shadow. For once I was just enjoying talking with a guy who treated me like a person, and not The Governor's Daughter. You weren't afraid to disagree with me and share your true feelings. Do I make any sense? I'm not very good at letter writing. The point I'm trying to make is that I guess we both had our reasons for hiding behind "masks."

He turned the paper over.

Matthew, I want you to know how much I enjoyed being with you. It was fun talking with someone who not only shared some of my interests, but felt as passionately about them as you do. You're different from any of the guys I know. You seem caring, respectful, and, I know this is going to sound ridiculous, but you made me laugh. By the way, the final scene in "Will You Be There?" <u>was</u> the greatest of all scenes and just accept that and move on!

Matthew smiled, recalling their brief debate.

I want you to know that I don't think any less of you for where you were raised. In fact, I admire you for what you've become. You're a gentleman—,

Matthew. You really are. I know my parents wouldn't exactly be thrilled knowing I was writing to you, which is why I'm sending this letter with one of the pilots. I know if they met you they'd see what a good person you are.

I just had to share my feelings with you, Matthew. I enjoyed the dance, sore toe and all, and hope there's some way we can keep in touch. Please don't forget me.

With love,
Becca

He read the letter at least ten more times on the ride home later that evening. And with Rollyn crammed right against his shoulder, sneaking peaks at the letter, he felt obligated to tell him all about the dance and Dirk.

Several times Rollyn jabbed Matthew in his ribs saying, "I told you dances weren't stupid. I told you." He also pestered him for a complete description of Rebecca, which Matthew surrendered, Rollyn oohing and aahing at every detail.

When they parted at the terminal, Matthew proceeded to read the letter again as he walked home. He couldn't get over the fact that *she* was asking for *his* forgiveness, that she actually found him interesting. He then struggled with how he was going to be able to write back. He couldn't simply mail a letter—not yet anyway. And then he wondered how a relationship of this kind would affect his mission for the Rebellion, if it was even possible to maintain. Given his present surroundings, it was obvious that they came from separate worlds. Did a relationship like theirs even have a chance?

As difficult as these issues were, Matthew willed them away for the time being; he felt happy, and . . . he just wanted to savor that for a while.

Carefully folding the letter, he slipped it back into his pocket as he turned the corner of a long row of shanties. He stopped, staring at his own sandwiched between the many others in the distance. He didn't want to be alone right now. The sight of his grandfather's cane and chair would only bring him down.

And then a thought came to mind. *The Smiths mentioned something about their roof leaking during the last storm. Maybe I'll go over and see what I can do.*

He smiled and looked skyward. "I don't want to start feeling sorry for myself, Papa. Time to sweat a little."

Having successfully completed his first mission for the Rebellion, with only a minor lecture from Warring, and realizing now that Rebecca truly *did* care about him, regardless of his being an Outsider, Matthew felt as though he were on top of the world.

He'd continue fulfilling his assignment for the Rebellion, because he knew it was the right thing to do. But somehow, somewhere, he would also see Rebecca again—Dirk or no Dirk. He was sure of it.

A newfound confidence began filling his chest over the turn his life was now taking, and with it the determination that nobody, absolutely nobody, was going to stand in the way of his success.

* * *

"Ah, Harris. Please, have a seat." Spire's CEO motioned toward the sofa with his hand.

"Thank you. Well, I must say, *you* look refreshed. I take it you *enjoyed* yourself?"

"I always do," he drawled, chuckling, in spite of himself. He then reclined in his chair and folded his arms across his chest, his voice becoming playful. "I haven't been completely out of touch, though."

"No?"

"I saw on the Information Network a few days back that we suffered a bit of an *accident* up north."

Harris's response was sarcastic. "Oh, yes! Terrible. Absolutely terrible. Thankfully only two men died in the explosion."

The CEO was enjoying this and continued playing along. "Anybody I know?"

"As a matter of fact . . . you *do* know them: a Corporal Lou Pierson and an Officer Jacob Saunders—two of our *finest* officers from the wall. A shame they never had the chance to enjoy their promotions as the plant's newest administrators."

"I hope you sent our condolences to their families. I'd hate for them to think of us as insensitive."

"It's all been taken care of," smiled Harris.

"Excellent!" His nephew had done a fantastic job tidying up the *problem* and he was proud of him.

The CEO's mood turned serious with his next question. "And what has our team learned from their search of the Tanner place?" Strangely enough, the murder had gnawed at him the entire week of his vacation. Now that he was back, he was determined to put the issue to rest.

"Nothing, I'm afraid."

That had *not* been the answer he'd been hoping for. "Nobody would talk, huh?"

"No—no, that's not it. Everyone our team talked with had seemed more than willing to share what they knew—surprisingly cooperative. It's just there wasn't anything out of the ordinary that caught anyone's attention that day."

"If I recall correctly, Tanner had been beaten and shot. The door had also been badly damaged by gunfire. You're telling me now that no one heard any of that?"

"He suffered two blows to the body, and one to the head—a blunt object of some kind was used, probably his own cane. He'd also been shot twice. Tanner probably struggled before being hit over the head, then beaten as he fell to the floor, and shot afterward. What *I* find interesting is that the door had taken more bullets than he had. Whoever did it also took the time to slice the door's top leather hinge."

"And nobody heard any of those shots?"

"An older, projectile weapon *was* used. A silencer would have been suffi—"

"But there still would have been some noise made when the bullets hit the door."

Our agents tell me it's pretty noisy over there—lots of babies crying, children playing, dogs barking. They tell me it's quite possible all of this could have been done without anyone hearing—"

"So what you're telling me is that we *still* don't know who did it?" The CEO was visibly frustrated; Spire had all of the latest advances in science on their side and it frustrated him that they still couldn't determine just who was responsible for Tanner's death.

"We have the shell casings from the floor and the bullets from the door. The lab's looking at them now."

The CEO took a moment to digest that, his fingernails rhythmically tapping the top of the steel desk.

Harris cleared his throat. "Besides, what does it matter anyway? You're aware of Tanner's record. I say good riddance!"

The CEO continued staring into space.

"Is there some *secret* you're keeping from me?" Harris asked. "Why are you so obsessed with his murder? He's dead. As far as Outsiders go, I would have thought that to be enough."

"Because I've had time to think about it," the CEO answered, irritated.

"The lab will let me know the moment they have—"

"He had a boy, didn't he."

It was a statement. Harris took it as a question. "Of course. His grandson. I don't recall his name offhand, but if you'll—"

"Matthew."

"What's that?"

"The boy. His name is Matthew. What's he up to these days?"

"I believe he's an ore hauler. Worked in freight for some time before that. In fact, I seem to recall him being the one—"

"The pirates tried to capture," finished the CEO, looking up at Harris. "A Tanner's a Tanner, Harris." He smiled at the look of confusion on his nephew's face. "Anything new on that attack since the last report?"

"I can check and see what Warring's come up with. *I'm* not aware of anything."

Silence followed again as the CEO resumed drumming his fingers.

"Sir, are you sure there isn't something I should know?"

The older man looked at his nephew, seeming to notice him for the first time. He smiled, realizing how distracted he probably appeared. "No, Harris. Forget about it for now. You're right; it's in the past. I'm sure I'm just being a bit paranoid."

"If it's this Matthew Tanner you're worried about, I can have—"

"No, Harris. It's alright. Just be sure and let me know if anything new develops—with either case."

"Of course," replied Harris, who began pulling out a set of notes from his silver attache case, only to stop in mid-motion. "You know, we've searched his home. All this Matthew has left is the freighter he flies. We could search it, run a diagnostic, look for anything unusual. Perhaps that would help to put your mind at ease."

The CEO sat back and looked directly into the younger man's eyes a moment before responding. "Yes. Perhaps that *would* settle me. Why don't you do that. I'm sure I'm being paranoid, but it wouldn't hurt to check. Thank you, Harris."

"My pleasure. Now, shall I fill you in on this year's earnings from the Harvest Festival?"

A more relaxed CEO nodded, leaned completely back in his chair, and clasped his hands behind his head as he prepared himself for the good news.

PART TWO

EVERLASTING LOVE

CHAPTER 15

They would be together in only twenty minutes and, for Matthew, the wait seemed unbearable. He wiped the sweat from his forehead onto the sleeve of his flight suit as he handed the Durin security officer his logbook.

"You check in *before* you unload your cargo."

"Sorry. I guess my mind's somewhere else. It won't happen ag—"

The surly officer stamped his book without showing the least bit of interest in his apology. "See that it doesn't, Tanner. Or next time I'll write you up."

"Right." Grabbing his log book Matthew sprinted for his ship. Normally he would have had at least four hours of down time. But the untimely delay of the previous hauler had forced Matthew into cutting his stay short. If he hurried loading his ore he would be able to attend at least an hour of the dance before his scheduled liftoff.

Hefting the first of several crates onto a dolly, Matthew couldn't help reflecting on how routine his ore runs had seemed lately in spite the ore dumps he was making for the Rebellion. Three months had gone by, and he hadn't encountered a single problem. In fact, he was finding himself becoming more and more relaxed with the each additional run.

But that was work. His personal life was an entirely different matter.

"Hey, Matt!" The hard slap on his shoulder made him jump every time. For the life of him he didn't know how someone as large as Dewy got to be so good at sneaking up on people.

"Dewy. How are you?"

"Fine, fine. A shame you won't be able to enjoy all of the dance this time, but I've read Warring's message and can understand his reasoning. Aft hold empty and ready to load?"

It still felt strange, Dewy talking to him in a more civil tone of voice, but over the last few months he had toned down his public hostility toward him. Perhaps he figured that everyone eventually learns to endure the presence of another, and if he did nothing but rail on him every time he saw him he was bound to arouse suspicion. Besides, most of the hangar personnel seemed to have forgotten all about the day Dewy had blown his top with him; they were used to it. As one mechanic pointed out on Matthew's following visit: "Don't let him get to you. If he gets irritated with you every once in a while, it means you're normal."

"It's ready to load, Dewy."

"Anyone inside?"

"Two guys. They're loading the starboard hold."

"Fine, I'll get started then."

Nobody had seemed at all suspicious of Dewy's desire to load only the aft hold of the *Wanderer*. After all, why wouldn't he stick to that particular hold? It was the smallest—less work on his part.

After half an hour the work was complete. And though he hadn't actually seen him do it, he knew Dewy had varied his load by a crate or two, had loosened the aft hold straps, and had loaded the scrambler with the new volume and weight total. There wasn't anything more to do; he was ready for launch.

He glanced at the hangar's chrono. The dance had started fifteen minutes ago. On any other day he would've caught a meal in the pilot's mess and rested for a few hours. But Matthew wasn't feeling the least bit tired or hungry. All he wanted to do was see Rebecca.

Grabbing a quick shower and a shave, he quickly dressed in the new suit he'd bought the week before, combed his hair, and critically inspected himself in the mirror. He combed his hair two more times before finally resigning himself to the fact that it simply wasn't going to get any better. *Well, what'd you expect, Tanner, considering what you had to work with?*

Stealing one final glance at himself, he suddenly became very nervous. He had been looking forward to this day for weeks, but now that it was here . . .

Shortly after receiving Rebecca's first letter, Matthew had written one of his own. He didn't want to involve Dewy in its delivery, feeling he was risking enough with the Rebellion already, so he sought help from the only other friendly face he'd seen on Durin: the door greeter from the first dance—Reuben.

Matthew happened upon Rueben, on his following visit, delivering food to the pilots' mess. After some conversation about his previous visit, Matthew discovered that Reuben was a full-time employee of the station's galley, and the one responsible for delivering the governor's meals throughout the day. It had been a gamble involving him, but he lucked out; Reuben seemed more than happy to help him. "Anything for love," he had said, his round face beaming. "Anything for love."

In that first letter Matthew apologized, himself, for not being more forthcoming regarding where he came from, thanked her for their dance, and expressed his desire to keep in touch.

Since then, many more letters had been exchanged. At first their letters had served as a form of introduction—an opportunity to get to know one another. Soon, however, they found themselves revealing more and more about themselves: hopes and heartaches, frustrations and dreams. And as they struggled to find just the right words to express their thoughts and ideas on paper, they were each taking more time to think through and explore new and budding emotions. Ironically, they were expressing themselves far better than they ever could have in person; their letters were bringing them closer together as physical distance seemed intent upon keeping them apart. But as open as their letters had been, Matthew still couldn't wait to see Rebecca and to talk with her face-to-face. Now, thanks to Rebecca, he would.

Governor Adams, for safety's sake, had always restricted Rebecca's movements to the family's end of the base, which provided them, after all, with all the amenities the rest of the base had to offer—though on a smaller scale. With the hangar on the opposite end of the base, complete with its own separate living area for pilots, there hadn't been any real chance for the two to *accidentally* run into each other. Another dance seemed like the only way to bring them together. Rebecca had succeeded in talking her mother into allowing her to host a dance of her own. It wouldn't include a fully catered dinner, or have all of the splendor of their first dance. But it would provide the two with the one thing they truly desired: the chance to see one another, the chance to talk.

Approaching the ballroom, Matthew suddenly felt extremely self-conscious. *What if she takes one look at me and realizes she's made a mistake?* Inwardly he had already decided he was going to retest his feelings for her when he saw her again, but it wasn't until now that he realized she might actually be preparing to do the same thing with him.

Taking a deep breath, he straightened his tie and passed through the door.

It was just as he remembered it, though the vines and potted trees that had added such contrast to the glass paneled walls and ceiling were missing, and a soundmixer, instead of a live orchestra, was providing the evening's music. To his left, just as before, was a refreshment table, though not nearly as filled as it had been.

What hadn't changed, he noticed, was the number of people in attendance. Apparently a dance, any kind of a dance, was always taken advantage of on Durin.

His eyes searched the room, his mouth dry, his heart beating with anticipation wild in his chest.

And suddenly, there she was—the young woman he'd grown to love through letters.

She was wearing a pale blue evening gown, her hair was pulled up, and she smiled as she spoke with friends. Before it had been her eyes he'd noticed first. Now, it was her. Standing before him, he now knew, was a woman who loved life, who enjoyed being with others, and who went out of her way to make people happy, despite her often cloistered existence. She spent a few months out of the year in Arcona, giving her the opportunity to visit with relatives and allowing her the chance to make and be among friends. But most of the year she had to remain on Durin, turning to her family and the arts for both entertainment and companionship—painting, reading, and studying the plays and performances of the past. In a way she had grown up very similar to Matthew—finding love and companionship at home, living outside the walls of Arcona.

Matthew smiled inwardly at how different Rebecca now appeared to him. He loved her. He was sure now; this was the woman for him.

A few seconds later, Rebecca turned and their eyes met once more. She smiled and politely excused herself from her friends, as both she and Matthew walked around the edge of the ballroom toward each other. Weaving by others they met in a quick embrace, so as not to draw too much attention. Rebecca had been perfectly willing to tell her parents all about Matthew, confident they'd be more open-minded toward him than Dirk had been. But Matthew had persuaded her to keep their relationship a secret for just a bit longer. Perhaps he was simply stalling, hoping the Rebels would soon make their move—a move that would theoretically place him on a more even plane with those from Arcona. Or perhaps it was simply because he felt they had a successful means of communicating with each other, and didn't want to see it suddenly come to an end.

"It's good to see you again, Matthew." And before he could get a word out Rebbeca offered her hand. "Now it's my turn. Would you like to dance?" Placing her smaller hand in his, Rebecca led Matthew out onto the dance floor. For several seconds they simply danced, each overwhelmed by the other's presence.

"I'm sorry I'm so late. I couldn't get here any sooner." Matthew glanced around the ballroom. "I can't believe you pulled it off, Becca." He chuckled. "Miller's been barking all week about having to prep the guest shuttles again."

"I just told my parents how bored I was, and that I really wanted to do something fun."

"And that's that, huh?"

"Well . . . alright, I confess. I waited until our last letter to tell you about all of this because I didn't want you to get your hopes up. What you see before you, Matthew Tanner, is the product of weeks of strategy, campaigning, and, in Dad's case, lots of begging and pleading. So I hope you like it."

"It . . . it looks great, Becca. Really, it does." Matthew forced a smile and pretended to focus on the music; after what she'd just said, how was he going to tell her that his leave had been cut short?

"What's wrong, Matthew."

Pulling her closer, he decided to keep that bit of information to himself a little while longer. "Thank you, Becca, for everything. Everything is perfect. *Everything.*"

Seemingly satisfied with his answer, Rebecca rested her head on his shoulder and moved with him to the music.

After two numbers, they both decided they could use a drink and headed toward the refreshment table.

"Doesn't it seem strange, Matthew?"

Matthew took a sip of punch. "What?"

"Us. I mean, I don't know. We've only met twice, have hardly even spoken and yet . . . "

"We feel as though we've known each other for years?"

Rebecca smiled softly taking a sip of her own. "Is such a thing really possible? I've seen it on stage, of course, but—"

Matthew reached out and took her hand. "It's a start, Becca. And, a good one I believe. I've needed you and . . . I've enjoyed having someone to write to—to talk to."

Rebecca rolled her eyes at the mention of her letters. "I hope my letters don't bore you. Sometimes I wonder if you think I'm just some silly girl who runs on and on and on."

"And I worry about you thinking that I'm some illiterate clod who talks as badly as he writes."

At that Rebecca laughed. "No. Believe me, Matthew. I don't think that for a minute. You're as sincere in your letters as you are in person. Really." She gave his hand a squeeze. "I just wish we had more than a few hours to share."

Matthew winced and glanced at the crystal clock that hung above the ballroom entrance, realizing he couldn't avoid the subject any longer. "Becca, I . . . "

"What is it, Matthew."

"I can only stay . . . twenty more minutes."

"What? But I thought you said we'd have three or four hours."

"I'm sorry, Becca. Really I am. You've done so much to put all of this together . . . I really do appreciate it. It's just that the freighter before mine had a bad thruster and has thrown the whole freight schedule out of whack." It pained Matthew when Rebecca's eyes slowly drifted to the floor. "Warring's using my run to help put everything back on track. I didn't find out about it until just before takeoff; otherwise I would have let you know. Believe me." He gently lifted her chin with his finger. "I'm sorry."

She shook her head. "It not your fault, Matthew. I just—" Her jaw clenched and then relaxed. "It just isn't fair, that's all."

Matthew was just as frustrated with the situation, but was determined not to waste what little time remained brooding. "Soon, Becca. We just have to—"

Just then Matthew spied the one person he'd managed to avoid for the last three months heading in their direction.

"Well, hello!" he called, flashing his trademark grin. "*What* do we have here?"

At the sound of his voice Matthew watched as disappointment fell over Rebecca's face. Realizing she'd just lost hours of their time together had been painful enough; the fact that she was now going to lose what few precious minutes remained, arguing with Dirk, appeared devastating to her. Matthew recalled her mentioning in her last letter that two of her friends were going to try to keep him occupied all evening. Apparently they hadn't been able to hold him any longer.

It was Rebecca who spoke up first, her face stern. "Dirk, I am *not* in the mood for you right now. Don't you have anything better to do?"

"I should have known. Clever, I must say. Very clever indeed. I suspected there was a more deceptive motive to those two friends of yours."

Rebecca flashed a wry smile. "Why? What gave it away? The fact that they'd actually *talk* to you?"

"Cute, Miss Adams. But the fact is I'm *here* now. And nothing's changed from the first time I broke you two up." He looked directly at Matthew. "I must ask you to leave . . . again."

Matthew stood straight, a defiant expression on his face. He had rehearsed this moment many times in his head, determined that if they ever did meet again he wouldn't run away with his tail between his legs. He *was* an Outsider, but he was also a pilot. "The *fact* is," he began, "this is a dance. And the invitation is open to anyone currently on this base. I realize you may dislike *who* I am, and *where* I come from, but as long as the governor's invitation is an open one, I'll stay."

Dirk stepped forward, gripping Matthew's arm. "I don't think you heard me." His grin had disappeared, giving his hard and chiseled features the angry aspect they'd lacked earlier.

Matthew struggled to keep his composure, trying to control the adrenaline rush. He looked down at Dirk's hand and back at his face.

Matthew wasn't particularly large, but he wasn't weak either. "You're holding an arm that's done nothing but lift and push for over eleven years now. Can you say that about yours?"

Dirk glared into Matthew's determined face, but from the brief twitch in his expression, and the quickness with which he started to laugh, Matthew knew he had him. He'd met up with guys like Dirk in the past. And like his grandfather always used to say, "No matter how big they are, show 'em you have a backbone, and, nine times out of ten, they'll back off."

Dirk removed his hand. "My, my, if the mongrel isn't a bit feisty. Well, we'll see just how *feisty* you can get. I should have reported you the first time." And with that he turned and left the ballroom.

"Matthew, he's going straight for my father."

"I know. I'm sorry, Becca. But I backed down last time because I didn't think we had a chance. Of course, now I may have blown *any* chance we might have had."

Rebecca looked softly, proudly into Matthew's eyes as they followed Dirk out of the ballroom. "Come on. Follow me."

She pulled him by the hand, through the crowd, to a small door just to the side of the ballroom's main entrance. Turning, she signaled two friends that were standing at the end of the room. Matthew then watched with interest at what appeared to be an orchestrated plan unfolding before his very eyes. It wasn't long before three more women joined the first two, walked over, and stood in a ragged line directly in front of Matthew and Rebecca, screening them from everyone on the dance floor. She quickly opened the smaller door and pulled him in after her.

Closing the door, she started to laugh. "We planned that this morning."

Matthew was smiling. "I don't understand."

"Take a look around you. What do you notice?"

He turned around to find them standing in what appeared to be some kind of holding room. In the dim light, coming from a tall rectangular window to their far left, he could see what appeared to be food-warming cabinets lining the wall on their right, while empty holding racks and storage cabinets took up the rest of the wall space directly to their left. Opposite the door was an elevator that Matthew guessed went directly to the kitchen; it was used by servers, perhaps, when catering larger parties.

And then it dawned on him: "We're alone."

She tapped him on the nose with her finger. "That's what I love about you. You're bright." Pulling him by the hand she led him over to the narrow window, where weak light from one of the many spot-lights used to light up the moon base's exterior was finding its way in. Taking hold of his hands she looked up into his gray-green eyes. "Matthew, I'm not giving up, and neither are you. Of course we have a chance. We have to."

"Why, because you always get your way?" asked Matthew with a smile.

Rebecca's face remained serious. "Because I can't think of anyone else I'd rather be with." Raising herself up on her toes, she kissed Matthew softly for the first time. And as Matthew returned it, he found himself amazed at how truly comfortable it felt. It wasn't a kiss between near strangers who'd only *seen* each other one time before; it was a kiss of sincere friendship, filled with understanding *and* love.

They parted and held each other, swaying to the music coming from under the holding room door—basking in their idealism, and, for a time, ignoring the reality of their situation. Thanks to Dirk, what had seemed like a tough relationship to hold together before, was *undoubtedly* going to become a lot tougher.

* * *

Matthew had mysteriously managed to avoid running into any of the trouble Dirk's comment had implied and was now scrambling toward the barracks. He was scheduled to leave in twenty minutes and knew his preflight check would eat up at least ten of them—which meant he had an equal amount of time to change into his flight suit and log out of Hangar Security.

It'll be close, but it was worth it.

After a parting hug and kiss, and a promise they'd keep writing, they had said good-bye. She'd had tears in her eyes when he left her, and he was sure the full impact of their farewell would hit him as well when he had the luxury of being able to think about it. For now, though, those tears meant only one thing to Matthew: she honestly cared about him.

He was elated.

Making his way into the hangar bay, he bounded up the steps that led to the barracks and rushed into the locker room. He changed, threw his duffel bag over his shoulder, and was rounding the wall of lockers when a fist slammed into the side of his head.

Matthew fell to the floor, unconscious.

CHAPTER 16

"Matt!"

No response.

"Matt! Come on, kid. Snap out of it!"

Responding to the mild slaps on either side of his face, Matthew slowly opened his eyes, and immediately sat up at the sight of Dewy's face.

"Easy, kid. Take it slow." He turned his head, addressing a scruffy-looking mechanic Matthew recognized from the hangar. "Jake, get Doc. He's at the dance."

"He looks alright to me," Jake complained.

"Get him!" barked Dewy.

Jake leered at Matthew, turned, and strode out of the room, mumbling something unintelligible under his breath.

Matthew reached slowly for the right side of his head; the skin was tender to the touch, undoubtedly bruised. "What happened?"

"I was hoping *you* could tell *me*," Dewy said.

Matthew winced from a throbbing headache, made worse by the bright lighting overhead. "I came in to change . . . so I could . . ." When Matthew noticed Dewy dressed in a formal suit and tie, his eyes shot open at the recollection of just what it was *he* was supposed to be doing. "I've got to get to my ship!"

Matthew started to get up, but was yanked back to the floor by Dewy's powerful arm. "Easy. Relax! Listen to me. I thought you'd be running late, with the dance and all, so I paged Jake earlier and told him to run your preflight and hang around the hangar until you showed up."

So that's why he's so upset.

"Hey, I was at the dance," continued Dewy. "I saw the way you and Miss Adams were eyeing each other." He gave the boy a peculiar wink. "I thought I'd do you a favor."

Matthew felt sheepish. "Thanks."

"That's alright. I was young once."

Matthew started to smile, but stopped short. "How long have I been out?"

"A few minutes I'd guess. I left the dance about five minutes ago to see you off—tradition, you know that." Matthew nodded. "But when I got here and saw Jake was still at the *Wanderer's* controls, I came to see how much longer you'd be. That's when I found you lying here. Jake followed after me a few minutes later; he's anxious to get to the dance."

Matthew started to get up again. Dewy pulled him down a second time. "Relax! We've still got eight or so minutes before your launch window completely closes." He then eyed him carefully. "Of course, if Doc says you're not in any shape to—"

Matthew's eyes darted to Dewy's. "I have to fly! You know that."

"But—"

"There're no buts about it. I've *got* to make this run. You weren't there when Warring lectured me that first time I was *delayed*. If he suddenly decides I'm more trouble than I'm worth, what would happen to . . ." he finished in a whisper, choosing his words carefully, ". . . our *shipments*?"

Dewy let out a noticeable sigh. "I can't tell you how glad I am to hear you say that, Matt." He helped Matthew to his feet and pounded the unsteady young man on the back, nearly knocking him headlong into the lockers. "Quick, Doc should be here any minute. Did you see who did this to you?"

Matthew shook his head while letting out a short laugh. "It's obvious, isn't it?"

"Dirk?"

Matthew nodded. "We had a bit of a *discussion* at the dance."

"Yeah, I caught that just as I showed up. So, you saw him before he hit you?"

"No. But who else could it have been?"

Dewy was shaking his head. "That snot nose . . ." He went on, letting loose a string of curses which, Matthew had learned over the last few months, made up a substantial portion of Dewy's vocabulary.

When he'd finished, his voice was menacing. "Don't worry, Matt. I'll take care of him."

"No, Dewy. Look, this is *my* problem, not yours."

"Not when it affects my pilots it isn't!"

"But there's no sense having him hold a grudge against *both* of us; breathing down *both* our necks."

"He's a pampered imbecile who—"

"And I agree with you, believe me I do. But he's still a Special Forces Officer, and you don't need his kind of attention. Besides, I doubt I'll have the chance to get to his end of the base anytime soon, anyway."

Dewy, a perplexed expression on his face, was about to say something when they both heard the door of the barracks slide open. Jake entered a few seconds later, the base's doctor trailing behind him.

"Doc" appeared to be in his mid-forties; a kind-faced man with strands of gray that stood out vividly amidst his closely cropped, coal-black hair. Matthew could tell by his formal suit he'd been pulled from the dance, but if he was upset about it Matthew couldn't tell. Unlike Jake, he appeared in complete control of his emotions—a professional. He immediately went to Matthew and inspected his swollen face with his thin, soft hands. "What happened?"

Dewy folded his arms and beat Matthew to an answer. "The pitiful puke says he tripped over his bag and fell into the lockers."

Jake shook his head, a quick and sudden snort escaping his throat. "Figures."

At that moment Matthew realized that his *friend*, Dewy, had disappeared, and, for a few weeks at least, he would once again have to play the role of the chagrined, younger pilot.

"Hmmm. Well, his pupils aren't dilated . . . and the skin isn't broken. How you feeling, son?"

Matthew opened his mouth to respond, but, again, Dewy intervened. "Can he fly?"

The doctor still had his eyes on Matthew. "I suppose so. I imagine he's got quite a headache, though."

The doctor started to reach into a small black pouch on his belt for a few pain relief tablets, when Dewy suddenly grabbed a handful of Matthew's flight suit. "Good! Thanks, Doc." And then to Matthew: "Come on. You've only got a few minutes left, and you *know* what Warring said about the schedule."

Matthew understood the need for Dewy to "keep up appearances," but deep down, he was going to miss the real Dewy.

The larger man pushed Matthew roughly toward the door as Jake picked up his duffel bag and followed from behind, all three walking briskly toward the *Wanderer*.

* * *

Matthew's return trip home was one of pure misery. Physically, his lack of sleep over the last twenty-four hours, in his anticipation of the dance, had finally caught up with him. And emotionally, he was struggling with what the ramifications might be now that Dirk had undoubtedly revealed Matthew and Rebecca's relationship to her parents. He successfully completed his run, however, managing to skim his load of ore to fill the vacant aft hold in near record time—despite the fatigue, a pounding headache, and a bruised heart.

Now, in the relative safety of the Arcona Spaceport, he concentrated on powering down his systems, trying desperately to will into his body enough energy to unload his cargo; a nauseating thought, to say the least. When his starboard hatch shot open, and Rollyn bounded inside, Matthew was now grateful he'd given into his pestering and given the kid his pass code; now he had one less thing that needed doing—even if it was simply opening the hatch.

A few months ago, Rollyn had started welcoming Matthew home after every flight. At first, Matthew had worried about the boy getting caught missing from his post. But Rollyn seemed quite adept at sneaking away and, so far, had avoided any punishment. Secretly, he wondered if the boy was doing it so that Matthew would know that he had someone to come home to, even if it was "just Rollyn," and not his grandfather. But then Matthew couldn't help also noticing a few new bruises on Rollyn's arms and cheek, and wondered if perhaps Rollyn was simply wanting to be around someone who cared about him, since it seemed his father had become a bit more abusive lately. Whatever the reason, he appreciated it.

When Matthew turned in the cockpit to face him, having toggled the final switch, the younger boy let out a long whistle. "Wow, Matt! You look—"

Matthew held up his hand. "Don't say it, Rolly. Okay? Just, don't say it." He brushed past him on his way down the narrow corridor.

"What happened to you, Matt?"

Matthew stopped at the open hatch. He really didn't want to take this outside and thought it best to get it over with before the unloading team arrived. "You remember me telling you about Dirk?"

"Sure. Sure, I remember."

"Well, he decided to give me a going-away present."

"Wow!"

Matthew couldn't help smiling, in spite of his fatigue; Rollyn's dramatic facial expressions were always fun to watch. "I'll tell you all about it tonight on the way home. I promise. Now get back to work before someone starts missing you."

"Me? You're kidding, right?"

Matthew mussed the boy's white hair as he passed him and, before he was out of earshot, called out, "Hey! Rolly!"

The boy spun around on his heals; his bright, round eyes wide and eager.

"Thanks for being here today. I . . . I needed it."

Rollyn simply smiled, gave a mock salute, and ran away.

Later that evening, on the transport ride home, Matthew kept his promise and shared with Rollyn the entire story. They had both derived great pleasure in coming up with different ways of getting back at Dirk, though, deep down, Matthew knew he'd probably never get the chance to actually carry them out.

The sight of his cot, beyond his doorway's thick evening curtain, though, pushed all thoughts of revenge, his mission, and even the future of his relationship with Rebecca aside.

Without securing his window curtain, or even taking the time to remove his clothes, Matthew walked numbly over to his humble bed and collapsed, exhausted.

Everything would simply have to wait until tomorrow. For now, all Matthew could think about was just how much he wanted to sleep.

"I hope you've learned your lesson, Matthew." Paul reclined in his *hide-back chair, folded his arms, and crossed his legs.*

"If you think I'm going to let that pompous idiot tell me what I can or cannot do, when I have every right—"

"No, no. Relax. Of course not. I'm not talking about Dirk, or your relationship with Miss Adams. I'm referring to that punch that has hopefully knocked some sense into you."

Matthew appeared lost. "What are you talking about?"

"Things have been going well for you lately, haven't they?" He didn't wait for an answer. "On the outside, it appears your involvement with the Rebellion has gone completely unnoticed. You're doing your part with the ore dumps, and Dewy's obviously doing his."

Matthew was genuinely confused as to where his grandfather was going with all of this. "Sure . . . But I still don't see what you're getting at."

Paul sat up, leaned forward, and rested his elbows on his knees—his fingers interlocked, and his expression became very serious. "What I'm getting at, Matthew, is that you're too relaxed. Before, you were wary and suspicious of what was going on around you, and you were careful with what you said and did."

"You're saying I should have known Dirk was going to pound me in the face?" asked Matthew, incredulously.

Paul sat back and assumed his previous position. "You've just validated my point, boy." He looked deep into his grandson's eyes. "How do you know it was Dirk who punched you?"

For several heartbeats, Matthew's eyes remained locked on his grandfather's. Finally, he slumped back in his chair; now he understood. "I'm letting my feelings for Rebecca get in the way, aren't I?"

Paul nodded slowly, pleased. "They've clouded your judgment, Matthew, and you've been letting your guard down. You have no idea who it was that punched you, or why. And, if you're not careful with the conclusions you jump to . . ." He stopped, letting Matthew fill in the blanks for himself.

Matthew recalled his forgetting to log in with Durin Security, and how he probably should have left the dance immediately after Dirk had. Perhaps he shouldn't have even supported the idea of another dance in the first place. And what about the letter writing? "Are you saying I should stop writing her?" Out of habit he ran a hand through his hair. "Because if you are—"

"Of course not, son. I'm sure you're careful in what you say. Besides, she's an incredible young lady, whom, I can see, you've grown to love very much. I wouldn't think of telling you to stop writing her, especially with all the loss you've had to endure in your life. You deserve it.

"Keep writing her, use her as your motivation for successfully completing your mission. Just make sure your thoughts and actions coincide with what you've been asked to do. After all, if your mission fails, if this revolution fails, what chance will the two of you really have of being together then?

"You're seriously involved with the Rebellion now. If your actions were ever brought to light, which they will be once all of the ore you've been dumping hits Zerith's atmosphere, I'd hate to think of what form of punishment Spire might resort to next. It's obvious banishment hasn't succeeded in putting out the flame of rebellion."

Paul reached over and gave Matthew's knee a squeeze. *"Son, fulfill your mission first—give it top priority. Only then will you have a solid foundation on which to build your life."*

Matthew looked hard into his grandfather's face. He could see the love, concern, and respect he had for him. *He's right,* he realized. *I have been careless.* *"I . . . I understand what you're saying, Papa. I'll do better."*

"Good!" Paul straightened. *"Now that we've got that settled, I think we need to discuss your safety."*

Matthew was still trying to digest his grandfather's first revelation; it took a moment for his new words to register. *"What do you mean?"*

"Do you remember that right hook I taught you years ago?"

Matthew smiled at the memory. *"Yeah, of course I do—so would Blake Mullins."*

"Good. Forget it."

Matthew's face fell. *"You lost me again."*

"I think you need something more to protect yourself with."

"What? A plasma rifle? You know I don't have any way of buying one. Civilians aren't permitted to—"

"Do you remember that small rise just beyond the cemetery? I took you there a couple of times to show it to you when you were younger."

"Yeah. I remember it. You said it was your favorite place to sit and think"

"That's right. Now, aside from the two trips we made there together, can you think of any other time I went there?"

Matthew's forehead wrinkled, his eyes revealing just how carefully he was searching his memory. *"No . . . I can't."*

Paul smiled. *"Odd, don't you think?"*

CHAPTER 17

"You killed the Tanners?"

The CEO had been standing in front of the great glass wall of his office suite, looking out at the city with his hands clasped behind his back. He turned around so that he could answer his nephew, face to face. "Physically? With my own hands? No. Though I suppose that's irrelevant, since I orchestrated the events leading up to their deaths, just as you did with the two guards from the wall."

"I see." Harris was silent a moment, seeming to process that information slowly. "And that's why you've been so obsessed, lately, with Paul Tanner's death?" From the look on his face, it was obvious he had failed to see the connection.

The elder man turned to look out the massive window again, finding it easier to express such weak thoughts when he didn't have to look his nephew directly in the eye. "For years, after their deaths, I had been . . . concerned . . . that Paul would discover the truth behind his boy's death, and feel the need to somehow . . . seek revenge."

"But he couldn't have known you were the one responsible for putting it all together. And even if he did, how could he possibly have reached you? He would never have made it into the city, let alone the front entrance of this building."

The CEO couldn't help smiling. "A silly fear, I guess."

"Silly indeed!"

At this, the CEO turned suddenly. He had had to swallow a lot of pride with this admission, and he didn't appreciate being slapped in the face with it. He glared at Harris. "Watch it! You have no idea what Tanner was like back then. And you weren't there on the day of their execution. *I* was." He turned back to the view beyond the glass. "We forced him to watch it, Harris, hoping it would teach him, and his followers, a lesson." His voice became softer with the vivid memory. "Before the moment of execution, Tanner had a look in his eyes . . . that would have melted steel."

"And a look he will never give anyone again," his nephew added, bravely.

The CEO turned and stared at him, unable to dispute the truth of the younger man's words.

He finally shook his head in defeat. "You're right. I should let it go, as I have for years now. But over the past few months . . . the news of his death . . . " He struggled to find the right words. "All of those old feelings have come back for some reason."

The CEO walked over to his chair, behind his desk, and sat down rubbing his tired eyes with his thumb and index finger. "Maybe now you can understand why I've been a bit impatient, lately, about that investigation. I just want to put it all behind me, for it to . . . go away." He cleared his throat. "Now, if—"

"You're concerned about his grandson now, aren't you? Concerned he might find out your secret, perhaps even mistakenly connect you to his grandfather's death, and finish what his grandfather wasn't able to. You've transferred your fear of Paul's vengeance onto him now, based on Warring's report on Matthew's bravery during the pirate attack."

He had intended to change the subject, and now regretted the fact that he'd even brought it up in the first place. But when Harris had appeared slightly frustrated at yet another of his inquiries into the progress of the murder investigation, the CEO thought it necessary to share with the young man the inner turmoil that had been building up inside him—hoping for some understanding. He could see now that Harris was beginning to understand his feelings *too* well.

Their eyes locked for several seconds before Spire's Chief Executive Officer finally answered, "I have always assumed that Paul's vengeance, if it existed, which I'm sure it did, had been curbed over the years by the stronger compassion he felt for those around him; concerned that any retaliation on his part might trigger a response that would directly affect the pathetic remnants surrounding him."

"And now he's dead."

"He was murdered!" shouted the CEO as his fist hit the desk. "Which is *precisely* what has been driving me crazy. He was surrounded by those he cared about, and was murdered. It just doesn't make any sense."

Harris broke the ensuing silence with a suggestion. "You've often reminded the council never to underestimate the Outsiders as a group. What if this was done in an attempt to distract us, prior to making a move against us?"

The CEO thoughtfully rested his narrow chin on clasped fingers, his elbows on his desk. "No. I've already considered that angle—believe me. I just can't convince myself that they'd be willing to sacrifice one of their own, especially Tanner, for the sake of an attack our informant believes they haven't the strength or firepower to win. It isn't in them to do that."

Harris got up from his familiar place on the couch and began pacing. "So, am I hearing you right? You're more concerned about a personal attack on yourself than the possibility that they might be organizing themselves for a combined attack on Arcona?"

The CEO's eyes rolled slowly in Harris's direction, his voice even and clear. "I'm not saying that at all, nephew. I've *always* said we should be watchful. If the rumors *are* true that they have supporters in Arcona, it would be very foolish on our part to let our guard down. I'm simply saying . . ." He wrung his hands in frustration—flashes of Paul Tanner's face relentlessly haunting him. "I don't know what I'm saying!"

Harris walked over to the polished desk and leaned on it with closed fists. "If they are unprepared for any sort of attack, then why not simply kill his grandson and put any . . . fears of vengeance you might have to rest? Granted, we have nothing to indicate that he is at all involved in any rebellious actions, and his death so close to his grandfather's could arouse suspicion, but I'm sure I can put *something* together."

The older man leaned back in his chair, a queer expression on his face. "Because contrary to the popular opinion of the Council, or even you, perhaps, while I have killed many in my lifetime, I don't simply kill to kill. I kill only when someone becomes an obstacle in my path, or needs to be taught a very *serious* lesson."

"But isn't he an obstacle? If you let this boy distract you to the point . . ."

The CEO knew what Harris was trying to say, deep down agreeing with the logic, but for some reason he couldn't bring himself to completely extinguish the Tanner line. He wouldn't hesitate killing the boy himself if he discovered he was in any way, shape, or form connected with rebellious activity, but there simply wasn't any evidence to suggest that. Even the diagnostic of his ship, three months earlier, had come up clean. He was a good employee; a solid flyer with a strong work ethic. And, in his opinion, given the lack of the latter attribute in Arcona over the last several years, was a valuable asset.

Besides, if Rebels truly did exist in Arcona, which he was sure they did, Harris had a point regarding the timing of such an *accident*; he didn't want the boy to become a rallying cry for . . . *For what? What* could *their puny number do?*

Maybe Harris is right. Maybe I am flinching at shadows. But on the other hand . . .

" . . . Don't you agree?"

The CEO turned and regarded his nephew, having only the vaguest idea of what he had just said. "I'll let you know when I become too distracted."

Harris, hearing this as more of a command than a statement, backed off, seeming to know he was pushing their familiarity with one another a bit too far. "Of course."

The chime of the desk intercom shattered the tension. "What is it?"

"Just a reminder to Harris, sir, about his three o' clock appointment with the agricultural reps."

"Thank you, Lori. I'll see that he's reminded."

Harris straightened, silently agreeing to a truce. "An efficient secretary, isn't she?"

"That she is," answered the CEO coolly.

Harris hesitated a moment before speaking. "I'll keep pestering our agents, but I'm telling you, the trail's now cold. We simply don't know who murdered Paul Tanner, or why." He paused a moment, awaiting eye contact. "Thank you for sharing your thoughts with me. I'll try to be more tolerant of your inquiries in the future."

"Thank you, Harris. That will be all."

"I do think, though, that—"

"That will be all!" growled the CEO through clenched teeth, making it clear Harris's presence was no longer needed, and that he had said all that he had wanted to say.

His nephew abruptly turned and left—the tall, wooden doors of the CEO's office sealing shut behind him.

For several minutes the CEO stared at the closed doors, knowing, deep down, that his nephew was right: He *was* becoming distracted.

But he wasn't there! He simply can't understand what I'm feeling.

He chuckled to himself. *Then again, I'm not even sure I understand what I'm feeling.* He rubbed his tired eyes once more, wishing he could get more sleep at night, and then reached for the monthly financial report that had been the reason for Harris's visit in the first place. The packet consisted of five pages that would turn black in forty-eight hours, preventing its information from ever being read, and he knew from the time it took with the last report that he was already cutting it close. Of course, he could pull the same information off of his own computer, inlaid in the right-hand corner of his desktop, anytime he wanted to. But he loathed the machine—the glare of the screen uncomfortable on his aging eyes.

He verbally unlocked his desk drawer and carefully removed the heirloom ledger. Setting it carefully on his desk he opened it and was preparing to begin transferring the report's figures when a thought suddenly came to mind—triggered, he guessed, from his conversation with Harris and the open book resting beneath his thin and bony fingers. *If there* are *Rebels among us, what's the one thing they would need to gain a foothold?* The question, of course, had been rhetorical. *Money. Money would* have *to be the necessary base on which to successfully build up anything.*

He stared blankly at the ledger's worn, brittle pages. *And all of Arcona's money is filtered through Spire, regardless of what the public believes.*

A theory began to develop as the ancient ledger seemed to be screaming at him.

Absentmindedly he flipped through a substantial portion of the ledger, realizing, if his theory proved true, he could have before him the lead that would finally give him the legitimate excuse he had been looking for; a lead that would allow him to permanently root out

Arcona's Rebels once and for all.

He considered sharing his theory with his accountants first and having them perform the necessary audit, but Harris's recent reaction to his earlier confession came to mind and he dismissed the idea immediately. *Perhaps it's already been looked at*, he thought. *It's too simple. Surely it has.*

No. He wanted something more concrete to support his feelings with this time before revealing them to anybody else.

No, this time, he'd do his own investigating first.

CHAPTER 18

It hadn't changed much from the day of the funeral, though Matthew could see that the harsh desert sun and dry wind were intent upon erasing and absorbing the half-buried wooden slab—the hand-carved letters of his grandfather's name, now bolder against the sun-bleached face of the humble grave marker.

He hadn't visited the grave since the day of the funeral. And while some may have interpreted this as being disrespectful, deep down he knew it was precisely what his grandfather would have wanted—looking forward, not back.

Oh, he was sure he wouldn't have minded an occasional visit, now and again, but Matthew himself had witnessed in several of the families of their shanty town how debilitating a death could be.

Some members of a family simply found the loss unbearable, spending their days engaged in daily pilgrimages to the graveyard, often shutting out the living around them—those still in need of their love and support. Matthew had come close to sinking into that despair himself; he knew firsthand how easy and natural the fall could be. But he had no desire to be sucked into such a consuming pit of grief.

With fondness Matthew recalled how his grandfather had been instrumental in rescuing so many from just such a "pit." Those with whom Paul visited knew his words of comfort were backed with true sincerity and honest sympathy—for all were very much aware of the losses he'd endured in his own life.

"You made it look so easy, Papa," said Matthew to the grave at his feet. "You made it look *too* easy."

Deep down, though, Matthew knew it had been anything *but* easy.

When his parents had been executed, their bodies were not permitted to leave Arcona. They were simply thrown into an unmarked grave with the other "traitors, dissenters, murderers, and thieves." The epithets were false, of course, and the pain of not having them buried in a decent resting place had to have been difficult to endure.

But his grandfather *had*.

Matthew remembered how many of the Outsiders, when they were banished from the city, had pleaded with the government to allow them to disinter loved ones so they could bury them in a graveyard of their own, so they could be, in some way, "close to family." All their requests had been denied—the complete separation from their ancestral past cruelly heaped upon the already heavy burden of their punishment.

Though quite young at the time, Matthew could still remember when the fever of these requests was at its peak. He could specifically remember a conversation between his grandfather and a Mr. Orme, who lived three doors down. The bearded, agitated man was trying to persuade his grandfather to join the others in their petition. Paul listened patiently to his friend and then calmly gave his memorable response: "Louis, I would like nothing more than to have my dear wife moved so that I could visit her from time to time."

Mr. Orme, thinking he had won Paul's support, had started to smile, but his victory proved fleeting.

"But she's buried in a beautiful coffin, with a marble headstone, resting in one of the loveliest graveyards Arcona has to offer. She deserves that, Louis. She really does. And I wouldn't think of taking that away from her."

Paul Tanner simply had a unique way of looking at things.

Matthew remembered what his grandfather had said after Mr. Orme, feeling both frustrated and angry, had left: "I feel sorry for him, Matthew. While some have taken comfort in my words, others seem incapable of accepting them."

Seeing Matthew's young face screwed up in confusion, he explained: "I meant what I said about your grandmother's grave. But, it's more than that. I'm *convinced* that death isn't the end of everything. In fact, I believe it's the start of . . . something wonderful. Our bodies remain buried in the ground, of course, but our . . . our . . . what makes us *us*, lives on."

"Lives on in the trees and in the animals and in the sky?"

"No, boy. I'm not a believer of any of that. Though I know there are many who subscribe to such ideas.

"No, we're people. And I believe that when we die, we remain people—only . . . on a *different* level." He smiled at the look of confusion on the boy's face. "What I'm trying to tell you, boy, is that I believe I'll see your grandmother *again*. And your parents. I don't *need* to hold on to the bodies they left behind; they've moved on."

He scratched at his chin. "I don't know why I feel so strongly about it."

At the time, Matthew, still quite young, had been confused, but he liked the thought of seeing his parents again one day. He moved beyond the specific words of his grandfather, to the basis of his belief. "How do you know it's true, Papa. For sure, I mean?"

Matthew's heart warmed now, remembering his grandfather's simple reply. Paul had looked away for several seconds and then looked Matthew straight in the eye, touching his chest. "I feel it here, son, in my heart."

After his grandfather's death, Matthew had often thought back on that conversation, and over the last few months had found the memory more and more comforting. And for reasons he couldn't quite put his finger on, he felt he was now beginning to understand his grandfather's faith; but, like his grandfather, he couldn't explain how or why he felt the way he did.

Matthew had shared his grandfather's belief with Rebecca in one of his letters. She had liked the idea, but really hadn't seemed interested in elaborating on her feelings. He wasn't surprised; death simply wasn't a topic many discussed on Zerith; death was to be feared, not pondered.

Returning to the present, Matthew took a moment to look around him. He noticed the elderly woman whom he had seen earlier still kneeling at a grave, weeping bitterly. At this distance he wasn't sure who it was.

It didn't matter.

He took a deep breath as he struggled to maintain control over his *own* emotions. Walking through a graveyard was healthy, he decided, for it grounded a person—reminding him of his own fragile and precious mortality. But too much of even a good thing could prove disabling, and he decided it was time to move on.

It had been a strange morning because he had expected to sleep in, given his fatigue from the day before. But at six A.M. he had found himself wide awake, feeling completely refreshed. Often on prep days—days on which he wasn't scheduled to fly—he took advantage of the free hours of the morning to rest up, or catch up on chores he needed to do before going into Arcona to prep his ship for his run the following day. But at the sight of his grandfather's chair, footstool, and cane, his plans for the morning had changed instantly.

Rather than spend the morning pondering his future, or the lack of a future, with Rebecca, as he assumed he would the evening before, he suddenly had an inexplicable desire to visit his grandfather's grave.

No, it had been more than that. Now, having visited the grave, *something* in the back of his mind began nagging at him.

He scanned the barren horizon beyond the graveyard, and tried to figure out just what that *something* was.

The horizon wasn't *completely* barren, he noticed, his eyes resting on a small, flat-top hill that rose out of the ground about a half mile away. He recalled visiting the hill a few times as a small child with his grandfather many years ago, and now suddenly thought it might be nice to visit it again. Perhaps it would help him feel closer to his grandfather—a desire that for some reason seemed particularly strong this morning. Strong enough, he realized as he began walking, to push even yesterday's panic over his relationship with Rebecca to the back of his mind. That was something he wouldn't have believed possible.

Reaching the top of the small rise, Matthew was instantly taken aback—the hill was much smaller than he had remembered it. But he was glad he had come, and began walking around its near-circular edge. The area on top of the rise had a rough circumference of a couple of hundred feet, dipping at its center.

Matthew stopped, looking toward the east at what he knew was the graveyard, the grave markers being too small to distinguish at this distance. The shanty town spread out beyond it, and, in the far-off distance, the wall and city of Arcona, sprawled across the horizon, its bristling skyline distorted from the heat waves rising from the sunbaked ground before it.

He turned around to admire the view opposite the city, but of course there was nothing but flat, arid wasteland as far as the eye could see.

"This is where grandpa comes to think, son," Matthew recalled his grandfather telling him, several times. "Your grandpa sits in the middle of this spot and thinks for hours."

Matthew remembered the words, but as he took in the pitiful view surrounding him, he couldn't help wondering *why* his grandfather would have picked such a place for a retreat. The view consisted only of those things he probably wouldn't have wanted to dwell on, visually rubbing in what life used to be, what it was now, and how it would *inevitably* end—all in one picture. There wasn't anything else to look at—no trees, no wandering stream, nothing one would normally associate with a place of meditation. In fact, the view itself was beginning to depress Matthew—the bleak and empty land before him producing feelings of hopelessness and despair.

Having made it this far, however, Matthew decided he'd at least give the place a chance. He tried to find its center so he could sit down. It took only seconds to discover, however, that the top of the rise really didn't have a true center. Its eastern slope, facing Arcona, was still intact, but its western edge, which received the brunt of the desert's occasional wind and rain, had been weathered into a more gradual slope that eventually ran even with the desert floor. The rise's center was actually situated just beyond the start of this gradual slope.

Deciding that it really didn't matter where he sat, he seated himself on the edge he had climbed up first, and dangled his feet over the eastern slope.

After several minutes had passed, Matthew again wondered why his grandfather had picked such a discouraging spot to do his thinking; it was depressing—a poignant, visual reminder of all that had been taken from his people, something he knew his grandfather wouldn't have wanted to dwell on. *So why this spot?*

And then it dawned on him: *When* did *he come here? Sure, he brought me here a couple of times . . .but I can't recall him ever mentioning coming here without me.* That wasn't to say his grandfather hadn't, but they had always tried to let each other know where the other was going to be. Matthew had always chalked this up to paranoia—a grandfather simply wanting to know where his grandson was at all times. But . . . *Maybe the rule didn't apply to him . . . No, he wasn't like that.*

Not finding the spot at all relaxing, and knowing he still had to fetch water from the well and dispose of the garbage before he met the transport at ten, Matthew started to get up.

As he placed his hands on either side of him, pushing his body upward, Matthew's right hand landed on a rock. Instinctively he moved his hand to another spot and stood, giving the obstacle a quick glance as he brushed the desert's powdery dirt from his pants.

Now that's strange.

The rock his hand had touched was about half the size of his hand, flat and smooth, with rounded edges. On top of the rock sat a smaller, more elongated one—also flat, though chipped on either side, creating a V-shape.

He picked up the smaller stone and studied it more closely, examining the chipped edges in particular. *Chipped with a tool.*

Matthew then realized that wasn't the only strange feature about the rock. The fact that both rocks were smooth and flat, unlike the surrounding material, suggested they had come from a stream or riverbed. Most of Arcona's water was brought in by shuttle from the forested regions and refineries, and the Outsiders pulled their water from an underground well nearly two miles from where he was standing; there simply wasn't any sign that a river had ever flowed on or near the rise.

Putting the smaller rock back in place, he wondered what the odds were of finding two smooth rocks, one showing signs of workmanship, on top of each other in the desert.

Pretty slim I'd imagine, he thought. *So why were they here?*

He walked around them until he had made a complete circle, finding himself standing behind the smaller, pointed rock.

Pointed . . . a pointer? For a brief second he entertained the idea of the smaller rock indicating a direction, but then, just as quickly, dismissed it. *You've been hanging around Rollyn too long, Tanner. They're probably left over from a couple of kids just messing around.*

He turned, then stopped. *But who?*

The fact was, Matthew couldn't imagine any of the parents he knew, given the inherent dangers of the desert, allowing their children to wander off *this* far. Even the older children of their community stayed close to home, rarely venturing beyond the graveyard.

He had come this far simply because his grandfather had brought him here years earlier.

Matthew studied the ground carefully. Other than his own tracks, there was no sign of anyone else having been here. But then rain, wind, and time could have accounted for that. He shrugged his shoulders. *Get a move on, Tanner. You've got a big day ahead of you, and it isn't going to start itself.* Turning on his heel, Matthew headed for the edge of the eastern slope.

At the base of the rise, however, he stopped suddenly. *What if it does mean something?*

Matthew found himself glancing all around him, needlessly making sure there wasn't a soul around to watch what he was about to do. *Why not? What have I got to lose?*

Quickly, Matthew scrambled up the rise until he once again found himself standing in back of the small, pointed rock. Cautiously he began walking in the direction indicated, paying particularly close attention to his footing—the vertical cave entrance near Rock Hill suddenly coming to mind.

After several paces he was stunned to discover another pair of rocks set up in the same manner as the first, with the "pointing" rock turned ninety degrees.

They are *pointers!*

Feeling much less ridiculous than he had before, he turned and walked in the new direction that forced him down the rise's more gradual, western slope.

After what felt like the same number of paces as before, he found yet a third marker—its "pointer" turned ninety degrees as well.

As he followed the third path, noticing that he was walking parallel to the first, he began to wonder if he had fallen for someone's idea of a practical joke. When he reached the fourth marker, turned, and found himself now returning to the point at which he had started, he was sure he had. *A square! I've just walked in a perfect square.* He started laughing, in spite of himself. *Well, whoever it was, they got me.*

Deciding he'd wasted enough time for one morning, he started back down the eastern slope of the rise when, suddenly, he recalled precisely what his grandfather had said about the place. He stopped. *Your grandpa sits in the middle of this spot. Could that be what he meant?*

He anxiously climbed the side of the rise and, in only a matter of seconds, had one of the smaller rocks in hand. Placing it in the dirt, near the side of the first marker, he kept his eye on the third marker and drew as straight a line as he could toward it. He did the same with the second and fourth markers. He then walked over to where the two diagonal lines he had drawn intersected—the middle of the square—"the middle" where his grandfather liked to sit.

From where he was standing, Matthew could no longer see the graveyard, the shanty town, or even the tall towers of Arcona. The inclining eastern slope blocked all of it from view. *And if I can't see them, then they can't see me.*

"No prying eyes," he muttered. "For what?" Just then the thought of something hidden sprang to mind. Falling to his knees Matthew began digging at the center of the "X."

Finding hard-packed dirt underneath the thin layer of sandy gravel, he grabbed one of the larger flat stones and used it to dig with. After removing about a foot of dirt, the rock hit something hard and hollow.

Minutes later, Matthew pulled a small wooden box from the ground. It had a metal latch on the front of it, tied with a long, thin piece of rawhide—looped where a lock was obviously meant to be. It crumbled when Matthew tugged at the knot. His eyes went wide as he lifted the lid.

Inside he found a large object wrapped in black plastic. Removing the plastic he found an oily rag. Pulling the ends of the moist cloth apart, Matthew sat stunned at what lay before him: an old pistol, a silencer, and a small plastic case filled with shells.

Picking up the gun, Matthew looked all around him, suddenly feeling very uneasy holding the illegal weapon in his hands. He knew how to load one, thanks to Miller and a pompous guard they had spoken with several years earlier, but he'd never fired one. Nor was he about to now.

Turning the pistol over in his hands, he studied every part of it, and a cold and sinking feeling formed in the pit of his stomach. When he screwed on the silencer, something the show-off guard had also showed him how to do, though with a slightly newer model, he realized a similar weapon had to have been used on his grandfather.

This gun, however, obviously wasn't the one used in the murder. Aside from the worn rawhide string still being intact, Matthew could smell nothing but oil—no gun powder. And, in spite of the oily rag it had been wrapped in, he could tell that the gun would need a lot of cleaning before anyone could safely use it again.

Scratched on the plastic bottom of the ammunition box, Matthew found the initials "P.T." He knew their significance immediately. He had found his grandfather's pistol—the one he must have had during the days of the first Rebellion.

He must have found a way to smuggle it out of Arcona. Matthew looked about him. *If he ever needed a weapon, he knew where he could find one.*

The two trips he had made to this spot when he was younger, and the fact that he couldn't remember his grandfather actually visiting the spot on his own, led Matthew to wonder if his grandfather might have wanted it to be accessible to *him* as well.

Matthew made up his mind, then and there, to clean it and hide it in an obscure place aboard the *Wanderer* for protection. If it was discovered, he could always claim it belonged to the ship's previous owner—it was old enough.

He buried the box and the oily rag and plastic, and threw the rock markers as far away as he could from the rise, using his foot to rub out the lines he had made earlier, knowing full well that the wind would soon take care of the rest. He removed his shirt, wrapped it around the gun and the ammunition, and held the shirt as if he'd removed it to cool off during his walk. He then headed for home, realizing he'd have to hurry if he was going to make the ten o'clock transport.

As he walked, struggling with numerous thoughts and emotions, he couldn't help voicing one particular question that had suddenly come to mind.

"Papa, why is it I get the feeling you're trying to tell me something?"

CHAPTER 19

Sealing the small white envelope, Rebecca turned it over in her hands, her eyes drifting to the rectangular window next to her.

She spied Zerith's distant star and put her finger to the glass. She knew at this very moment Matthew was somewhere in between her and that star, and knew he'd be on Durin by morning. *Sixty, seventy yards away*, she thought, and her hand dropped as she looked at the envelope. *And I still won't see him.* Again she eyed the distant star. *Might as well be a hundred million.*

Shifting her weight on the divan, Rebecca leaned back against the wall of their living room, staring at nothing in particular. She hadn't gone anywhere on the base all day, choosing instead to lounge around in her favorite blue shorts and T-shirt—her hair in a ponytail, her face without makeup.

Just then the living room door swished open. Startled, Rebecca jumped in surprise and quickly tucked the envelope under her leg at the same moment her mother entered the room. She was dressed in one of her flowing day robes and was obviously frustrated about something. "Honestly, you'd think I was the only person on this station who knew what color taupe was." She made her way to several shelves of antique books that lined one of the walls of their richly furnished living room and began sifting through them. A few seconds later she threw up her hands and hurried for a curio cabinet at the far end of the room, glancing quickly from one figurine to the next. "I could have sworn I had something taupe in here. Honey, where's that book of color swatches we were looking through yesterday?"

Getting up from the divan Rebecca made her way to the large
fabric sofa in the middle of the room, her hand behind her back. "I
don't know. Is it on your nightstand?"

"*That's* right." Her mother carefully closed the glass door of the
curio and made her way to her bedroom. "Thanks dear," she said as
she passed Rebecca, hardly giving her a glance.

Rebecca hurriedly slipped the envelope under a small silver platter
resting on a narrow table behind the sofa. With her father visiting one
of the mining sites and her mother busily working on her latest redec-
orating project, she hadn't felt at all rushed to get her letter into place
all afternoon. But if her mother suddenly decided to stay a while she
didn't want to miss what might be her only opportunity before
Reuben's meal delivery later that evening.

Flopping on the thick cushions of the sofa, she continued to
mope as her mother came out of the bedroom, book in hand. "You
should have seen the doctor's eyes, dear. He just *loves* my suggestions
for the sick bay."

Rebecca rolled her eyes. Her mother had successfully managed to
redecorate a third of the base in the past two years and had considered
the doctor's surrender a positive sign that she was truly making
progress—that people loved what she was doing. She knew her
mother was simply trying to keep busy and that this latest project was
helping her to do just that, but Rebecca couldn't help wondering if
the good doctor had surrendered to her voluntarily or if her father
had had a hand in it.

Her gesture hadn't gone unnoticed, for her mother stopped as
she'd passed the arm of the sofa, a sympathetic expression instantly
crossing her face. She set the book down on a side table and sat next
to her. "Honey, I'm sorry your father got as upset as he did the night
before. He's just . . . He's worried about you, dear, that's all."

Rebecca looked up into her mother's face; it was a face that nearly
resembled her own, though her features appeared more mature and
matronly. "Mom, does Dad think I'm some silly child who doesn't
think? Does he honestly believe I'd fall for just any guy?"

"Of course not, honey, it's just—"

"He's never even met Matthew! He has no idea what he's like.
He's only going by what Dirk's said. He's not even listening to me."

Rebecca could tell from the expression on her mother's face now, as well as the night before, that *she* wasn't particularly keen on the idea of her being interested in an Outsider either. Still, Rebecca appreciated her mother's willingness to at least talk and listen; her father simply forbade her having anymore contact with Matthew and stormed out of the room.

"Honey, you've only met him twice. And there's more to this than you realize. Outsiders are . . . well, they can be *dangerous* in some ways. It's best you realized this now, before you found yourself getting too attached."

In her heart, Rebecca wished she could let her mother know all about what she *had* learned of Outsiders—that while they may have only met twice, they had shared so much through their letter writing, and that she was already *attached.*

Over the last three months Rebecca had been appalled to learn of just how poorly the Outsiders had been and were being treated, how they were living and surviving. At first she'd felt sorry for Matthew and all of the others forced to live in such desperate conditions, but as she'd read more of Matthew's letters, and as he attempted to explain their history and just why they had chosen to remain where they were despite their conditions, her simple sympathy had evolved into a genuine respect.

"Honey, look, I don't want to reopen everything we discussed last night. It's time to move on. Just understand that your father doesn't want to see you hurt. This *Matthew* apparently doesn't want to live by all of our laws. Your father's simply concerned whether or not a man such as that can be trusted." She leaned in and hugged her. "Oh, honey, I had several crushes at your age before I finally met your father." She gave her another squeeze. "He's a good man, and he loves you."

"I just wish he'd realize I'm not a child anymore. When I take my placement test next year he'll have to let me go. I doubt any career I'm assigned, even if it is in politics, will have room for an overbearing fa—"

"Over*protective*, dear. Not overbearing. You've had quite a bit of freedom here on Durin if you'd stop to think about it: trips to Arcona, dances, tutors to address whatever tickled your fancy at the time—most girls aren't as fortunate." She ran a hand though Rebecca's bushy ponytail, brushing a few wayward strands aside.

"Believe me, your father knows how old you are. I think *that's* what's scaring him." She laughed and then gave Rebecca a final hug. "He loves you, honey. Know that, alright?"

Rebecca nodded.

"The problem, my dear, is the two of you are too much alike." She stood. "You're both *stubborn*." Rebecca grinned at the oft-repeated phrase, and found herself drawn to her mother's smile. She desperately wished she could open up completely with her and share everything she'd learned and how she truly felt. Rebecca was almost certain she'd understand.

"Look, we'll talk again later, okay? I've got to get these colors to the doctor. He's so excited about the changes. I'm sure he's waiting for me." Rebecca watched her mother leave, her garish robe struggling to keep up, and winced in sympathy for the doctor.

After several minutes of silence she stood up, dimmed the living room lights, and returned to the divan.

Spying Zerith's star she marveled again over how different life seemed lately. What was it about Matthew that she found so appealing? She'd never acted this way with any *other* guy she'd met.

He was very attractive, but so were a lot of the other guys she knew. She knew she'd been drawn to his genuine sincerity and honesty in the beginning, but now it seemed as if there was something even deeper she was being drawn to.

She laughed, realizing their long-distance romance topped anything she'd seen in a play or book. And with the thought of plays, she was suddenly reminded of a tutor from the year before. They had been studying some of the more classical plays of Zerith's past when Rebecca expressed an interest in wanting to write a play of her own. Her tutor had simply patted her hand and reminded her that her place in life had yet to be determined, and that it would be best to wait and see what the placement test revealed before wasting her time on something she wasn't meant to do. The tutor had been brought in to satisfy a curiosity she'd had, and for that she'd been grateful. But Rebecca remembered well the hurt she'd felt at not even being encouraged to try. And the fact that her efforts would have undoubtedly been viewed as a waste of time dashed the budding interest she'd had.

Was that it? she wondered. Matthew had fulfilled a dream of his by becoming a pilot, and without having to take a placement test. He'd simply done it by getting his hands dirty and taking a risk.

Rebecca brought her knees to her chest and hugged them, glancing around the room and taking in all of her fine furnishings. *And even though I have all of this, I'm told not to dream at all.*

She realized then just what it was that attracted her to Matthew the most and what truly set him apart from those around her: *He's not afraid to dream; he* makes *them happen.*

Rebecca made up her mind then and there that she *would* try to write a play of her own. She wouldn't have to show her work to anybody; she could do it for her own personal satisfaction—test or no test.

Her eyes returned to the glass and to the apparent emptiness of space. "You're lucky, Matthew," she whispered. "You may be an Outsider, but you're richer than you realize."

* * *

"Ah, Matthew! Good to see you." And then in a whisper, "I just stocked the barracks mess with fresh fruit. Grab some while you can."

"Thanks, Reuben. I will."

Matthew moved out of the way as his friend worked at getting the awkward food cabinet down the small set of steps, his round face beet red under the strain.

I still don't understand why they just don't put in a ramp, thought Matthew, thinking at the same time how good it was to see Reuben again, his greeting much friendlier than the one he'd publicly received only minutes earlier from Dewy—but then, he had expected that.

"So . . . how are things, Reuben?" he asked, with a certain degree of anticipation.

The heavyset man had finally reached the bottom of the steps. He looked up, fighting to keep a straight face. "Oh, fine, fine. Can't complain." He swiped at his brow with a worn handkerchief he'd yanked from his back pocket. "Of course, I wouldn't mind having someone to care about me the way you do." He gave a quick wink and pushed his cart toward the base's business wing, back to the galley.

That's what I wanted to hear!

When the door of the barracks had slid shut, Matthew took a moment to ensure he was alone—the sound of a closing locker telling him he'd need to wait awhile before retrieving what he so anxiously desired.

Collins rounded the wall of lockers, rubbing a towel over his thinning, gray head of hair. He was dressed in his faded gray flight suit and getting ready to head out. "Hey, Matt."

"Hi, Collins. Switch runs with Billings?"

"Yeah. Poor guy's got the flu. It's going around you know." He tossed his wet towel into a small hamper sitting against the wall and quickly ran a comb through his hair while Matthew laid down on one of the bunks and pretended to fall asleep.

A minute later, Collins, respecting the young man's need for rest, left without a word.

The moment the door was shut, Matthew bolted from his bed to the fourth bunk along the far end of the wall. He reached underneath it, feeling around its center—the spot he and Reuben had long ago agreed upon—until his hand brushed against something taped into place.

He quickly returned to his bunk and anxiously opened the small, white envelope.

Rebecca began her letter by thanking Matthew for the wonderful evening she'd had the night of the dance, even though it had been short, and then went on to explain just what had happened with Dirk and her parents after he'd left.

He learned that Dirk *had* in fact gone to her father, but that Governor Adams, to his credit, had decided to handle the situation behind closed doors, rather than barging into the ballroom and confronting his daughter that night.

Exactly the opposite of what Dirk wanted, I'm sure. Probably explains why he decided . . . for some reason, he corrected himself . . . *why he might have wanted to take his frustration out on my face.*

Rebecca had been genuinely surprised at how her parents had handled the news, revealing sides of them she'd never really seen before—her father very displeased, forbidding her to see the "Outsider" again, and her mother, who usually sided with her husband, suddenly showing restraint. Rebecca guessed her mother could see how strongly she felt about Matthew and that she would need *someone* to talk to. She had been there for her before, and Rebecca believed she wanted to be there for her again. Both, Rebecca figured, were probably hoping it was simply a crush and, given the distance and lack of communication they would have with one another, would probably dissolve within a matter of weeks. She assured Matthew in closing that their letter writing was still a secret and that nothing, not even time, was going to change how she felt about him.

Matthew rechecked the date. *Yesterday's date*. He refolded the letter and carefully slipped it into the lining of his worn flight jacket.

As he pulled out a slip of paper from his duffel bag with which to write a letter of his own, he decided he wouldn't tell her about being hit after the dance; he was embarrassed enough over his carelessness and now realized he needed to be more cautious. With the mission for the Rebels, along with the unorthodox relationship he was having with Rebecca, he knew if he *didn't* remain more vigilant, he risked the destruction of both. Instead, he focused on more of the daily, trivial matters of living in a shanty town.

Through such anecdotes and sketches, Matthew had tried to paint as accurate a picture as he could of who he was and where he came from. Deep down he knew he ran the risk of scaring her off, but at the same time he knew he couldn't deny his past. He believed in his grandfather's sacrifice and, short of exposing his role in the Rebellion, had begun clarifying, lately, just what those beliefs were. By being honest and up front, removing what she had referred to as their "masks," Matthew deeply believed that Rebecca could then make up her mind as to whether or not he was really worth holding on to. And if, after all he had shared, she *was* still interested in him, then he'd know it was because she truly cared about him, Matthew Tanner— nothing more, nothing less.

* * *

A week later Rebecca made a startling confession. She had shared a few of Matthew's letters with her mother.

I needed someone to talk to, Matthew. I hope you can understand. I've been trying to put on a happy face around here, but it's hard when you have no one to share your heart with. I can talk to you in our letters, but I simply

*needed someone to lean on here. You have come to mean so much to me and
have really caused me take a closer look at my own beliefs, my own dreams. I
hope you're not upset. I really believe we can trust her.*

Her mother, thanks to his vivid descriptions, had found the treatment of the Outsiders deplorable, and expressed shame at knowing they existed, but like most Arconians, never taking the time, nor having the interest, to learn what was *really* going on.

*Mom is impressed with how well you've learned to read and write
without formal schooling. She also thinks your grandfather had to of been a
very special man for not only bringing you into his home, but taking the
time to raise you as well as he did. She's often said, "Anyone can have children, but it's a completely different matter to raise them properly." If you
want to know the truth, Matthew, I think she's beginning to understand
just what it is I see in you. Who knows? Maybe she'll start working on
my father.*

At first, Matthew had been embarrassed knowing someone other than Rebecca was reading his letters. The whole process of writing even a simple letter frustrated him; he struggled with every word he put down on paper. But he understood Rebecca's reasoning, appreciating how difficult it must be not having anyone around to share her feelings with—at least he had Rollyn. He also couldn't help admiring her craftiness in using his letters as a tool to chip away at her parents' prejudice.

Nearly a week later, he was beginning to see just how powerful a tool his letters were becoming.

*My mother appreciated your news about Doreen, Matthew. Thank you
for taking the time to look into that. I guess they were really good friends as
children and then went their separate ways when they got older. They'd tried to
keep in touch, but after they were married, their lives became more complicated
and they simply lost track of each other. After the banishment order was given
Mom tried to look her up again, wondering (knowing her personality) if she
was part of the rebellious group. But she never found her.*

When you told us she'd died of malnutrition several years ago, focusing on her son's health rather than her own, Mom broke down in tears and left the room. I think she's really beginning to understand just how horribly all of you have been treated over the years. Doreen's death drove it home. It made it personal.

I can't help but believe she's sharing some of what you tell me, in a roundabout way, with my father. I know she hasn't told him about our letter writing. She promises to work on him though. I hope so. I'd really like to see you again.

Oh, my play is really beginning to take shape. I hope one day I can let you read it. It helps to keep my mind busy. But I have to be honest with you, Matthew. It's hard.

As powerful and uplifting as her letters were, Matthew could sense Rebecca's resolve beginning to wane as the weeks went by. More and more, her letters began focusing on the fact that they hadn't seen each other for quite a while and, after having shared many memories from their past, a natural desire to want to create a present, as well as a future, was becoming more and more apparent.

At first, Matthew began to wonder if they were simply writing too much. There really was only so much a person could say three times a week, living the way that they were—Rebecca, within the confines of the mining base, and Matthew, carrying out the monotonous routine of a hauling schedule.

Please don't take this the wrong way, Matthew, but sometimes I wonder if I'm really writing to an actual person.

Perhaps I could watch you from the hangar door sometime. I'm sure I could come up with some excuse to be there. What do you say?

Matthew dearly wanted to see her again and had even toyed with the idea of having Rebecca try out her plan. But if her father found out about it and reported his dislike of Matthew to Warring, it could jeopardize everything he was doing for the Rebellion. Deep down, as much as he truly wanted to see her again, to talk with her, to feel her hand in his, to hold her close, he knew his mission had to remain his first priority.

She'd been upset with his response and quite curt in her reply. And that had troubled Matthew greatly.

For the hundredth time he'd considered telling her about his mission as a means of helping her understand just why it was he was so unwilling to take a risk. But he knew he had no right to place that kind of burden on her. If the Rebels failed, if in fact he was one day discovered, he didn't want her caught in the middle. He lived amidst the consequences of those who had chosen to rebel, and watched daily as they struggled to survive. The person he loved was in a good place already—a very good place; how dare he run the risk of having all of that taken away?

He decided after receiving two curt letters in a row that he'd spice up his next letter with a gift. Most people assumed that the majority of his dockins had been spent on the various improvements that had been made to the *Wanderer*, not knowing they were Dewy's, and not his own. Consequently he had accumulated a precious stash of savings nobody knew about. Using some of that stash he bought Rebecca a small, heart-shaped pendant from a booth that specialized in trinkets and souvenirs for pilots and visiting guests.

The idea of a "genuine" souvenir from Durin always seemed ridiculous to Matthew, since the vast majority of the items actually came from Zerith; he had hauled several of the cases himself from time to time. But it allowed visitors to take something back with them, and helped in a small way to supplement a few of the station's more exotic amenities.

He carefully scratched, "I am with you," on the back of the pendant, hoping with all of his heart that she would like what to her could only be seen as a *simple* gift.

In addition to being filled with thanks and appreciation, Rebecca's return letter also overflowed with contrition.

Matthew, I'm sorry. I truly am. I feel horrible you spent as much money as you did on this beautiful necklace. I know how hard you work for the dockins you get.

I do appreciate it, Matthew, and know how hurt you'd feel if I insisted you take it back, though I want to so much.

Forgive me for complaining. I realize now I have nothing to complain about. You are the most sensitive and caring guy I've ever met, and have taught me so much about what really makes life important.

    Regardless of our current situation, I'm lucky to have you. I need to be patient—it's that simple. You keep telling me that in time we'll have a chance, and I need to believe in that. I'll try to remember this every time I wear your beautiful gift—which, by the way, will be always.

Satisfied with how well his gift had been received, Matthew truly felt they were headed in the right direction.

* * *

Having spent the better part of her morning writing and rewriting a particularly stubborn scene in her play, Rebecca had decided to clear her head by going for a swim. Normally she found the family's private pool sufficient, but today she had wanted a change of scenery and had enjoyed the openness of the station's larger, public pool.

Dressed in a blue swimsuit covered loosely by a white, knee-length robe, Rebecca drabbed at wet hair with her towel as she triggered her living room door—surprised to find Dirk standing near the sofa. Her eyes went immediately to her manuscript she'd left on the end table, now in Dirk's hands.

"Rebecca, I'm surprised by this. You can write."

Rebecca might have been slightly flattered by the compliment had Dirk's eyes not been scanning her from head to toe while he'd said it. "And you can read." She pulled her robe tighter around her body.

Dirk laughed at the jab. "You always were a witty one, Rebecca. I guess I shouldn't be *too* surprised by this."

Rebecca stepped forward and held out her hand. "Could I have that back, please? It's personal."

"It's a play, Rebecca. How can a play be personal?"

Rebecca took another step closer. "I'd like it back, please."

Dirk held her gaze for several seconds before finally relenting, taking in her form a second time.

"Thank you." She held it close to her chest. "So, do you often come by and pick up things that don't belong to you?"

Dirk's trademark smirk returned. "Just relax, Miss Adams. Your father asked me to meet him here. My visit is strictly official."

Rebecca's chin raised slightly. "Indeed. Well in the future I would appreciate it if you wouldn't touch what doesn't belong to you when you *do* visit . . . *officially.*"

The edge in Dirk's smirk faded a bit as Rebecca began making her way to the hallway that led to her bedroom. Dirk hurriedly blocked her path. "Come on, Rebecca. What's going on? I told you what I read was good. Don't you believe me?"

She looked up and softened ever so slightly. "I'd just appreciate it if you wouldn't—"

"Alright. Alright, Rebecca. I apologize."

"Thank you." As she proceeded to walk, however, Dirk continued blocking her path. "Look, Rebecca, would you be interested in a game of Rotku later on tonight? I seem to recall a time when you enjoyed that."

"I . . . I don't think so, Dirk. Maybe another time." She made a move to pass him, but was again blocked.

"What is it, Rebecca? Are you still upset about that Outsider hauler?" She didn't look up.

"That's it, isn't it?" He rested his hands on her shoulder. "Rebecca, forget him. You deserve far better than *that.*"

Rebecca's eyes shot upward. "You don't know anything about him!"

Dirk released her, but held her gaze without flinching—his jaw set. "And neither do you! Let me tell you something about him and Outsiders, Miss Adams. They are a miserable, worthless lot who can't seem to get it through their thick skulls that they lost a battle they shouldn't even have started!"

"Why? Because they believed in the freedom of choice?"

"Oh please, Miss Adams. Spare me. I think you've been on this *rock* too long. Our planet was dying before our government took control. If it hadn't been for our leaders and their wisdom, we wouldn't even be having this conversation. Think about it. Do Arconians appear miserable to you? No. Are your friends miserable? No. Are *we* miserable? No. All of us have our place in this world—it's that simple—and *everyone* is taken care of. Everyone."

"And what if we're capable of more than what's *expected* of us?"

"What, like you being able to write a play?" He threw his head back and laughed. "I said it was good, Rebecca. I didn't say it was *that* good."

As she attempted to push her way past Dirk he forcefully grabbed her shoulders, surprising her—her manuscript spilling to the floor.

Dropping to one knee she grabbed at the pages while Dirk simply stood by, watching her from above. "Besides," he continued, "what business is it of yours, anyway? Don't tell me you've actually fallen for that mangy mutt. He's ancient history, *Miss* Adams. He *will not* get near you again!"

Having collected all of her pages, Rebecca stood and glared at Dirk. "To you he may be a mutt, but let me tell you something, Dirk. He's *ten* times the man you'll *ever* be!" She could see his eyes beginning to harden, but paid no attention to them. "And *yes*, I would rather be with a mangy mutt like him, then with an arrogant, self-absorbed shell of a man like you!"

For a brief moment Rebecca expected a slap. Dirk's face reddened under her words, and his upper lip twitched with anger. But then he softened suddenly, again taking her by the shoulders. "That's Rebecca Adams—witty *and* feisty." His eyes then traveled down her neck and beyond, her robe having loosened when she'd retrieved her papers. She started as his hand went to her chest. "Well, well. What's this?"

She glanced downward and saw her pendant in between Dirk's thumb and forefinger. She reached up and grasped it. "A gift from Mother." She stepped backward.

Dirk continued staring at her closed hand, his face unreadable. "It's very nice, Rebecca. Though I am surprised she didn't have it professionally engraved."

She'd had enough of Dirk, and Rebecca tried once more for the hallway, but Dirk was gripping her solidly by the arm. "Where'd you get it, Miss Adams?"

His grip was firm, but Rebecca stood her ground. "My mother, Dirk. If you don't believe me, ask her yourself. Now, my father's due here any minute, correct?" She didn't bother waiting for an answer. "Should I tell him you refused to let his daughter, dressed in as little as she is, get to her bedroom?"

They held each other's gaze for several seconds before Dirk finally released her, allowing her into the hallway and into her room. When

the door had slid closed, she locked it and slowly walked to the foot
of her bed and sat down.

Pulling her robe tightly around her, she mentally replayed what had
happened, biting her lip, and wondering just what it was she had done.

* * *

*He asked me where it came from and I told him it was a gift from my
mother. Mom's been telling Dad the same thing. Dad hasn't mentioned
anything about it tonight so my guess is there's nothing to worry about.
Besides, even if Dirk thinks it came from you, what can he really do about it?*

Though slightly concerned over Rebecca's run-in with Dirk, after
a few more letters, Matthew, too concluded there was little point in
jumping to any rash conclusions.

Then—the unexpected.

On his way to the barracks, he saw a complete stranger—not
Reuben—wrestling with the infamous food cart on the small but
obtrusive flight of steps.

Matthew felt the blood drain from his face, and the next several
minutes felt more like a dream than a reality.

Not caring if anyone saw what he was doing, he raced up the
steps and through the door, sprinted to the fourth bunk, dropped to
the floor, and thrust his hand beneath it.

Nothing!

He slumped to the floor.

Painfully, Matthew realized that the one and only link he and
Rebecca had with one another had unmercifully been cut.

CHAPTER 20

"Thank you, Mr. Lowoski, for that very *thorough* report on District Six." The sarcasm in the CEO's voice was obvious.

"I *always* try to be thorough in my reporting."

"We can tell. And there's not a soul in this room, awake, or otherwise, who would disagree with you on that point."

The eleven council members had been called together for an unscheduled meeting. Each, in turn, had been asked to give a status report on their respective districts and assigned businesses.

Large, round faces lined the oval edge of the council room's massive oak table, their corpulence physically supporting a conclusion the CEO had arrived at weeks earlier—they had become fat and lazy, all of them, while their subordinate officers to whom they delegated their work (and ultimately the Rebels) had become stronger.

He knew that now. And, in only a matter of minutes, so would they.

He stood and walked to the head of the table while Lowoski glared at him, undoubtedly murdering him, creatively, over and over in his mind.

The CEO smiled, well aware of the desire each of these men had to be where he was now; they could not be trusted—greed was the only glue holding them together.

And yet, despite their thirst for his power and control, he now had to depend on them for assistance. And, given their lust for what they *did* have, he had a feeling that after hearing what he had to say he would get it.

"Gentleman, I've called this emergency meeting to share with you the results of a month-long investigation I've been conducting. And I assure you, if you have felt your time wasted with what has taken place so far, you will feel otherwise in a matter of minutes."

He smiled inwardly as each of the council members began to fidget and squirm in their own unique way—no doubt suddenly mindful of the skeletons in their closets, curious whether this was the day they would suddenly be brought out into light.

"Harris, lights please."

Harris, standing against the wall, triggered the dim switch that significantly reduced the enormous room's interior lighting, at the same time lowering heavy curtains to block out the unrelenting sunlight streaming in through the many windows lining the eastern wall.

The CEO then lowered a white screen at the front of the room and activated the projector.

"It's a graph," muttered one of the council members, who was obviously expecting more.

The CEO was enjoying this. He was feeling like his old self again—the nightmares of Paul Tanner fading as he'd buried himself in his research. "It *is* a graph—a spline chart, to be precise. It shows the trend of our yearly earnings."

"According to those gridlines, the data's thirty years old."

"All I see is a wavy green line."

The CEO took a deep breath, digging deep for the patience he so desperately desired. "This particular slice of the chart *is* thirty years old. And the *wavy green line* you see before you is actually two lines."

He tapped a button on the tabletop, zooming in on the lines. "If you look carefully at some of the edges of the peaks and troughs, you'll notice the blue and yellow lines do part occasionally, though only slightly. When the two align, they appear as one line. And, yes, green." He reached for a glass of water, allowing the men a few moments to soak in the chart's layout.

Setting the glass down, he continued. "The blue line represents the actual quarterly totals of a given year. The yellow line represents formulated projections; projections, mind you, taken for granted as we've become more and more stable in our growth and development. Given how controlled our economy is, it isn't surprising to find that our projections almost match precisely the actual gains; natural resources are the only data points that occasionally fall out of sync."

He was pleased to see several heads nodding; they appeared to understand what had been explained so far. Several, though, including Harris, seemed confused—not so much over the information, he guessed, but about his reason for sharing it.

He tapped a second button on the tabletop and the image before them slowly began scrolling from right to left, plotting out the passage of time. "As you can see, our green line remains consistent—a tribute to our . . . *hard* work and *determination*." The comment, tongue in cheek, produced a few chuckles.

"Now, keep your eyes on that green line, gentlemen. Notice what happens to it."

All eyes were riveted on the slightly wavy line rising and falling with the passing of each year. After several moments of nothing but green, the two lines suddenly separated, ever so lightly; the image halting before the point of division had completely cleared the left-hand side of the screen.

The change sparked an immediate rumble of speculation. The CEO spoke above it. "As you can see, life as we know it has run predictably well up until about three years ago. Then, suddenly, the two lines parted. Not much, as you can see, but enough to tell us that something is askew."

He then permitted the image to continue scrolling until finally the two lines merged again, at the beginning of what was the current year's last quarter. The image froze and the CEO adjusted it so that only the three years of separation were visible on the screen.

"It has taken me quite a while to put all of this together, gentlemen." He didn't feel it necessary to mention that it had taken a week alone to assemble the chart they were currently viewing. He had discovered just how rusty *he* had become with computers over the years and had relied heavily on his secretary for help in putting it all together. "But we now have the proof we've been looking for. I had you stand up earlier to show you that what you *think* has been going on in your respective areas, *isn't* really the case. And, for over three years now, it has all happened right under our very noses."

A long pause followed. Lowoski spoke up first. "Just what are you suggesting the gap represents?"

The CEO was sipping water from his glass. He set it down and took a moment to look each one of them in the eye. *They're clueless.*

he thought. *Genuinely clueless.* "Embezzlement, gentlemen. Rebel-guided embezzlement—pure and simple."

The room exploded in shouts of disbelief.

"Order, gentleman, let me ex—"

"Surely our accountants would have alerted us to any discrepancies in our monthly or quarterly figures!" shouted one.

"They're stored in secure, closed-system computers. We receive them every month for review. Who could have tampered with them without anyone noticing?" added another.

The others quieted down as the logic of the two comments gradually hit home.

The CEO patiently cleared his throat. He chose to begin by addressing the last question first. "'For review,' you said? How many of us have *really* taken the time to review them? How many of us over the years have simply taken the numbers we receive at face value?

"We've become lazy, gentlemen; we've assumed tomorrow will be the same as today." His voice rose in volume. "How many of you had your advisors quickly produce the reports you've presented to us today, without so much as even glancing at the raw figures yourselves?"

An uncomfortable silence followed.

"I thought so." He pointed at the graph. "Not all of the numbers I've used in this chart came from our *precious* computers, but from my own family ledger. The very ledger whose existence all of you have feared for so long.

"In this particular graph the projected yellow line you see before you shows where we would be had the numbers not been tampered with—based on the numbers recorded in *my* ledger. The blue line, the actual line, on the other hand, is based solely on those figures found in our computers."

From the expressions on their faces he knew he had their undivided attention. Now he would demonstrate the wisdom and value of his leadership.

"The figures you received every month and quarter *were* accurate; the Rebels simply removed a small portion of our profits later."

"But because the algorithms of any projected line are based upon the computer's actual figures," began Lowoski, "without the previous values from your ledger, any projected line we called up would have always aligned with the new totals."

He's not such a fool after all, thought the CEO, genuinely surprised. "Correct. The mistake they made was pulling the dockins *after* the monthly figures had been posted."

"Not counting on," Harris interjected, "the record you and your ancestors have diligently maintained for years now."

"Precisely. It began three years ago, and appears to have ended shortly after the end of last quarter. I suppose they were hoping we would simply forget about them—toss past figures aside as yesterday's news . . . just as we *have* been doing. Bottom line: they've been banking on our complacency with the numbers." He worked his way to the control panel at the head of the table. "Watch closely. Had I merely relied on the data from our computers, *this* is what the line would have looked like."

He hit a third switch on the desk, and slowly the yellow line dropped to merge with the blue one . . . becoming green once again.

The men exploded in renewed anger.

The illustration had been predictable given all they had discussed, but it visually solidified his theory, and had completely brought to a head the one emotion he had been looking for. *Now, all I have to do is channel their fury.*

"Gentlemen! Gentlemen!"

The room quieted down after several more shouts for order, though it was obvious, even in their silence, how frustrated and irritated they felt at being played for fools.

"Gentlemen, I know how you feel, but now is not the time for emotion; it is the time for action."

The councilors remained quiet, their eyes locked on their leader.

"The numbers I showed you today represent our industry's *combined* totals for each quarter. I will assign each of you a particular set of numbers, before and after the split, to break down, to try and determine exactly just where the money has gone."

He swallowed hard, hoping each of these callous and angry men would appreciate the sacrifice he was making with his next statement. "I can't do it alone, gentleman. I need your help." He didn't feel it necessary to mention that this sudden show of trust was based upon a thorough examination of each of their personal and professional bank accounts. "After what I've managed to put together so far, I am convinced the research would take too much time to do on my own. And, for now, all of our accountants are suspect. The fact that the figures are now back to where they should be indicates, to me, that the Rebels now have what they feel is sufficient for their needs.

"Others of you will be taking a closer look at our accountants, to try and determine which of them surely had a hand in this."

"I'll take that assignment," called out Harris from the other end of the darkened room.

"No, Harris. I've already selected an assignment I feel you'll find more to your liking." His eyes returned to the council. "Gentlemen, we now have the hard evidence we've been looking for—*evidence*, I believe, that will finally lead us to the Arconian Rebels and sympathizers we've speculated about for years. Before we step forward to reprimand anybody, though, I want specifics. I want only those responsible to pay for their crimes."

He pounded his fist on the table. "I am convinced we can pick out this cancer without disrupting the stability we now enjoy. Anything rash could stir sympathy. We have to be cautious!"

The CEO paused a moment as several councilmen voiced their agreement.

A moment later he stepped in front of the graph, the green line streaking wickedly across his face. "Together we can unravel whatever it is these Rebels have put together. They may have a head start, but I do not believe, by any means, we are at all too late."

He leaned on the oak table with both fists as his voice rose to match the fierceness burning in his eyes. "I want their feeble, traitorous plans exposed for all to see, and those responsible rooted out and destroyed . . . once and for all!"

CHAPTER 21

"But I need your help, Papa! I haven't seen any sign of Reuben, and it's been nearly a week since Rebecca's last letter."

"Just what is it you'd like me to do?"

Matthew stammered, trying desperately to come up with a single answer as a flood of desires filled his heart. They came in a rush. "Does Rebecca know what happened? What happened to Reuben? How long until I'm able to see her ag—?"

"Easy, Matthew, easy. Believe me when I tell you that I'd love to answer all of those questions; it pains me to see you this upset. But . . . I'm simply not allowed to."

Matthew just stared at him as his heartache was replaced with frustration, which quickly gave way to anger. "Papa, I've tried to be patient, haven't I? I've tried to be understanding. But I can't stand it any longer! Who or what prevents you from answering me?"

"What to you might appear as prevention is in truth—"

"I don't need more philosophy, Papa! I need answers!"

Matthew looked around at their bright and familiar surroundings. "Why is it we only meet in my dreams? Why always here? And . . . why can't I see Mom and Dad?" He looked directly into his grandfather's face. "Why, at the very least, can't you help me find out if the one person who truly cares for me knows what's happened? If she . . . still loves me?"

"Matthew, listen to me." Paul ran a hand through the boy's hair. "I can only give you counsel—remind your heart and mind of that which you know to be right and true. Ultimately, all of the decisions you make, and all of the consequences that follow, have to be your own."

"But why—"

"Was it any different when I was alive? In no way could I live your life for you, foretell the future, or tell you what could be found in the hearts of others. It's no different now. I'm here to advise and to guide. Beyond that, there's nothing I can do."

"And the pistol! You call that advising? You practically placed it in my hand!"

Paul cringed. "Yes. I crossed the line on that one. Chances are you'll never need it. I promised I wouldn't let it happen again." Before Matthew could ask him who he had made that promise with, he added, "Be patient and trust me when I say that if you hold fast to what you know is right, you will *be rewarded."*

"But how will I know Rebecca will be there when all is said and done?"

Paul looked tenderly into his eyes. "You don't, boy. You don't."

"Then how can I be expected to go on? I—"

"Because deep down you know that what you're doing will have an enormous impact on our people. And that impact, the reward, extends far beyond simply having the chance to live within the walls of Arcona."

Matthew's expression was one of fatigue—not of mind or body, but of heart. "But I suppose you aren't allowed to tell me exactly what that reward is?"

Paul, sensing the boy's turmoil, turned his eyes away. "I can't, son. It's simply not time yet."

The silence that followed was palpable.

"I see."

Paul wrung his hands in frustration and bit at his lower lip. "Matthew, trust me, if I—"

"No, Papa. Enough! I've heard enough!"

"But you must try to—"

"I'm not going to lose her! I can't."

"Matthew . . ."

"Papa, I'm not going to play these mind games anymore." He glanced around the room and started to laugh—a laugh that unknowingly tore painfully at his grandfather's heart. "You know," he began, seeming to study his surroundings with a keener eye, "perhaps none of this is *real. Maybe you really* are *nothing but a dream."*

When Matthew's eyes returned to those of his grandfather, he noticed that Paul's body seemed transparent; the back of his chair was now visible through his chest.

"Papa?"

There were tears in the older man's eyes.

"Papa, what's going on?" Matthew's voice became frantic as Paul faded, his image almost indiscernible. "Papa! Come back! Come back!"

Soon, all Matthew could see was a lonely hide-back chair sitting directly across from him.

"Papa!"

With a start, Matthew awoke—the creaking of his cot loud in the evening's silence.

He put his hands to his face, and was genuinely surprised at the tears he found running down his cheeks; he'd been crying . . . and he had no idea why.

CHAPTER 22

Though he thought his mind had been made up, he was now having second thoughts. It had been well over an hour now, and he was scheduled for departure in twenty-five minutes.

Impatiently Matthew walked the length of the barracks, desperately wondering if he had made a mistake.

He couldn't help it. It had been weeks since Rebecca's last letter, and he had to know how she was feeling—if she still cared. The fact that he was always running into Reuben's replacement only intensified his desire. When he'd tried to casually find out what had happened to Reuben, all the replacement would divulge was that he'd been transferred to one of the dig sites—short and to the point.

Finally, after much consideration, Matthew worked up the nerve to ask him if he would deliver a message to Rebecca. Unlike Reuben, however, this man was all business; he would deliver the message, alright, but for a price.

They settled on twenty dockins. It was expensive, but Matthew believed if he could finally get word to her it would be worth it.

A few days ago Matthew would have felt completely uncomfortable with the whole idea; as a matter of fact he had been feeling unusually irritable and insecure all day. But he was now determined to let Rebecca know that for him, at least, nothing had changed; he loved her, and wanted very much—impossible as it seemed—to build a life together.

No sooner had he sat down on a bunk at the far end of the room when the door slid open. The last person he had expected to see sauntered into the room.

"Well, well. What's the matter, loverboy? Aren't I good enough for you?"

Matthew stood slowly, now understanding why the new food server had been around as often as he had—it had been a setup.

Dirk removed from his pocket the letter Matthew had written. "It's a touching letter, Matthew. Really it is. And it gives me *just* the evidence I needed. It's a shame it'll never be delivered."

The shock of Dirk's appearance was beginning to wear off. "What business is it of yours anyway?"

Dirk began walking toward him, slowly—grinning. "My job is the personal safety of Governor Adams's family. You're a threat to that safety."

"A threat? How?"

"Conspiracy. I really don't believe Governor Adams will appreciate all this sneaking around behind his back; it undermines his authority as a father; it puts the stability of his family in jeopardy. Therefore, you *are* a threat."

Matthew stood his ground as Dirk came to a stop, arm's length, in front of him. "It's all how you look at it, Matthew, I suppose. Of course, fathers have always been irrationally overprotective of their daughters." He laughed. "Reuben was the only one who delivered food to both the governor's quarters *and* the pilot's mess. Once I had him pulled, all I had to do was wait."

"So you're going to make sure not even a letter gets through to her? Am I that much of a threat to you?"

Dirk smiled, crumpled the letter in his hand, and tossed it over his shoulder. "The truth is I care very little for the letter. It would only muddy up what I already have in mind. As for you being a *threat* to me, you're *nothing*. And you're going to stay that way."

"Why do I get the feeling you're here to give me more than just my letter?"

"You're bright, Matthew. The fact is, I'm tired of you. I'm tired of you upsetting my own plans. And I'm here to make sure you understand just *how* I feel about you."

"And I suppose you intend to pound my face in."

"Something like that."

"How will you justify it?"

Dirk reached into the same pocket the letter had been in and removed a large, golden brooch. He tossed it to Matthew, who instinctively caught it, turning it over in his fingers. "What's this?"

It belongs to Mrs. Adams. I'll simply tell her and the governor that I caught you trying to steal it—that you put up a bit of a struggle when I confronted you about it."

"And you expect her to believe *that*? That's ridiculous!"

"Why? It has your fingerprints on it."

Matthew looked down at his hands, realizing how easily he'd again fallen into another of Dirk's traps . . . unprepared for the smashing right hook that followed.

He dropped the brooch as Dirk's left fist slammed into the other side of his face.

Dodging another right, he leaped past Dirk, trying to give himself some space in which to gather his senses.

Dirk, anticipating the move, swept Matthew's right leg out from under him as he brushed by, sending him to the floor.

Despite Matthew's earlier bravado, he now suddenly realized just *who* he was up against: a Spire security officer; a man trained for action.

But then Matthew wasn't completely without *experience* either.

He dodged Dirk's incoming foot, grabbed it, and twisted, sending Dirk crashing to the floor. Both got up quickly, Dirk even more outraged than before.

Stay calm, thought Matthew. *Stay calm.* "At least your attack's out in the open this time," he began, stepping backward toward the showers. "That was a cheap shot last time."

"What are you talking about?"

Matthew watched Dirk's face closely. *He honestly doesn't know what I'm talking about!* Matthew found himself having to force back all of the questions that were suddenly coming to mind.

They eyed each other, both looking for an opening.

Without warning, Dirk rushed forward, throwing a right and then following up with a low left, striking nothing but air as Matthew successfully dodged the wild punches.

And then it happened: Dirk took a deep breath and seemed to find the focus he'd been lacking. He stepped toward Matthew with a new determination in his eyes—a look born of long and strenuous training.

Matthew, cleverly drawn into striking first, threw out a fake left and followed through with his practiced right hook. Both missed their mark as Dirk deftly grabbed Matthew's trailing right arm, swinging him around, and driving a powerful knee into his stomach.

Matthew bent over, gasping for air as Dirk hammered another fist into the side of his head.

Matthew staggered backward, clearly shaken. But when Dirk came in for a second blow, he was caught completely by surprise with a vicious uppercut to the face; his nose crumpled under Matthew's clenched fist.

Blood flowed as Dirk growled in rage. Like a savage beast, he charged.

Matthew disappeared around the wall of lockers.

Dirk followed him around the corner, coming to an abrupt stop as the door of an upper locker slammed into his mouth—driving the broken cartilage of his nose even deeper into his face. He let out a shriek, shook off the pain, and continued charging.

Matthew continued throwing open upper and lower locker doors, trying to slow him down. Seeing they were having no effect, he held his ground and braced himself for the impending attack.

Dirk came in swinging.

After several minutes both had blood streaming from their faces. Matthew's right eye was nearly swollen shut from an earlier hit. And while Matthew succeeded in evading most of Dirk's blows, landing several punches to the officer's grisly, battered face, he found he was no match against Dirk's well-practiced, side-thrust kicks and back fists.

In the end, it was an unexpected jump kick to the head that sent a defeated Matthew crashing to the floor.

Dirk moved in immediately for the kill, kicking unmercifully at Matthew's head, chest, and stomach.

Matthew curled up, instinctively trying to protect his head and midsection as his brain struggled to piece together what was happening.

The kicking stopped and Matthew could hear Dirk's laughter. It wasn't filled with as much energy as before, but he clearly sounded pleased at the sight before him. "I've got to admit . . . you're good." He was breathing heavy, his voice sounding bloody and strained. "Given training . . . you might have won."

Matthew wanted to tell him to look in one of the many mirrors lining the wall across from them, adjacent the shower stalls, to take a good look at just how *good* a job he *had* done, but he kept silent and focused instead on simply remaining conscious.

Dirk took a step backward, taking a final look at his prey before commencing his final blows. "I'm going to finish it, Matthew. You're going to die." He let out another laugh. "Don't worry. I doubt anyone's really going to miss an *Outsider* anyway. And if they do . . . they'll get over it."

Before Dirk could take a step, Matthew, still curled up on the floor, gave one final kick with both his feet, catching Dirk in the shins. He fell forward, toward the lockers, his head meeting with the corner of an open locker door.

He landed on top of Matthew, who cringed—expecting body blows that surprisingly never came.

Painfully he pulled himself out from underneath Dirk, and checked for a pulse. He was alive, but Matthew felt he had to get out of there before he regained consciousness.

He slowly, carefully, brought himself to his feet, using one of the sinks for support.

As he stood, he looked at himself in the mirror above the sink: his right eye was swollen shut, his face was covered in blood—trickling from his nose and several cuts—his skin split by Dirk's powerful punches. He looked himself in the eye. *What have I done? I've . . . I've ruined everything!*

He spit blood, mixed with saliva, into the sink and ran his tongue over a tooth that had been knocked loose.

Matthew's thoughts were a jumble.

No! What happened here was personal, he thought, finally confronting the selfishness he'd been experiencing lately. *It doesn't have to affect the mission. It can't!*

Turning on the water, Matthew quickly rinsed his cuts. He wiped his face dry with a towel, grabbed his duffel bag, and stumbled toward the door.

It had been a good lunch, but now it was time to get back to work.

Dewy passed through the door, into the hangar bay, and saw that he had timed things just right; he would be able to see Matthew off before prepping the bay for the next, incoming freighter.

In the distance he noticed Matthew seated in the cockpit of the *Wanderer*. He couldn't make out any facial expressions, but caught the rapid thumbs-up sign from Matthew as he raised the ship above the docking bay floor, turned, and set a steady burn toward open space, beyond the docking bay's shimmering energy field.

It was a routine they had followed for months now, and he gave little thought to it.

Walking to where the *Wanderer* once stood, he noticed what appeared to be drops of drive coolant running in a line along the bay floor.

Dewy was a stickler when it came to his hangar bay; everything had its place, every section of the bay was clean and orderly. It was a standard Dewy adamantly enforced—no exceptions.

He dropped to one knee and wiped a finger over the drops, which he intended to show the maintenance supervisor immediately.

Something made him stop.

He sniffed at his finger—his firm, determined expression suddenly replaced by confusion. *This isn't coolant.*

He tasted it. *Blood?*

Dewy looked to where the *Wanderer* had stood only seconds earlier . . . his mind racing.

Getting to his ship without anyone noticing him hadn't been a problem; everyone in the hanger bay had been preoccupied with their respective projects and therefore hadn't paid any attention to him. Walking in such a way as to *not* arouse suspicion, however, had been an entirely different challenge. Aside from an immense headache, and a stabbing pain coming from his ribs, the floor seemed to shift with every step. But he *had* made it, had even acknowledged Dewy as he usually did before takeoff.

Matthew had performed these tasks so many times in the past they had become second nature, requiring little thought. Which was good, considering how sluggish his mind was now.

He had rested fitfully in his cabin for the first three hours of the flight, awakening and adjusting to the new course and speed with little problem. The two hours that followed the correction, however, found Matthew keeping a close vigil over his instruments, fighting off waves of nausea and pain.

Soon, he reached the drop coordinates.

Matthew adjusted his speed and relative altitude and eyed the button that controlled the outer door of the *Wanderer's* aft hold, feeling a desperate inner need to see this run through.

As bad as the fallout of his fight with Dirk might become, he couldn't let it spill over into his mission for the Rebellion; he was determined to right what appeared a hopeless situation. And though he knew deep down there was something he was overlooking, his mind was too clouded and disturbed to isolate it and think it through; he was reacting, nothing more.

He watched through his half-closed left eyelid as his altitude leveled off. He jabbed the button and listened to the familiar hissing of the hydraulic unit, letting him know that the ore was being dumped.

With the drop complete, Matthew closed the outer door and proceeded to change course and arc back to the standard flight path. He fought desperately against his body's longing for sleep until finally he was back on course, in light space, his autopilot engaged. Then he couldn't hold out any longer. Slumping over his control panel, Matthew fell into a deep and fitful sleep.

"Papa? Can you hear me?"
Silence.

When his eyes opened, it took a moment to figure out where he was.

Slowly, painfully, he righted himself—the sight of the blinking green light on his course grid bringing everything back into a fuzzy, but understandable focus.

The ore!

He glanced at his ships chronometer. The *Wanderer* had already completed its second course correction and would soon complete its third. He had only about three hours to skim the ore from the other two holds.

I've done it in less . . . haven't I?

Carefully he stood up, and using the walls of his ship's corridor for support, made his way to the aft hold. He triggered the door release and the change in air pressure with the accompanying ear popping sent him to the floor.

He stood up and opened the door of the starboard hold, unfastened the dolly, and loosened the cargo's restraining straps. He then reached for the first crate at the top, his ribs and sore, stiff muscles screaming in protest as he struggled to free the heavy crate.

Fifteen minutes later, when he had finally shimmied the crate loose, a sharp pain in his side made him cry out, the full weight of it too much for his ribs and muscles to bear. Fortunately he managed to roll out of the path of the falling crate and watched as it fell harmlessly to the floor—breaking open and spilling its contents all over the *Wanderer's* narrow corridor.

Deep down, he had known it would be impossible, but his heart simply refused to accept it.

With his back against the wall he slumped to the floor, the sharp ore cutting and scraping his hands and wrists. Tears filled his eyes as even more unwanted pain shot through his wounded body.

Wiping his brow as well as his face, Matthew noticed blood trickling from the small cuts he'd suffered from the fight—reopened under the recent strain.

His head fell into his hands. *I've failed.* The ore had already been dumped, and there was no way to transfer what remained. He knew that if he triggered the scrambler now, it would account for the missing ore, but wouldn't explain the spilled ore, nor the empty aft hold. His throat tightened. *And if I don't activate the scrambler, the weight and volume scan will give me away the moment I land.*

Matthew cleared his throat as he wiped the blood and sweat from his hands onto the legs of his flight suit. *Maybe if I can put it back . . .*

He struggled to get to his feet, but soon realized that he lacked even the strength to do that. And if he couldn't stand, how would he possibly put the ore back into the crate? —let alone back into the starboard hold?

He considered cutting his gravity and moving the ore that way. But if he passed out, unable to reestablish gravity when the *Wanderer's* emergency breaking procedures kicked in, he'd be killed instantly.

Slowly he lay down on his side, the dizziness too much to endure. *Instead of making things better, I've made them worse. I'll be discovered, and the Rebels . . .*

He closed his eyes in despair.

"Papa? I'm sorry for what I said. Please help me. Please . . ."
"I'm here, boy. I'm here."

"I'm in a lot of pain, Papa."

"I know, son. Just be still. Be still . . . "

The blaring of the *Wanderer's* emergency klaxon slowly began registering in Matthew's mind.

He knew what it meant.

Dragging himself to his feet, gritting back pain and dizziness, he slowly got up and plodded his way through the spilled ore toward the cockpit. Every step he took was filled with pain, the simple act of breathing now excruciating.

Reaching the pilot's chair he punched in the computer's landing subroutine which halted the squawking of the ship's alarm; had he waited any longer, the emergency braking procedures would have engaged—automatically freezing his systems and locking him in an orbit around Zerith until help could arrive. *It's not going to be* that *easy!*

Slowly he made his way to his cabin, removed a panel from inside his closet, retrieved his grandfather's gun, and tucked it into the belt of his flight suit. He knew it would be useless to try and defend himself if Spaceport Security suddenly decided to storm his ship, but he felt better knowing he could at least try.

Catching sight of Arcona, he allowed the ship's computer to bring him in closer to the spaceport.

As the buildings and landmarks became distinct, he wondered how long it would take for security to notice the results of the scan. How long would it take them to react? After all, he couldn't remember anyone failing the scan in the past—nobody had dared to! How would they handle such an unprecedented event?

His mind was becoming clouded once again as he fought hard against the pain brought on by the mere act of sitting upright.

Finally he took over the controls and steered the *Wanderer* through the spaceport's large hangar doors. As he brought it in slowly to rest in his assigned pad, Matthew knew, at that very moment, that the scan he'd been dreading had already taken place. *This landing will be my last.*

He didn't bother powering down, but instead headed toward the starboard hatch. *If I can get to Miller's motorbike, maybe . . .*

He hadn't even made it past the pilot seat when its headrest caught him in his side. A jolt of pain shot through Matthew like a knife, plunging him into unconsciousness.

Regaining consciousness, Matthew could hear sniffling, crying. Slowly he turned his head in the direction of the sound; it was Rollyn— he could have predicted that. What he could never have predicted, though, was the gun the young boy now held in his shaking hands, taking aim at Matthew's heart.

"Why, Matt?" he sniffled. "Why couldn't you have just died?"

Matthew tried to reach for his own gun, but the mere image of Rollyn with a gun was too much for his strained senses. He passed out again. But not before hearing a shout, and feeling, with a sudden jolt, a bullet tear into his body.

CHAPTER 23

Flashes of bright light, the sensation of being carried, bouts of pain, and the taste of warm broth sporadically assaulted Matthew's senses as he continued drifting in and out of consciousness. Sensing he was being cared for, he did his best to follow the dull sounding, unintelligible directions being given.

Finally, his eyes opened.

"Miller! Miller, he's waking up!"

Matthew turned his head to the side as Miller's large form emerged from the darkness. "Considering we're the only three people in this cavern, why is it you find it necessary to *shout* all the time?"

"You're the one who's shouting!" countered Patch.

Miller glared at him.

Patch's syrupy voice went on, undaunted, "You're just jealous because you weren't the first one he saw when he woke up."

Miller stomped in his direction.

Patch, knowing he had pushed too hard—again—quickly leaped to his feet, his left foot knocking Matthew soundly in the side of the head.

Miller stopped his advance. "Oh, great! We've waited two days for him to wake up, and when he finally does, you kick him in the head!"

"Sorry, Matthew," and to Miller, "I was just going to bring the lantern closer so he could see us better," Patch lied.

Miller shook his head as he lowered himself to the floor while glaring at Patch's back. "What do you say we just beat him with a stick now?" he called out.

"Guys, please."

Miller looked down at Matthew, seeming to have forgotten he was even there.

"Where am I?"

"You're safe, kid. You're in Rock Hill Cave."

Matthew craned his neck from side to side, the small lantern on the floor revealing nothing familiar. "The pile of straw?" he asked, weakly.

Miller hooked a thumb over his shoulder. "It's back there a ways. We're actually in a side cavern. We figured we'd be safe here."

"What's . . . I . . ."

Patch squatted easily beside him. "What's the last thing you remember, Matthew?"

"I . . ." he hesitated, unsure of what to say.

Miller's hand rested on his shoulder. "It's okay, kid. We know you're part of the Rebellion. So . . . so are we."

Matthew's eyes widened. "What?"

Patch started laughing. "Hard to believe, isn't it? I only found out about Miller's involvement a few days ago. Here we've been working together for years, and only *now* does it come out."

"But then . . ." Suddenly it all made sense: the ease with which he had become a hauler, the rebuilding of the *Wanderer*, Dewy's possession of his ship's wiring schematics, the installation of the secondary hatch switch, and the fact that neither of them had ever questioned him about the modifications made to his aft hold.

Finally, he found his voice. "How long have you two been involved?"

Miller, somehow picking up on his train of thought spoke up first. "For quite some time, Matthew. But, please, don't get the wrong idea about us." He suddenly appeared uncomfortable expressing his feelings. "You . . . you got under both our skins . . . long before the idea of involving you *ever* came to mind."

Patch nodded, flashing a wide smile on his thin and kindly face.

Miller continued. "The ore idea is quite old, actually. I wondered for years just who I could trust to handle that aspect of the mission—that was part of *my* assignment. I'd watched you grow up and knew just what kind of person you were. When the Rebellion decided to put their plan into motion, I was sure you'd be perfect for the job. So, I, along with several others, I'm sure, did our best to steer you in that direction."

"I often wondered if Miller was involved," confessed Patch, "but we were each told never to bring it up, unless absolutely necessary—less problems should either one of us have been caught.

"*My* job was to make sure your ship's electronics would hold up, and to ensure the modifications we'd make in the future were possible, and . . . unnoticeable."

"The added hatch switch?"

Patch smiled at Matthew. "Part of it, yes. I also designed the hydraulic drop system, as well as the scrambler. Though you were led, I'm sure, to believe otherwise."

In the silence that followed, Matthew's mind was spinning under these new revelations. But even as he struggled to put all of these new pieces together, the stark realization of what had happened suddenly hit him.

He tried to sit up, the sharp pain in his wrapped chest and leg pinning him to the floor.

"Easy. Easy, kid! Relax."

"But, Miller, I've blown it! I wasn't able to make that last drop!" A weak and latent memory flashed through his mind. "Rollyn!"

Again Miller tried to settle him, patting him on the shoulder, convincing him to lie still.

Patch again asked, "What's the last thing you remember?"

Matthew's eyes darted in all directions as he desperately tried to recall everything that had happened. He told them of his fight with Dirk and how clouded his mind had been afterward, how, without really thinking it through, he had gone through the motions of trying to complete his mission. He then related how he thought he remembered seeing Rollyn standing over him with an old gun, similar to the one he had, silencer and all, pointed at his chest. "He was crying . . . I think he shot me. Everything's a blur after that until . . . until I opened my eyes and—"

"Saw a face only a mother could love?" teased Miller, trying to lighten the situation for Matthew by injecting a little humor.

Patch's serious expression remained unchanged as Miller burst into laughter. "You're just jealous because I not only have talent, but looks as well."

"Talent? Oh, please." Miller's eyes brightened. "Such as picking locks?"

"Precisely," answered Patch, appearing oblivious to Miller's trap.

Miller roared with laughter. "If you're so talented, just why was it you couldn't even find your way out of a locked bathroom?"

Patch patiently waited for a lull in the laughter. "And I *would* have gotten out—in seconds, mind you—if you had given me some *tools* to work with!"

The serious tone in Patch's voice caused Miller to laugh even harder.

"I don't recall," continued Patch, patiently, "ever seeing you tighten a C-bolt with your mouth. It's big enough, though. Shall we try it now?"

Miller, hearing the implied threat, quieted immediately. He started rolling up his sleeves. "Why you little—"

"Guys, please!" Both were startled at the sound of Matthew's voice. "You've been together in this cavern for two days? I'm amazed you haven't killed each other!"

"Don't think it hasn't crossed my mind," grumbled Miller. "I'll get you some water." He disappeared into the dark shadows, beyond the light of the lantern. The clanging and shuffling sounds of supply packs being moved were sharp and distinct in the cool silence of the cavern.

"You *were* shot, Matthew."

Matthew peered into Patch's face. "Rollyn shot me?"

"Don't be too hard on him, kid. It's kind of my fault." Miller returned and placed a cool tin cup to Matthew's lips. "Drink slow. That's it. We'll get you some warm food in a minute."

He placed the cup on the dirt floor. "When I saw you fly in, I could tell immediately something was wrong; you weren't coming in as straight as you normally did. And then when I noticed how long it was taking for you to power down, I knew something was up.

"When I got to your ship, the starboard hatch was open. I looked inside and saw Rollyn standing over you. I shouted, and it scared him. He fired, but he was looking in my direction when the gun went off; he'd been spooked is all.

"The bullet went in and out of your thigh. We cleaned the wound later. You were pretty banged up: four cracked ribs, several cuts, and a concussion. But you're healing well. I haven't seen any sign of infection."

Patch picked up where Miller left off. "I came up behind Miller after he shouted. Rollyn had dropped the gun and was sobbing over you when we got to him.

"You should have seen the look on our faces. Both of us knew the significance of what we were seeing with the spilled ore and all—"

"But neither one of us knew what to say," finished Miller. "Patch here squared his shoulders and said, 'I'm part of the Rebellion, Miller. Are you going to get in my way?'"

"Miller just smiled," Patch continued. "When he told me he was also part of it, we raced to get both of you out of there before security had a chance to react. I'm just relieved they were slow on the uptake; the officer probably stepped out of his booth for something during your ship's scan, otherwise—"

"So Rollyn's . . ."

"I took you on my motorbike to a safe house I've known about for years; now *there* was a challenge. But my bike was more maneuverable so . . . anyway, after cleaning your wounds and taping your ribs, we agreed to bring you here—to rest and heal.

"Patch had followed me from the spaceport, with Rollyn, on his skimmer. He stayed with him awhile at the safe house before meeting up with us here. Since our covers were shot, our regional director thought it best if we stuck together—figured it was safer that way." He chuckled, glancing at Patch. "I guess he doesn't know us very well."

Matthew smiled, knowing it was only a joke; they would die for one another, and they knew it.

"Matthew." Patch waited until he had his undivided attention. "I was there throughout most of Rollyn's questioning." He paused.

"What is it?" prodded Matthew.

Patch took a deep breath before answering. "Rollyn's father . . ." He glanced at Miller, who silently nodded his approval for what he was about to say next. "Matthew, Rollyn's father killed your grandfather."

Matthew's eyes remained locked on Patch's. "What?"

Miller took over. "Apparently his father was a link for Spire—an informer. He'd been promised a fortune for keeping an eye on Outsider activities.

"He was only a year away from receiving compensation. It seems that a few of the Outsiders over the years have been offered the same deal; Spire promises a substantial reward if you simply act as their eyes for a time. Whether or not Spire honors their end of the bargain when all is said and done . . ." He shrugged his shoulders. "As far as the informer's concerned, the reward is supposedly far more than what they would have received had they simply defected, abiding by Arcona's basic terms of citizenship."

"And . . . Rollyn's job . . . was to watch me," surmised Matthew; he was stunned.

"Yes. His father encouraged your friendship, demanding the boy keep an eye on you and your grandfather, in case either one of you were ever approached by Rebels."

Matthew appeared confused. "But I became involved quite a while ago. Wouldn't Spire have moved in earlier if—"

"My guess is," continued Miller, "while his father may not have approved with how your grandfather had led the first rebellion, in his heart he still believed in its fundamental ideals. Rollyn said that when a close friend of his father's defected, he let him in on the agreement he'd had with Spire. That friend then recommended him for the job, and Rollyn's father became their new informant. But when you told your grandfather about your involvement in the Rebellion, his father became concerned that a new revolution was just around the corner—your grandfather possibly serving as the rallying point."

"Putting his compensation at risk," added Patch.

Miller nodded and continued. "Deep down I think he would have liked to have seen a new rebellion succeed, but he was more anxious to have a slice of the Spire pie first."

"But why kill him?"

"Rollyn says his father knew how committed your grandfather might be to the basic philosophy of the Rebellion, and how respected he was by most Outsiders. I guess he feared the potential of that combination."

"He wasn't involved in any of it!"

"*We* know that, kid. But *he* didn't. So when he went over to talk with him, to threaten your grandfather to drag his feet on any involvement, or risk having you exposed, the argument that followed must have gotten out of hand. Your grandfather, it seems, was very upset over the idea of being threatened, blackmailed. He apparently got in a few body blows with his cane when he tried forcing him out of his house. That's when Rollyn's father completely lost control."

Matthew closed his eyes. "He didn't see the gun."

"Rollyn says he didn't mean to kill him. But I don't think his father felt he had any other choice. Who knows? Maybe past resentment finally found its way to the surface. But my gut tells me that by eliminating your grandfather, he felt he could slow down whatever the Rebels had put together. Not having a part in it himself, he didn't understand just how different the organization of the new Rebellion was—is.

"He tried to make it look like an outside attack, muddying the water for both the Rebels *and* Spire. Until now."

"And since he sometimes came by our place whenever he needed Rollyn, nobody would have considered him out of place that day," concluded Matthew.

"Right."

"So, it wasn't Spire *or* pirates."

Patch stood up. "No. Tell him what we've decided about all of that, Miller."

"*Our* guess is that the pirate attack was purely coincidental. Given your description of their ship, it sounds to us like those who attacked you are all that's left of the pirates. We're guessing they'd banded together in an effort to merely survive."

"Explaining their cobbled-together ship."

"Right. Even if they'd combined their fuel and supplies, it couldn't have been much. Even *I* shiver to think how they've managed to survive all these years. Anyway, they probably decided to start raiding again and picked you because of the size of your ship; they'd start small and use the information from your computers, as they had in the past, to obtain what they'd need to go after bigger fish."

"And the lock bypass?"

"I'm willing to bet Patch's salary that they got it off a Durin security officer in exchange for a cut of any future spoil."

"My pay? Why my pay?"

Miller rolled his eyes. "Will you stop your whining? If you took a moment to think about what I just said you'd realize you'd have nothing to lose!"

Patch fell silent, trying to figure out if he had, in some way, just been insulted.

Miller gave Matthew a wink and continued. "The officer could have received the offer over a secure line while on patrol above Durin, dumping a bypass into space for the pirates to pick up. That would help to explain why Durin security wasn't watching your departure as closely as they should've, prior to the attack."

"But why not get their information directly from Durin's computers?"

"You know how long it takes for information to get to Durin. Besides, Durin's on the receiving end of information. *Your* ship would have carried the spaceport's latest flight information—more accurate. Anyway, would you want to run the risk of physically being caught by Dewy with *your* hand in the cookie jar—so to speak?"

They do *know Dewy.*

"When their attack failed, their contact probably cut his losses and quickly concentrated on covering his trail."

"What's left of the pirates," concluded Patch, "will probably surrender soon, or die off. They can't possibly survive much longer. Especially after the blow you dealt them."

All were silent as Matthew struggled to sort out all of the new and disturbing information.

"Anyway, kid, Rollyn was ordered to take you out the moment an opening presented itself. Or, I should say, when it appeared obvious you were involved."

"To slow things down."

"Exactly."

"That explains why he was always the first one to greet me when I landed. He was waiting for me to slip up."

"I guess when the kid saw you wounded, with ore scattered all over, he knew it was precisely the kind of situation his father had described.

"But, Matthew, Patch and I don't believe he had it in him to go through with it. We believe he was more frightened as to what would've happened if his father had found out he had passed up the opportunity."

Silently Matthew recalled the bruises Rollyn had been receiving from home and wondered now if they'd actually been signs of resistance.

"You lost a grandfather," added Patch, "but he lost his father . . . long before this."

Matthew nodded. "But what's going to happen now? With all three of us exposed, and the ore spilled all over the *Wanderer*, surely it won't take them long to put it all together—maybe even trace it back to Dewy." He suddenly found himself wondering if he'd *ever* see Rebecca again.

Miller chuckled. "I think you're giving them far too much credit. But if it helps, before we left the safe house we were told that the *physical* part of the Rebellion was going to begin sooner than expected anyway.

"Spire's discovered the missing dockins. You knew about those, didn't you?" Matthew nodded. "Up until now we've managed to remain several steps ahead of them. Now it turns out that's all changed. We'll have to act soon, before they have the chance to catch up to us."

"What about—"

Matthew was cut off at the sound of running footfalls, and the jerky flashing of a hand light coming down the corridor that led to their cavern.

Patch and Miller sprang to their feet, both taking up positions on either side of the cavern's entrance. They each pulled a gun from behind their back.

Matthew recognized the pistol in Miller's clenched hand as belonging to his grandfather, and presumed the one in Patch's hand, matching it, belonged to Rollyn's father. *His father must have held onto* his *gun, too.*

Matthew, wrapped in a blanket and lying on the dirt floor, never felt more vulnerable in his life.

A man called out what had to have been the agreed-upon call sign, for both Patch and Miller lowered their weapons and stood aside as a young man, whom neither of them had ever seen before, came to a dead stop directly in front of them.

He was breathing easily, despite the fact he had been running. The sweat, streaming down his face, indicated he'd been running, or jogging, for quite some time. He had on a bright colored jogging outfit and appeared to be only a few years younger than Matthew. His message was short and to the point: "Tomorrow, between eight and eleven in the morning. Those directly involved know the specific time. Stay put." He turned on his heel and jogged back down the darkened corridor, the beam of his light bouncing erratically down the linking shaft.

"Be ready? A meeting?" asked Matthew.

Miller turned from the entrance, returning to the brighter light of the lantern. His face was grim. He glanced back at Patch, who, Matthew guessed, wore a similar expression.

"No, kid. The Rebels have decided to make their move in the morning."

Matthew couldn't believe his ears. "Are we ready?"

Miller walked over and sat down on the dirt floor, his elbows on his knees, as he rubbed his thick bottom lip with the back of his hand. "I sincerely hope so, kid . . . for all our sakes."

CHAPTER 24

10:10 A.M.—Arcona Spaceport

Tossing his clipboard onto his desk, Warring turned to the young man who'd served as his assistant that morning. "Give me a few minutes alone, will you? I'll call you when I'm ready."

The young man nodded and left, the door sealing shut behind him.

Resting his elbows on his cluttered desk, Warring ran his hands over his bald head and began massaging his temples with his fingers. For the past three days he and his team of technicians had been working around the clock dismantling the *Wanderer*, looking for anything "out of the ordinary" and trying to retrieve its flight data—orders from the top. He knew his men were doing the best they could, but for the hundredth time he wished Patch and Miller were here to lend him a hand.

Warring still had no explanation for the spilt ore and empty hold discovered on Matthew's ship, nor had he any idea where his two prize technicians might have taken the boy. He was well aware of Patch and Miller's fondness for Matthew and was certain they were helping him now, but was at a loss as to just what kind of help that would be. While putting together his initial report of the incident, he learned Miller had been seen carrying Matthew out of the building, with Patch and Rollyn Carlton, from Shipping, following closely behind. But two calls to both of Arcona's hospitals had turned up nothing.

He glanced out the wide window of his office that gave him a panoramic view of the shuttle and freighter bay. On its distant pad sat the small freighter in question. With most of its inner and outer hull plating now removed, Warring fancied it resembled a dead carcass, the few technicians now on duty appearing to pick off and clean what remained of its meat.

He rubbed his eyes laughing at his imagination. "Warring, old boy," he muttered to himself. "You've been up *too* long."

When he pulled his hands away, however, he was surprised to see several workers from Shipping and Receiving running into the hangar, their orange coveralls quite distinct from the blue ones he and the other workers wore. As he looked closer, he could have sworn one of them was carrying a rifle. He stood to get a better look when his door slid open.

Two young men, both in orange themselves, made their way into the room—the first presenting a rifle of his own, the second sealing the door and locking it from the inside. The young man with the rifle was the first to speak. "Mr. Warring, sir. Believe me, we don't want to hurt anyone."

Warring slowly raised both of his hands. "That's fine, son. You'll get no argument from me there. What do you say you put that rifle down and we can talk about what's troubling you."

"I can't do that, sir." It was clear the young man still respected Warring, in spite of the orders he seemed intent upon carrying out; Warring was firm, but fair, and those attributes had clearly not been forgotten now. "I need you to ground all flights and order all employees into Receiving."

Warring sized up the young man carefully. "And if I don't?"

Whatever reservations the boy had shown earlier left him that instant as he brought his rifle to bear on Warring. "Then I'll be forced to do it myself, sir."

From the expressions on both of the young men's faces, Warring had little doubt the boy meant what he said.

Turning to the small microphone at the edge of his desk he keyed the PA system, noticing, at the same time, that most of the employees far below were already in the process of being herded into Receiving. "Attention. Attention. All port employees and pilots, I need *all* of you to report to Receiving immediately. I repeat: All flights and projects are be terminated and all port employees and pilots are to report to Receiving immediately. We have a bit of a situation here that we need to address. Let's all be cooperative and I'm sure no one will get hurt." He released the button and eyed the two young men at his door. "Will that do?"

"Thank you, sir. That was just fine. Now, if you'll step away from the desk and follow us, we'll head down to Receiving ourselves. There's something on the Information Network we'd like everyone to watch."

Warring nodded. He had no idea what this was about but couldn't help wondering if it had something to do with Matthew and his ship. Before he stood, however, he glanced out his window once more, determined to get word to someone that they needed help; he had a responsibility for the safety of his employees and knew what needed to be done. Gripping his desk, he prepared to stand.

"Your hands up, sir, away from the desk."

Warring slid his right index finger a few inches along the desk's edge until it found the security button.

"Your hands up, sir!"

Warring pushed the button. "Son, when you get as old as I am maybe you'll under—"

The butt of the rifle to the side of Warring's head instantly cut short his reply.

10:13 A.M.—*Special Forces, Dispatch*

The taller of the two rogue guards rechecked the intensity level of his plasma rifle and glanced at his partner, who had his rifle in hand and was flattened against the wall on the opposite side of the doorway. "Remember, if there's resistance, arms and legs; Lars and Phillips are on duty and I don't want any kills." He checked his wrist chrono. "Alright, Nate . . . on two. One . . . two!"

Nate slapped the door panel just as the taller guard got into position and fired a high intensity bolt above the heads of the six operators, taking a huge chunk out of the wall directly above the mounted rifle case. "Hands up! Everyone! Hands up!"

The stunned operators threw up their arms and backed away from their terminals as Nate ordered them to sit on the floor at the opposite end of the communications room.

The taller officer quickly checked each monitor to make sure none of them had had the chance to send out a warning message and then positioned himself in front of the rifle case.

"Nate! Halls! What's going on here? Have you two lost your minds?"

Halls turned an eye on Lars as he lowered the intensity of his rifle. "Just sit back and relax, Lars. We don't want anyone to get hurt."

Halls then glanced over at Nate who was alternating his attention between the stunned dispatch operators and the massive electronic map of the city that took up the entire wall behind the dispatchers' monitors. At that moment two lights, at nearly opposite ends of the city, lit up. Nate called out the areas being indicated. "Water refinery, and . . . the armory."

Lars's eyes went wide as he began standing. "Halls, you know procedure. I've got to get word to our officers in that area. Look, there are problem—"

"Lars, if you haven't noticed, I believe *you* have enough to worry about already."

Just then one of the operators, who had managed to work one of his feet underneath him, lunged for Nate—earning him a quick shot to his right thigh from the taller officer.

Nate's rifle swept the line of men in warning as the wounded man dragged himself back to his spot. It was only a slight burn, but enough to let all of the operators know that the two men before them *were* serious.

"I said it before and I'll say it again," shouted Halls as he made a show of increasing the intensity of his rifle by two clicks, "We don't want to hurt anyone!" And then to Nate, "Key up the Information Network on one of those monitors." He eyed the operators. "Everything will make sense in a few minutes, believe me." A short burst from his rifle melted the rifle case lock, sealing it shut.

Halls then walked over to the doorway and secured the door. He and Nate were the only two officers assigned to their building level, and had already blocked off access to the entire floor, but he didn't want to take any chances. He then glanced at the map board, the voice of the Information Network's anchorman suddenly dispelling the room's uncomfortable silence. A few more lights began to glow, but for the most part, most key sites remained unlit—either successfully secured, or at the very least unaware of what was actually taking place. He smiled; they had successfully taken control of Special Forces' dispatch center, effectively shutting down, at least temporarily, Arcona's ability to effectively mobilize its military and law enforcement officers. A small step, really, but one of incalculable importance to say the least.

One particular red light then caught his attention: the spaceport. He hoped the others had managed to gain control of it without any casualties.

He turned to Nate who had noticed the light as well.

"Well," drawled Nate. "I'd say we made it just in time."

Halls eyed the operators on the floor, expressions of shock and confusion alternating on their faces. "We shall see, Nate," he replied. "We shall see."

* * *

"That's it, gentlemen. Just line up against the wall over there."

The five men staggered through the plush surroundings of the high-rise office suite. Their bloodstained shirts were mere ribbons from the lashings they'd received, their faces bruised and swollen.

"That's it. Very good." The CEO appeared overly pleasant. "Well, I must say, you're looking *lively* this morning." He chuckled to himself as he walked up to the first man in line. "How'd you sleep?"

The man simply stood there, swaying slightly on his sore and torture-worn feet, weak from hunger.

Cruelly, the CEO grabbed a shock of the battered man's thinning hair and violently yanked his head backward.

The two guards who had accompanied the prisoners lowered their rifles, prepared just in case one of them miraculously found the strength to strike back.

The man winced from the pain, and through clenched teeth rasped, "We . . . haven't slept . . . in days."

Satisfied with the answer, the CEO released his grip, shaking the loose strands of hair free from his hand. He smiled and returned to his polished steel desk, leaning on its edge, his arms folded. "That's right, you haven't. And I must confess, all of you have held up remarkably well. I was certain you would have broken days ago,"—he eyed a man with burn marks and blisters running up the lengths of his arms—"considering what you've been through."

He turned. "Harris?" He was standing just behind the CEO's desk, data tablet in hand, an uncomfortable expression on his face; an expression that hadn't gone unnoticed. *He's used to others doing his dirty work for him*, thought the CEO. *Well, this will be good for him. It will be just like old times. He's got to learn that sometimes you simply have to take matters into your own hands . . . regardless of how ugly the mess might be. I learned it from my father, and now he'll learn it from me.* "Have they undergone all forms of torture?"

Harris cleared his throat. "Not all forms, but a majority of them."

"And these traitorous accountants have still refused to reveal just who they've been funneling the stolen dockins to?" He knew the answer, of course; he just enjoyed watching them squirm.

"That's correct."

"And the chem-serum?"

"They've admitted to the embezzlement charges, but each insists they don't know the name of the collector."

"What about a physical description?"

"Each of them have given entirely different descriptions. Either they're lying, which I find hard to believe, considering the grade of serum we used, or we've had *several* Rebels coming here to collect it."

The CEO glared at each of the beaten men in turn. "Doubtful. Using that many men, for *that* particular task, would've been too risky. Disguises?"

Harris nodded. "It makes the most sense."

He's telling me they're dead ends—all of them. I can hear it in his voice.

The CEO focused on the blood stains that now marred the plush white carpet of his office, undoubtedly coming from the soles of the prisoners' bare feet. Harris was convinced that the reason they weren't coming up with anything solid was because there *wasn't* anything solid. He believed the Rebels had simply stopped their leaching, for a time, over the fear of getting caught—that they really weren't as prepared as they'd thought.

Harris was also convinced that they had been caught early enough, before they'd had the chance to rally and organize an attack. All Spire had to do now, in his opinion, was keep a careful eye on all inventory levels and business transactions, capturing members of the Rebellion, one member at a time, until eventually they would come to believe that their every move was being monitored; ultimately they'd realize how futile any plan of retribution would be.

There was only one thing that kept the CEO from embracing Harris's logic: the incident at the spaceport three days ago. Just as he'd feared, somehow a Tanner was in the middle of this mess.

And though that aspect of the Rebel plan had been exposed, and was no longer a real concern, it raised some interesting questions: Just what were they planning to do with such a small supply of ore? Was this the first time they had tried this, or was it only now that they had been caught?

With two of Warring's best technicians *and* Matthew Tanner still missing, the CEO couldn't help believing that the smuggling had been going on for quite some time. But if that was true, where was the ore being stored? How and when were they going to use it?

The most curious part of the investigation, thus far, had been the computer diagnostic Warring had personally performed, hours after their escape. The scan had triggered a complete crash of the *Wanderer's* computer systems—something that hadn't happened earlier. And while Warring had assured him he would do his best to recover the computer's memory, the CEO knew it would take days, if not weeks to restore.

Yes, they had discovered the means by which the Rebels had been secretly funding themselves, but thus far, they had been unsuccessful in really determining if and where those dockins were being spent. And, deep down, the CEO couldn't help wondering if the information in the *Wanderer's* computer, along with yet undiscovered physical evidence that perhaps might be buried within Tanner's ship, would provide him with the answers he was looking for.

Until Warring finished his report, however, the pitiful group standing before him was his only lead. And, unlike Harris, he wasn't quite ready to claim victory yet.

Reaching the end of the ragged line he turned to address them. "Each of you had a good life. You had solid jobs with all of your needs provided for. Now, for some *ridiculous* reason, it seems that isn't good enough."

He paused. "A pity, really." Two of the men looked up, perhaps they had wanted to protest, but their tired eyes revealed how physically incapable they were of doing so. "Therefore, I find all of you guilty of treason. And since you refuse to cooperate in our efforts to root out the true source behind your actions, you leave me little choice but to hand down your sentence.

"My assistant, Harris, was given the responsibility of planning and organizing your *executions*." He smiled. "Or should I say, your *accidents*.

"Harris, tell each of them how they will die."

Harris rounded the desk and cleared his throat as he approached the men. He tried to disguise how uncomfortable he felt by pretending to intently study the information on his data tablet. He began by reading three of their names, struggling to maintain a strong and determined-sounding voice. ". . . you will be on assignment in the forested region, assessing the cost of a new refinery project we've been considering. There you will contract a deadly disease and will die. Your bodies will be discovered later, and the area will be quarantined. A few weeks later a new vaccine will be developed to prevent further spreading of the *disease*. We will then offer free immunizations against the dreaded disease to all of Arcona's citizens; Spire will again be viewed as the savior of Zerith."

"Death with a purpose, gentlemen," interrupted the CEO. "A great honor—more than you deserve, I can assure you."

Harris indicated the other two. "A midair shuttle collision will claim *your* lives. Each of you will be in a private shuttle. A faulty thruster will cause your shuttle," he pointed to the man at the end of the line, "to plow into his. The resulting fireballs will leave hardly anything behind."

While Harris was returning to his position behind the desk, the CEO added, "Your deaths, aside from making us look good, will also send a clear and powerful message to the instigators of your pitiful plan—a reminder of what happens to those who attempt to question Spire's authority. Blood well spent, wouldn't you say?

"Of course, all of this needn't happen if you could share with us *something* that we would find useful. After all, the serum is only rewarding when the right questions are asked. Perhaps you have information that has remained untapped, that you would like to share with us now."

All five remained silent, each one, by virtue of the Rebellion's organization, truly incapable of revealing anything more.

As bothersome as these Rebels had been over the last few weeks, the CEO appreciated what they *had* done for the council. They'd been an eye opener, a wake up call so to speak. Those assigned the task of weeding out the embezzlers had done an impressive job, sifting through and analyzing months of computer logs and registries in only weeks—their efforts quite telling; they enjoyed living at the top and would do anything to remain there. Perhaps now they wouldn't take for granted the posh lifestyle they enjoyed. In the end the CEO concluded that if the stumbling Rebels had managed to alert the council members to the danger of their complacency, then all of this trouble had been well worth it.

But that didn't mean he was willing to give up on these prisoners just yet.

As the CEO walked along the northern wall of his office, glaring at the silent and pitiful forms standing before him, he decided he would make one final attempt at getting some answers.

"Guard, remove the first three and return them to their cell. I want to talk to the other two."

The three men were ushered out of the room through the same hidden door they had passed through earlier—a door that would lead them back to their cell, where only the guards and prison officials were aware of their existence.

The door sealed, the southern wall appearing solid and uniform.

Walking over to his desk, the CEO called out a series of numbers that triggered open a drawer on the right-hand side of his desk. Tapping the left leg of his desk caused the wall behind the prisoners to lower, revealing a black, oddly pitted surface.

The CEO removed a small revolver from the drawer, its gleaming surface cold and polished. He made a show of checking its cylinder, though he already knew it was loaded. He rounded his desk and approached the first man who seemed fully aware of the impending danger, yet mindful of the hopelessness of trying to resist or escape.

"What's going on?" asked Harris, confused at this sudden turn of events.

"Well, Harris, I have another lesson for you. Considering a midair collision has a horrible tendency of reducing its victims to ash, I really see no harm in pushing our threats with *these* men a bit further, to the next level."

"What do you mean?" Harris had moved to the side of the desk, the data tablet still in his hand.

"It's simple. Watch."

The CEO approached the shorter of the two traitors and rammed the business end of the gun into the man's stomach, the man's head coming to rest against his shoulder. He then spoke calmly into the man's ear. "This antique of mine belonged to my great grandfather. A pity they're seldom used these days—barbaric, yet effective." He pressed it harder against the man's stomach. "This will be the last time I ask you. At this very instant you're facing your own mortality. If you don't give me the answer I am looking for, I'll *personally* end your life. And a bullet isn't as kind as a plasma bolt; you'll die slowly, holding your gut . . . and bleeding to death."

"You're just going to shoot him? Here?"

The CEO glanced at Harris over his shoulder. "Of course. But don't worry. The black wall you see will absorb the bullet, just as it has the thousands of others over the years."

Suddenly, the wall's noticeably pitted appearance took on an eerie and disturbing quality. "It's how my father, and his father, handled many of the more *stubborn* obstacles of the past."

He looked down at the head of the man he was about to destroy; he was sobbing, mumbling something unintelligible about his wife and children. The taller prisoner was staring at the nightmare, his swollen eyes wide with terror.

The CEO merely smiled at him. "It's been a while." He pulled back the hammer of the weapon with his thumb. "And I've missed it."

Harris approached him, a strange smile working its way onto his face. "Let me do it."

As the CEO considered the offer, his desk intercom chimed.

"What is it, Lori?" he called out over his shoulder, his eyes still holding his nephew's gaze.

"I think you'd better take a look at the Information Network. It's . . . just take a look." He hadn't failed to notice the fear in her voice.

The CEO pushed the sniveling prisoner off his shoulder and against the black pitted wall. Given his weakened state, he crumpled to the floor.

Uncocking the pistol, the CEO set it on the corner of his desk and slapped a button. A large viewer screen lowered from the ceiling in the middle of the room.

An anchorman was struggling to share with the viewers all of the latebreaking changes that were coming across his desk. Behind him, runners could be seen scrambling to organize and post the numerous incoming field reports. After listening for only a few seconds, the CEO muted the volume and called for the remaining guard to remove the two prisoners, leaving him free, with Harris, to catch up on the unfolding events without any distractions.

When the door had sealed shut, he quickly restored the viewer's volume.

". . . runners confirm that water and sewer departments have also been taken over. It is estimated that these filthy Rebels have now taken possession of nearly ninety-five percent of Arcona's utilities. Five fatalities, from the armory, have been confirmed so far.

"Inside support has reportedly been the key to their success, though I doubt . . ."

Suddenly, the anchorman's eyes widened and the camera began to shake. The screen went black for several seconds before a new face appeared—his expression calm, his voice soothing. What followed was a plea for all citizens of Arcona to listen closely to what he had to say.

The CEO's eyes remained glued to the face in front of him, though the shock and anger over what he was witnessing made whatever the man was saying completely unintelligible. "What is this?" he shouted. "What's happening?"

"They're doing it. I don't believe it!"

The CEO thought he'd detected a hint of admiration in the young man's voice. "Support from inside? It can't be!"

"Support from across the board, it would appear," clarified Harris.

The CEO slapped the viewer's power button. "It has to be some kind of a trick. It's impossible!" He glared hard at the viewer's blank screen. "We can still retaliate." He turned to the intercom. "Lori, get me Special Forces—Tactical Division. I want a full report on what's *really* going on."

"I can't!" He could hear her private viewer blaring in the background. "All inside and outside lines have been cut. Even the computers are jammed."

"Don't give me excuses!" he yelled. "Find a way to reach them!"

He pounded his fist on the intercom, breaking the connection. "This is ridiculous. It's impossible! How far do they really think they'll get?"

The *click* of the revolver's hammer brought the CEO's head around.

"Harris?" The gleaming revolver was pointed squarely at the CEO's chest.

"From where I'm standing, it appears we've made it all the way to the top."

CHAPTER 25

The physical occupation of Arcona by Rebel forces had come as a complete shock; a fragile and potentially dangerous emotion for which the Rebellion's leadership had conscientiously done its best to prepare.

In addition to replacing the Information Network's biased anchorman with a spokesman of their own, a team of criers had sprung up throughout the many districts of Arcona in an effort to clearly state the Rebellion's objective, to ensure their message had the chance of being heard—complete, unfiltered, and unbiased.

At the heart of their message was a desire to once again establish on Zerith an even playing field, giving all citizens a voice in how their world should be governed and shaped.

They wanted a world in which all, not just a few select families and individuals, would have the opportunity to advance themselves monetarily, academically, and in a career of their *own* choosing—advancement dependent upon individual effort and desire. In doing this *all* of Arcona's citizens would be expected to once again do their fair share of the labor necessary for survival—enjoying, once more, benefits they'd inadvertently lost with the acceptance of their current government's debilitating handout. They would have the opportunity to develop, grow, and *feel* success.

What followed next was an explanation of how complete the takeover had been. Arconians were assured that leaders at the highest level had temporarily been silenced until the citizens of Arcona could have the chance to decide, for themselves, in what direction they as a people were willing to go.

A vote would be taken once the Rebels had been given an opportunity to explain and defend their position, which, they believed, would in turn justify the need for having taken such forceful action in the first place. If the overwhelming majority were still in favor of maintaining their current lifestyle, and system of leadership, their opinion would be respected. All the Rebels wanted was the chance to be heard.

In the days immediately following that first broadcast, Arconians were enlightened about the hidden corruption and greed of their leaders. It began with the contents of a personal family ledger, belonging to the Chief Executive Officer of Spire. It was opened for all to review and examine; its thousands of entries revealed just how many businesses and government officials, including their president, Spire had purchased and controlled over the years.

The actual living conditions of the Outsiders were revealed next. Cameras captured and broadcast images of the inhumane treatment handed down to a people that had simply wanted to be heard.

Another team of Rebel reporters revealed the truth behind many of the refineries dotting the forested region and exposed them for the pleasure palaces that they were. This, of course, naturally put into question the government's original decision to leave the forested region in the first place. The demand for a new study naturally followed.

Two former guards from Special Forces reappeared from the *dead*, so to speak, to share how they had been secretly rescued by the Rebels, shortly before the disaster of Northern Outpost G6 months earlier—an explosion that was to have been their death sentence.

Compelling and heart wrenching testimony also came in the form of five accountants, who shared with all who would listen the horrible ways in which they had been tortured, and the coldness with which they, too, were to have been executed.

As enlightening and disturbing as all of these witnesses had been, interviews with Joel Harris, nephew and assistant to the CEO of Spire, had had the most dramatic effect on public opinion. His chilling description of life inside the monopolizing machine of Spire was given in the most vivid detail, with facts and figures wholly corroborated by the CEO's own family ledger. His mother's younger sister had at one time had been involved in the first Rebellion. When she had mysteriously disappeared, Harris's mother began to take to heart many of her sister's earlier ramblings. She kept them to herself, and it wasn't until Joel was chosen as the CEO's successor that she began sharing her feelings with her son; Joel Harris listened.

Once they had the facts, it didn't take long for an overwhelming majority of Arcona's citizens to accept the Rebellion leaders' message.

And though there were several who expressed doubt and concern over whether they could honestly survive on their own, they couldn't deny the incriminating evidence before them: a few greedy and corrupt individuals had helped to collapse an entire society, causing it to fall into overwhelming dependency—and its citizens had *let* it happen. Now they were being given the opportunity to fight back, to stand on their own feet. The fear of living life without a safety net for many *was* frightening, but deep in their hearts, they knew it was right.

Those few who opposed the Rebels in the debate struggled to justify their lies and deceptions by pointing out how long their system of rule had successfully kept their society alive. The fact that all of Arcona had just been given the opportunity to peek behind their leaders' curtain of wealth and power, however, allowed them to see them for what they really were—slothful and powerful bureaucrats who were suddenly fearful of losing their absolute power.

Citizens of Arcona were free to express their thoughts and opinions, but Rebels vowed that if Arcona ultimately voted for change, no one would have the right to crush, harm, or use others to get what they wanted. In short, those who went beyond verbal opposition to the new order would be given the choice of imprisonment or one of the many shanties beyond Arcona's wall—soon to be made vacant with the proposed welcoming of the Outsiders, citizens who, in light of the evidence being presented, had been wrongfully mistreated for so many years.

A few desperate council members tried latching on to this threat, pointing out how similar the Rebels' proposed actions were to what had happened before—that while they were being portrayed as close minded and harsh dictators in their banishing of the rebellious, the Rebels, in fact, were no better. The difference, of course, was obvious: those that would end up going to prison, or living in a shanty, under the Rebellion's proposed system, would do so by their own choosing. It would be a decision rooted in choice, not tyranny.

After a week of continuous revelation, discussion, and debate the ballots were cast. And while the citizenry of Arcona overwhelmingly agreed to the complete rebuilding and restructuring of their world's government, all were well aware of the hard work that lay ahead. Coupled with the freedom to once again dream, however, the prospect of hard work seemed only to bind and unite, rather than rend and destroy.

Among those struggling to make sense of this new and exciting atmosphere of change, was a young man by the name of Matthew Tanner—well aware of the enormous challenges that lay ahead, yet unsure of *his* place in this new and uncertain frontier.

* * *

"It's been awhile, Papa."

"That it has, boy."

"Listen, I . . . I'm sorry again for the things I said. It's just—"

"Stop, son. Believe me, I can understand how you felt. In fact, it turns out I went through the same kind of struggle, years ago."

"What do you mean?"

"For years I wondered how I'd found the strength to get past her death, your parents' deaths, and the failure of the first Rebellion. At first I was bitter—filled with resentment. But, somehow, I managed to move on.

"Your grandmother, I've learned, had been doing the same thing with me that I've been doing with you—listening, counseling, helping me to look beyond my own problems, to focus more on the needs of others. Without her help, I'd hate to think what would have become of me," he slapped Matthew's knee, "or you."

Paul went on. "Now I finally understand why I'd always felt so strongly about an afterlife.

"She's a remarkable woman, who's had to put up with a lot," —it was said with a grin.

"I wish I could remember her and Mom and Dad," said Matthew. "All I have are bits and pieces. I was too young I guess."

"Oh, she's awfully proud of you, boy! Your parents, too."

Matthew's smile faded as his eyes fell to his feet. "I only wish I had listened to you earlier, Papa. Maybe things would have—"

"It was hard not being able to tell you more, Matthew. You have to believe that. But I couldn't deny you your freedom of choice. You had to

make your own decisions based upon the information you had at the time. That's something else I've come to discover here: Our free agency is essential to this life. But don't feel bad, boy. The other person I was assigned to fared far, far worse."

Matthew's head rose in surprise.

"You weren't the only one I was visiting in their dreams."

"What do you mean?"

"Believe it or not, I was also assigned to the man responsible for arranging your parents' death."

"What? Who was it?"

"Well, I'm sure that will be revealed in time. I'm not allowed to give you his name. Suffice it to say, all of my attempts to turn him failed. Normally a vivid recollection of one's guilt is a powerful force for change. But, in his case, he'd already given too much of his soul over to the other side. Besides, it's hard to compete against the influences of one's own family."

Matthew was confused with the explanation, but decided to respect what little his grandfather had shared, trusting and admiring his restraint.

"There's a phrase, in fact, that I've come across here that seems to apply very well in his case."

"What's that?"

"He's 'past feeling.'"

Matthew found the phrase both cold and frightening.

"He's chosen his path, and must now suffer the consequences of his actions. For you it was a beating, but for him it will be far worse."

Paul sat back, folding his arms. "I pity him now, which surprises me. But then life itself has taken on a whole new meaning for me here."

"I still wish I would have listened to you. In some ways I feel as though I've failed."

Paul leaned forward with a look of surprise. "Matthew, you know now that the Rebellion's schedule had only been pushed up by a week and a half. Besides, the discovery of the embezzled dockins preceded your decision by several days. Sure, the freighter that picks up the ore has to travel a few hours more to retrieve it, but look at how valuable it's been. Durin's dragging their feet, and who knows when they'll finally accept everything that's happened. The fact that the leaders of the Rebellion had shown such foresight helped convince many that they weren't a bunch of wackos. Their sheer organization has boosted their credibility immensely.

"*Matthew, if those leading the Rebellion had not planned ahead, had failed to anticipate Durin's reluctance to simply believe a bunch of recorded voices and images, I shudder to think of how many lives would have been lost in the chaos that would have followed. The fact that none of the Rebels lost their life has sent a powerful message to the fence-sitters.*

"*Son, you* have *succeeded! You've fulfilled your part of the grand mission. It might not seem like much to you now, but in retrospect, years from now, it will. No, you didn't single-handedly save the world, but you did fulfill your calling. It would have been impossible for any of the Rebels to have come this far on their own; that's why the first Rebellion failed. It's taken unity, patience, and perseverance.*"

Paul paused, choosing his next words carefully. "*Matthew.*" *He waited until he looked up.* "*You did it. You can look in the mirror with honor tomorrow, because you succeeded.*"

Matthew felt a calmness settle over him. They were precisely the words he had wanted to hear, and his eyes filled with tears.

"*And as far as Rebecca's concerned, believe me when I tell you that your feelings toward her had already been anticipated. She's always been a critical part of the plan.*"

Matthew wiped away the tears, suddenly incredulous. "*So you're telling me that the fact that I would write her so much had already been known?*"

"*You could say that.*"

Matthew gave a short laugh. "*Well you lost me, Papa. If what I do before I do it is already known, then how can I possibly* really *be free to choose?*"

Paul grinned. "*Now there's the old Matthew I know and love! Always questioning. Never lose that quality.*" *He took a deep breath.* "*It's not as difficult to understand as you might think. The fact that my attempted interference with my pistol failed, yet succeeded, has shown me how . . . Well, here, I have a better idea.*"

Paul turned and grabbed his cane that had been leaning against his chair. "*What's this?*"

"*Papa!*"

"*Come on. You asked me a question. At least give me the chance to answer it. Now, answer me.*"

Although he appeared frustrated at what was obviously going to be another Paul Tanner lesson, he was genuinely pleased; it had been a long time. "*It's your* cane."

"*That's right. I'll hold it like this, so that it's perpendicular to the floor. Now, about how high would you say it is from the floor?*"

"*From the top of the cane, or the bottom of the cane?*"

"*From the bottom.*"

Matthew looked at the floor and was surprised to find a hard-packed dirt surface. Up until now the floor had always seemed solid, though extremely bright. "*How did you—*"

"*Matthew, stay with me.*"

Matthew collected himself and gave his answer. "*About two feet.*"

"*Good. Now, tell me, what's going to happen when I let go of this cane?*"

"*This is ridiculous, don't you think?*"

"*I'm waiting.*"

Matthew pursed his lips and, in a tone of resignation, said that it would hit the floor, probably bounce once, and then fall flat on its side."

"*Will it lie flat?*"

"*Of course.*"

"*And what about the curve in the handle, will it curve toward the ceiling, or lie flat against the floor as well?*"

"*Flat against the floor,*" he answered with suspicion, wondering if he'd inadvertently fallen for a trick question.

Satisfied with the response, Paul said, "*Alright, let's see what happens.*" He released his grip and both watched as the cane did precisely what Matthew said it would do.

"*How'd you do it?*" asked Paul.

"*Do what?*"

"*How did you make the cane do exactly what you said it would do?*"

"*It just happened.*"

"*So, you're telling me you knew precisely what the cane would do, did nothing to influence it, and it naturally did as you said it would?*"

Matthew's eyes then brightened as he suddenly understood just what his grandfather had been getting at.

Paul leaned over to retrieve his cane and placed it back where it had been before. "*Yes, Matthew, we can be free to choose, to act, in spite of the fact that our actions have been anticipated. We're placed on this world and used according to how we'll behave—all of us.*

"*Soon, Matthew, a beautiful plan will be introduced, presented to our people. And this truth, along with a multitude of others, will be taught. You've had a hand in preparing our world for that great message. Other worlds already have it. Now, it's our turn."*

At the mention of the future, and recalling his grandfather's earlier reference to Rebecca, Matthew couldn't help asking, "What about Rebecca? I know the fact that she may be a part of this plan doesn't necessarily mean her part would include me. But can you at least tell me if she's safe or not?"

Paul stared at Matthew for nearly a full minute, then closed his eyes. After several seconds, they fluttered open. "She's safe."

Matthew released a breath he hadn't realized he'd been holding. "Thank you, Papa. Thank you very much."

After a moment of silence, Paul leaned forward and took hold of Matthew's hand. "Boy, this will be the last time I'll be able to speak with you like this."

Matthew's eyes filled with shock. "What? But, Papa, I . . . I need you!"

Paul looked tenderly into his grandson's face. "What special day is only a few weeks away?"

Matthew was clearly confused. "I don't know."

Paul smiled. "Your birthday."

Both started to laugh.

"I'd completely forgotten about it. So much has been happening lately. I—"

"I know, I know. But the point is . . . you're a man now, son. My . . . my job is done."

Matthew's eyes watered at the sight of his grandfather's tears and the sound of his halting, gravely voice. He stood up, helping his grandfather to his feet, and embraced him in a powerful hug. "I won't plead, or beg, Papa. You've already done so much for me. You sacrificed your life for me. I . . . I couldn't possibly ask for more." He fought to suppress a flood of tears as he buried his face in Paul's broad shoulder. "I'm going to miss you," he whispered.

Paul patted his back. "I'm going to miss you too, boy. Believe me I will." He pulled back from Matthew and looked him in the eye. "But remember, we'll . . . we'll see each other again one day. Follow your heart and be good, and we'll have an eternity together. I promise."

The moment Paul let go of Matthew his image began to fade.

Matthew struggled to maintain control of his emotions. "I . . . I love you."

"I love you, too, Matthew." He pointed a finger. "Remember what I've told you!" Paul's image was nearly transparent.

"But, Papa, I've never been able to remember these dreams!"

Paul's fading smile suddenly appeared as radiant as ever. "This one, you will."

And with that, his grandfather was gone.

Paul gazed at Matthew's sleeping face, proud of the man he'd become. He fondly recalled the day the boy had permanently entered his life, after the death of his parents. He'd wondered then if he really had what it took to raise the boy as his own. At the time all he did know for certain was that they had each other. He made up his mind to do his best. It was all he could do—his life enriched because of it.

After several minutes, Paul looked over to his right. "I want to thank you for allowing me the chance to honor the vow I made with his parents. It's meant so much to me, to them."

His eyes returned to Matthew's sleeping face, and a grin emerged. "If it's alright with you, though, I have just one final request . . . "

CHAPTER 26

Matthew squinted his eyes against the bright sunlight pouring through his shanty's small square window; dust motes danced amidst the bright light of yet another new day of freedom.

Surely it had to be a dream, he thought. *It* had *to be.*

His hand lingered on the raised window curtain as he struggled to bring his mind into focus. *The detail . . . everything was so* clear.

He walked back to his bunk and sat on its edge. *It felt so real!*

He rubbed his eyes with the heels of his hands and tried to shake off the confusion clouding his mind.

Beyond the shanty walls he could hear idle chatter mixed with the low droning of a small transport as the few families that remained excitedly worked at securing what few possessions they had. They were obviously looking forward with great anticipation to the new life awaiting them beyond Arcona's wall—several Arconians had graciously opened their homes to the refugees as they strove to find work and a place amidst a population stirring with the wonder and excitement of change.

Matthew glanced at his clock. He'd slept in, but had no regrets; this was to be his last morning in the shanty, and he planned to enjoy this last opportunity to bask in the memories of the only home he'd ever known.

The sound of a passing skimmer jolted him from his thoughts. He suddenly remembered he'd promised one of the widows up the street to help her load a few pieces of her furniture. He would have liked to be able to do more for his neighbors, but his ribs and leg wound were still tender, and he'd promised his doctor he'd take it easy. It had been difficult being shuffled from safe house to safe house throughout the past two weeks, especially when he knew his friends had begun moving several days ago. But yesterday morning he'd finally been permitted to return—all those who might have felt inclined to retaliate against him for his role in the Rebellion, including Rollyn's father, had been arrested only a few days earlier.

Today was also his turn to move, and he knew the two transports assigned the task had only a few dozen families remaining until they reached his place; he knew he had to get a move on.

It wouldn't take him long—a cot, two chairs, and a few articles of clothing were all he planned on taking with him. It wouldn't take long at all.

He stood, stretched, and walked over to the washbasin; every move he made this morning felt strange and awkward. *Pretty soon I'll have running water*, he thought, as he filled the basin. *How will that be?* He could feel the excitement beginning to churn within him, restrained at the same time by the huge degree of uncertainty that now surrounded his future. It was thrilling, yet humbling, all at the same time.

After he had washed and dried his face, he then decided to take a moment to examine his healing eye and cuts. On seeing his reflection, however, his eyes went wide, not at the yellow shade his bruised eye was now sporting, or at the scabbed over lines that seemed to criss-cross his cheeks and forehead, but at a sudden remembrance that pierced his heart and warmed his entire soul: *"You can look in the mirror with honor tomorrow, because you succeeded."*

Tears welled up in his eyes. "It *was* real! I *knew* it was!"

He closed his eyes, not sure of how to express his thanks for what he now knew to be a reality; his grandfather *had* been with him—had been for quite some time—watching over and guiding him.

Then came the vivid recollection of their parting.

But Matthew wasn't upset. He clearly remembered his feelings at the time, recalled his grandfather's sacrifice, and was overwhelmed with feelings of gratitude, not sadness.

His eyes then studied his reflection a second time—his entire being filling with renewed determination. *We've succeeded. Now, I'll make the most of it.*

He thought of Rebecca. *No matter what.*

As he rinsed his face off again, his ear picked up the sound of the skimmer that had passed by earlier. It sounded as if it had stopped just out front.

Odd. Maybe Patch decided to give me a hand? He dried off his face and walked to the thick evening curtain covering the door. Pulling aside the heavy leather, he froze at the sight of Dewy opening the passenger door of a skimmer. Rebecca stepped out.

"Becca?"

Matthew could hardly believe his eyes. There she stood, dressed more casually than he'd ever seen her before—blue, calf-length pants with a simple white T-shirt, her hair done up in a ponytail. She was beautiful.

At Matthew's wide-eyed expression, Dewy exploded with laughter. "You got him, Miss Adams. That's for sure. Hey, Matt! Don't forget to breathe!"

As Dewy's laughter faded, Matthew found himself unable to move. *This can't be happening!*

By this time Rebecca was standing directly in front of him, her smile switching to concern at the sight of his healing face. She reached a hand toward his eye, which Matthew intercepted with his own, to see if in fact she was real.

Convinced that she was, he pulled her in for a hug. It was a gentle hug, one filled with relief, with surprise, with thanks.

As they held each other, Rebecca began to cry. "I was beginning to wonder if I'd ever see you again." She pulled back. "When I heard what Dirk did . . . I'm sorry, Matthew."

Matthew's eyes closed as he pulled her close and fought to hold back tears of his own—she still loved him. "It wasn't your fault, Becca. Believe me. It wasn't your fault."

"I missed you so much."

"I missed you too."

When they finally stepped back and looked into each others' eyes, the reality of the situation brought a flood of questions to Matthew's mind. "How'd you find me?"

Dewy, who'd been leaning on the skimmer with his arms folded, enjoying the sight of their reunion, chuckled loudly. "Wait till you hear what she has to say about that! But, as far as bringing her here was concerned, it was my pleasure."

He walked up to Matthew and shook his hand. "Besides, I felt I owed it to you."

"You don't owe me anything, Dewy," said Matthew. "I'm just glad you're alright. I've been worried sick about you."

Dewy suddenly appeared embarrassed, rubbed his large hands together, and avoided eye contact. "Ah, close your mouth, Matt. I feel guilty enough as it is."

"Guilty?"

"Look, you're bound to find out about it soon enough anyway. I just . . . "

"What's wrong?"

Dewy finally met his gaze. "Do you remember the day I found you near the lockers, knocked out?"

Yeah."

"Well . . . look. Dirk will probably be in enough trouble as it is, and before you start getting a lot of questions . . . there's something you should know . . ."

Matthew smiled at the sight of this mountain-of-a-man stammering and stumbling over his own words. "What is it, Dewy?"

Dewy shut his eyes for several seconds, then opened them. "I'm the one who hit you."

"What?"

"Look, I saw the way you and Miss Adams were dancing that night. I also caught Dirk's reaction. I got a little concerned about the attention you were drawing to yourself. So . . . so I wanted to scare you a bit, just to keep you on your toes—in case he was planning something for you."

"Couldn't you have just *warned* me?"

"That's just it. I needed an excuse to pull you aside . . . to also make sure you still had your eye on our objective. We hadn't talked forever, really. I . . . I didn't have a whole lot of time to think up an excuse . . . so . . ."

"So you knocked me out."

Dewy looked sheepish. "Yeah."

"What if I hadn't come to in time for the launch?"

Dewy appeared offended. "Hey, watch it. I am a professional, you know."

All three burst into laughter.

"Well," said Matthew. "Hopefully we can be ourselves from now on."

Dewy nodded. "I'd like that."

"Say, what happened to Dirk anyway?" He turned to Rebecca, still surprised she was actually standing next to him. "I suppose your father wants me arrested now. Dirk set me up for the theft of your moth . . . What's so funny?"

Both Dewy and Rebecca were looking at each other, all smiles.

"Tell him, Dewy."

"Well, after you left I discovered some blood on the bay floor. I went back to the barracks and found Dirk unconscious near the lockers. After a quick search I discovered your letter, as well as the brooch. After reading the letter, and knowing Dirk the way I do, it wasn't hard putting two and two together."

"So what did you do?" asked Matthew, genuinely curious.

"I decided to turn the tables on the pompous jerk. I pocketed the letter, polished the brooch and placed it in his hand."

Dewy fell silent.

"And?"

Rebecca picked up where Dewy left off. "So when he woke up and found the brooch—"

"It had only *his* fingerprints on it!" Matthew was impressed.

"Exactly," answered Dewy. So whatever story he'll make up about you will be meaningless—unless of course he's prepared to explain why only *his* fingerprints are on the brooch, and how he got it. You two may have fought, but he can't prove you're a thief. It would be his word against yours. I'll bet he remains quiet about the whole thing."

"So I'm not a wanted man on Durin?"

"Of course not."

"But the fight—"

"A hauler—an outsider, no less—successfully beating up a guard of the Special Forces? Trust me, Matt, he'll be trying to keep everything as low-key as possible. In fact I'll be real curious to find out how he's explained his injuries."

"How is he anyway?"

Dewy smiled. "He was still in the sick bay when we left. They hadn't started really questioning him yet—too much medication. Oh, he'll have himself a nasty scar on the side of his head." Dewy touched a finger to Matthew's scar running just beneath his lower lip. "But, hey, no one gets through this life without a few of those. Ain't that right?"

My scar, thought Matthew, as he turned to look into Rebecca's smiling face. *So much has happened since my run-in with the pirates.*

"I imagine once we've come to terms with Durin, he'll answer for what he did to you." Dewy smiled. "Look, there were some people with a transport down the road that looked as if they could use a hand. I'll leave you two to catch up for a while." He gave a quick wink that made both Matthew and Rebecca blush. "When I get back, I'll help you get your stuff into my skimmer. You can come back to Arcona with Miss Adams and me. What do you say?"

"Sounds good." Matthew offered his hand once more to Dewy who gladly accepted it. "Thanks, Dewy, for everything."

Dewy was noticeably embarrassed. "Ah, that's alright, Matt. It was a pleasure working with you," his smile was sincere.

The moment the skimmer had left, Rebecca gave Matthew another hug. "I've missed you so much!"

Matthew enjoyed the embrace. He pulled back, and kissed her.

Rebecca then gave him a careful once-over. "Well, I must say, you do look terrible."

"Well thank you, Becca. If it's one thing I've always been able to count on it's been your honesty." He ran a hand through his morning-tousled hair, making a sincere effort to flatten a few of the rooster tails he knew were there.

"I'm kidding, Matthew. You look . . . kinda cute like this. How are you feeling, though? Be honest."

"I'm feeling much better. Miller arranged for some hospital treatment, and that's really made a difference. I can't imagine how many of us here would've really benefited from the facilities I saw in that hospital. I won't be able to do any heavy lifting for awhile, but I'm feeling better every day.

"But, tell me, Becca, how did you get back to Zerith? How long have you been here?"

"You can thank Dewy for that. As a matter of fact, he's planning on heading back to Durin tonight to see if he can help persuade my father to accept what's taken place here; I know if Father could just sit down and talk with the provisional leaders, face to face, he'd understand and sympathize with their intentions. I'm sure he's just leery of jumping too quickly. All he's received are video clips from the Information Network. How's he to know if what he's seeing is real or not? He needs to know just how much change has actually taken place. Dewy told me this morning that there's talk of a . . . a constitution—that's what they called it—now being drafted. I guess it officially declares the laws that will govern our world. Dewy feels very strongly that my father should be here to offer *his* input."

After a few more questions, Matthew learned it had been Dewy who had gone to Rebecca's mother and persuaded her that she and Rebecca should leave on the last outgoing freighter, prior to the Rebellion's scheduled takeover. He'd received his warning two days after Matthew's fight, and knew that if he could get the governor's family to Zerith, he had a better chance of finding a safe place for them to hole up until the dust settled. On Durin there wasn't any way to tell what the reaction to the takeover would be, or how long they might go without supplies.

Dewy left a time-delayed message for Governor Adams, in which his family assured him they were leaving of their own free will; and Dewy gave his word as a respected friend of the family that he would personally ensure their safety. Then they left Durin, arriving on Zerith nearly twelve hours before the takeover began.

"Where have you been staying?"

"With family, mostly."

"But, how'd you find me?"

Rebecca fell silent and asked if they could go inside to talk.

When they passed through the door curtain, Matthew suddenly felt self-conscious. "I'm sorry you had to come and see this. I—"

Rebecca was still holding his hand. She gave it a squeeze. "Matthew, don't apologize. After everything you've written to me, I *wanted* to see where you lived." Her eyes took in the cots, chairs, and the broken piece of mirror above the wash basin. "I only regret you were forced to live like this in the first place."

Matthew guided her to his cot where they could sit next to each other. He was sure she could smell the urine and rot that naturally permeated the air and, despite her assurances, couldn't help feeling embarrassed. *She's too beautiful to be sitting in a place like this.* He remained silent, waiting for her to speak first.

"I really don't know how to begin." She bit at her lower lip. "When I woke up this morning I . . . I just *knew* where you lived." She then glanced around the room. "I knew what all of this looked like before I got here. I know it sounds crazy." She paused, running her fingers over their clasped hands. "Dewy and I drove by once earlier, before I realized we'd gone too far but . . ."

Matthew recalled hearing the skimmer but wasn't quite sure how to respond. He gave Becca's hand a squeeze. "Well, I'm glad you found me. When *I* woke up this morning I was wondering if I'd ever see you again."

"So when do we start?"

Matthew was confused. "Start what?"

"Come on, Matthew. Letter after letter, all we ever talked about was having the chance to be together—to date, to talk, to take long walks together. Don't you remember?"

"Of course I remember."

"So, when can we begin building our future?" She was smiling. Matthew wasn't.

He stood up, let go of her hand, and walked to the other side of the room.

"Matthew, what's wrong?"

Silence.

"Matthew?"

"Becca, look at me!"

"I am. You've seen better days, but for the most part—"

"No." He shook his head in frustration. "Becca, I'm being serious. *Look* at me."

Rebecca offered a gentle smile. "I am looking at you, Matthew. Just what is it you want me to notice?"

Matthew swallowed hard before speaking. "Becca, what you see me wearing, what's in this room, it's all I've got." Before Rebecca could respond, Matthew rushed to finish his thought. "Oh, I'm moving to Arcona, alright, but to a tiny apartment—a hole in the wall."

"Matthew—"

"I mean, I have been fortunate in some ways. For months I've been burying a lot of my earnings under the cot you're sitting on, saving for . . . I don't know, for the future I guess. Most people have found old friends or family to stay with—until they can establish themselves. Patch offered, but . . . I don't know. I've never been one to—"

"Matthew, what are you trying to say?"

"Becca, the point I'm trying to make is I don't have anything to offer you. I'm not even sure if I still have a job! I'm sure I could continue running freight once all of the dust settles, but . . ."

"But what?"

"But . . . Becca, I just don't think I could ever give you the kind of life you're used to."

Matthew was surprised to see a touch of anger flash across her face. "And just what makes you think I'm expecting any of that?"

"Well, I—"

"Do I come across as spoiled, demanding?"

"No. I—"

She stood up. "Then understand this, Matthew Tanner. I love you for who you are, not for what you aren't. And I don't love you for what you have. You're thoughtful and caring, but just a bit insecure. And I love you for that, don't get me wrong." She turned, her arms wide. "Okay, you don't have a lot. So what! It's *you* who's taught me how little one needs to survive and be happy." She move closer and jabbed a finger into his chest. "Are *you* telling me now that everything you've written in your letters was a lie?"

"No, it's just—"

"Then I would suggest you reconsider our dream of beginning a life together, because it seems to me that the only one keeping us from fulfilling that dream, now, is you!"

Matthew was staring at her in shock. He'd never seen this side of her before. Suddenly her finger dropped and she leaned closer to give him a kiss on the cheek. "We'll build our life *together*, Matthew. Just like everybody else is doing right now." She then gave him an even longer kiss on the mouth. "Together."

Matthew embraced her. "How did I ever find such an understanding person?" he whispered.

"Easy," she said, nuzzling his ear. "You asked me to dance, and I said yes."

Holding her close for several minutes he kissed her once more and straightened. "Will you let me answer your question again?"

"And what question was that?" asked Rebecca, smiling.

"'So when do we start?'"

"Start what?" she teased.

Matthew laughed. "You sure do make it tough on a guy, you know that?"

Rebecca's face suddenly became very innocent. "Why, Matthew Tanner, I have no idea what you're talking about."

But as Matthew leaned closer, Rebecca's face gradually became sincere once more.

"Rebecca Adams . . . will you marry me?"

Rebecca's eyes started to tear up and she hugged him close. A moment later she looked up into Matthew's eyes. "Yes, Matthew. Yes." And they kissed once more.

Several minutes later it was Matthew who spoke up first. "I suppose if we're ever going to start that life together, we'd better get moving. Dewy will be here any minute now."

"I can't wait to tell my mother, Matthew. She was really impressed with your letters. I think she's going to be so excited it all worked out."

"What about your father?" asked Matthew dryly. "He barely even knows I'm alive."

"I don't know how *he'll* take it. You'll have to let me know what happens when you ask him for my hand."

Matthew rolled his eyes. "Thanks a lot!"

Rebecca laughed as Matthew walked over to his chair and grabbed his grandfather's cane, handing it to her. "Why don't you take this outside and I'll move the chair. We'll put all of the stuff out front so that . . . Becca? Becca, what's wrong?"

Rebecca was standing with the cane in her hand, staring at it, holding it as if it were something hot. "Where'd you get this?"

"It belonged to my grandfather. I know he would've wanted me to give it to someone who could *really* use it, but I guess I haven't had the heart to part with it yet. Why?"

"It's . . . it's coming back to me, Matthew."

"What is?"

"How I knew where to find you."

"What do you mean?"

"Your grandfather." Squinting her eyes, Rebecca appeared to be concentrating on the door across from them. "Your grandfather told me where to find you." Matthew's eye went wide. "He . . . he showed me *all* of this, the inside *and* the outside."

Rebecca then proceeded to give Matthew a thorough description of Paul, and by the time she had finished, he had no doubt that she too must have experienced a vision similar to his own.

Matthew reached out and took her hand. "What did he say to you?"

Her eyes then went from the cane to the rest of the room, seeming to recognize everything at once. As she walked around it, touching things here and there, she answered him. "Nothing much, really. He introduced himself, told me not to be frightened, and . . . and then gave me two messages."

She met him! She actually met him! Matthew's heart felt as if it would explode. "What were they?"

"He . . . he said," she closed her eyes, concentrating. "'Trust that whatever happens . . . happens for the best. When we do this . . . that's when we recognize all of the miracles that surround us.'"

Matthew smiled as her eyes opened. "That sounds like him alright."

But Rebecca hadn't paid any attention to him. She gasped, and then blushed.

"Becca, what is it?"

Her features softened, and she appeared embarrassed.

"What is it?"

She bit her lower lip. "He said that after you proposed to me in . . ."

"What?"

"He said after you proposed to me in the morning, I'd remember the second message I was to share with you. We're both supposed to remember it."

Matthew's heart was pounding within his chest, the sound loud in his ears. "What? What was it?"

"He said . . . 'Teach your firstborn well. He's . . . he's part of the plan . . . a teacher of many.'" Rebecca blinked several times then turned and faced Matthew. "What plan is he talking about, Matthew?"

Matthew felt a powerful burning in his chest, and he swallowed at the implication of the message.

Ignoring her own question, Rebecca then asked, "How could he have known when you were going to propose?"

At this, Matthew grinned. He had every intention of sharing with her the dream *he'd* had, but decided he'd start with something else first.

Taking the cane from her hand he held it perpendicular to the floor.

"Becca, about how high would you say this cane is from the floor?"

CHAPTER 27

Matthew couldn't believe it. He *honestly* couldn't believe it. A year ago he would have scoffed at the idea that he would even be living in Arcona, let alone getting married! Now, here he was, standing in the middle of Arcona's beautifully decorated outdoor arena, amidst a throng of people, celebrating not only a new birthday, but his wedding as well.

"I love you."

Matthew looked down into Rebecca's beautiful brown eyes, marveling at how lovely she looked in her flowing white wedding grown. It reminded Matthew of the first gown he'd seen her in—close fitting, trimmed in delicate lace, its cut and lines drawing one to her face . . . and those eyes. "I love you, too."

"Cold feet?"

He smiled. "No, of course not. I just can't get over how many people are here. There must be a thousand, at least!"

Rebecca grinned. "I know you tried to convince Dad to have a small ceremony, but you have to understand that—"

"That you're their *only* daughter, and they wanted to do it *right*. *Believe* me, the message came through *loud* and *clear*."

"He can be stubborn." Rebecca ignored Matthew's sidelong glance and changed the subject. "I hope you're not feeling *too* uncomfortable though."

Matthew could have brought up just how tight and painful his shoes were, or how terribly uncomfortable his tie and starched collar felt around his neck, but decided to keep those complaints to himself. "No, no. It's just . . . overwhelming, I guess."

The truth was, he was pleased to see how well her parents were supporting their decision, how hard they were trying to show and demonstrate their approval.

Dewy had successfully managed to convince Governor Adams to return to Zerith, offering to stay behind to maintain order at the base in spite of the fact that he was a Rebel. Governor Adams knew, from years of personal experience, that Dewy was a man of honor, and someone who wouldn't take advantage of the situation—a man he could trust. Besides, when it came to maintaining order and discipline, who could possibly do a better job than Dewy?

Matthew wished Dewy was here now, but appreciated what he was doing in the effort to bridge the gap between Zerith and Durin.

During the first few days of his visit, the governor had met with the Rebellion's provisional leaders. A few of them had been acquainted with Adams in the past and very much appreciated the opportunity to share their message of change in a peaceful setting, and to offer him the chance to become a voluntary member of their leadership council.

Aside from being an overprotective father, he was the antithesis of Spire's councilmen. He had been selected as governor of Durin years ago, simply because Spire's CEO couldn't trust anyone else with such a distant assignment. He had in Adams a man he could depend on, someone who was honest and would work hard—ironically, someone who wasn't in any way linked to his corrupt ruling council.

Patiently, Governor Adams listened as the new council carefully outlined their objective, sharing with him the working draft of their constitution. Adams listened to, analyzed, and observed all of the suggested changes to do away with a system of corruption he'd secretly grown to detest over the years. He ultimately agreed to the terms and principles of their agenda and, just as Rebecca and Dewy had predicted, it wasn't long before he began offering helpful suggestions of his own. He was involved now—wholeheartedly committed to the cause.

When Matthew had first been introduced to Adams, only a few days after his arrival, the governor had seemed distant, leery of the young man. But the more he got to know Matthew, the more he learned of just how right the Outsiders had been all those years ago, the more accepting he had become. When Matthew's role in the

Rebellion had been revealed—the fact he had been skimming ore right from under his nose—Governor Adams appeared more impressed than upset, noting the courage and dedication it took to successfully pull off such an incredible stunt.

Two days before the wedding, Governor Adams pulled Matthew aside. He revealed how prior to his departure from Durin, Dewy had tried to prepare him for Matthew's proposal, assuring him that Matthew was a good man—that the governor couldn't hope to find a better husband for Rebecca, nor a better son-in-law for himself. Offering his hand to Matthew, the governor assured the young man that he too had reached that same conclusion and, to everyone's relief, offered the two his blessing.

Sometimes Matthew wondered what would have happened if he'd never met Dewy, if he hadn't had his support.

His eyes found Rebecca's parents now as he surveyed one of the long rows of chairs, three deep, that formed one side of the large octagon of chairs surrounding them.

Rebecca's mother waved to him, already in tears. Matthew was sure they still had their concerns about him. After all, he *was* almost a complete stranger who'd practically come out of nowhere. And now he was taking their only daughter away from them to live on a shoe-string budget at best. But he was determined to prove that he had what it took to provide and care for Rebecca—to make her happy. They seemed to respect his dedication, and so far had done their best not to interfere.

One by one, Matthew then began picking out of the crowd those contacts he had known only by sight over the past several months. Only a few hours ago he had begun learning their names. All of them seemed relieved that their life of secrecy was over, and Matthew now looked forward to getting to know each one of them a little better. For now, though, he was glad to see that they had come, glad they were safe.

Earlier he had also run into an abashed Warring, as well as an elated Patch and Miller, but the vast majority of those in attendance were strangers to him, and he couldn't help feeling a bit self-conscious.

And then, his eyes found Rollyn. When they had run into each other, earlier that morning, Rollyn had dramatically, but sincerely, pleaded for Matthew's forgiveness. He assured Matthew that while their friendship may have been arranged in the beginning, it had long since become something genuine to him. It had been an emotional reunion—for they hadn't seen each other since the day of the shooting—and it was still unclear as to what Rollyn's father's fate would be. It was good to see Rollyn without any bruises, though. And Matthew was pleased to learn that the Leelands had decided to take him in, promising to look after him, regardless of his father's fate. He had hugged the boy and assured him that he loved him; that he was in no way holding him responsible for what had happened. Rollyn had appeared relieved, grateful. Matthew now gave his young friend a wink, causing his large brown eyes to brighten under the powerful influence of his own smile.

Out of all the familiar faces he had spotted, though, Reuben's was beaming the brightest. Citing poor performance in the Pilot's Mess, Dirk had managed to have Reuben temporarily transferred to one of Durin's mining sites. Because he'd had no time to verify the specifics of Dirk's report, the governor had simply taken the officer at his word. Once the governor had learned of Dirk's jealousy and his dark intentions, though, he'd deeply regretted the oversight. Dirk would soon answer for his crime, but by way of apology, Governor Adams had sent for Reuben and ensured him a place at the ceremony. It was now clear that Reuben had more than accepted the apology—his round, smiling face said it all: "I was there in the beginning, and I wouldn't have missed this for the world."

Balloon bouquets were scattered throughout the crowd, while tall sheets of wooden lattice surrounded the group as a whole. In the center of the octagon of chairs stood an arbor; assorted flowers and bands of red silk woven throughout the fragile, white lattice, created a romantic and airy feeling amidst the packed assembly of well-wishers.

Matthew caught sight of Mr. Jacobs, dressed in his simple black robe, making his way through one of the narrow aisles that cut through the crowd—those in attendance now grew quiet as they gradually became aware of his presence.

Matthew was pleased Mr. Jacobs had agreed to perform the marriage ceremony, and, unlike his experience at his grandfather's funeral, intended to pay close attention to every word this dear man would have to say.

But it was *this* thought that suddenly reminded Matthew of the one person who *was* missing; his face fell, ever so slightly.

"Are you happy, Matthew?" whispered Rebecca. Mr. Jacobs was nearing the arbor.

"Of course I am, Becca. It's just . . ."

"What?"

Matthew looked into the crowd. "I only wish Grandpa could see me now. That's all."

When she didn't respond to his comment, Matthew looked down and found her gazing past him.

Something in her eyes made him turn to see what she found so fascinating.

At the end of one of the rows of family members he immediately noticed an empty chair—an odd sight, considering every other chair was full. Some guests had been forced to stand along the lattice walls in the back.

Rebecca gave his hand a squeeze. "I think he can, Matthew," she whispered.

Matthew's chest warmed, and his mind felt at peace.

She looked up, her eyes shining. "I think he has a front-row seat."

Matthew smiled at her with tears of his own . . . and could almost sense his grandfather's smile—a smile belonging to a man who had proven, to both of them, just how *everlasting* love could be.

ABOUT THE AUTHOR

Jeff graduated from Utah State University with a degree in elementary education, and has been involved in a variety of teaching and mentoring experiences. He is an avid reader who enjoys learning from books as well as people.

This is Jeff's first book, and it originated as a story he wrote for his children to enjoy when they are older. Jeff and his wife, Kara, are the parents of four children, and live in Rexburg, Idaho.

An Excerpt from A Novel by Jeffrey S. Savage:

CUTTING EDGE

Travis stared at the lines of code on the screen in front of him. For some reason the second variable in the record was resetting itself. Obviously something was wrong with the order that they were being read into the table. Maybe if he switched the second variable with the first? As he leaned forward to change the code, he felt a strong wave of déja vu wash over him. At this time of night it always felt a little like he was typing the same lines over and over, but now he was almost sure he had tried this combination before. Glancing at his scribbled notes on the legal pad in front of his keyboard, he realized why.

He leaned back in his chair and buried his face in his hands. It wasn't the second time that he had reversed those variables in exactly the same way—it was the third. His head throbbed and his mouth felt like he had been sucking on sweat socks. If he hadn't committed to get this out to the guys in testing by tomorrow, he would have given up and gone home hours ago. He grabbed a couple of aspirin from the open bottle on the shelf above his monitor and washed them down with a flat root beer.

He should probably call Lisa again, so she wouldn't worry. Checking the clock in the corner of his screen though, he decided that he would only succeed in waking her up. When he had talked to her at 11:00, she was getting ready to go to bed. He was startled to see that nearly three hours had passed since then. Even if she had waited up and read for a while, she would have given up and gone to sleep long before now. The thought of her lying in bed made his eyelids start to droop, and he rubbed at them fiercely.

Quickly Travis stood up from his chair, and tried doing some deep-knee bends. If he could just stay awake, he knew that he could have this done in less than an hour. He would do fifty knee bends and then sit back down and knock this thing out. Resting his hands on his hips, he counted each bend out loud. At least he could close his eyes, while he was exercising. The repetition of it was actually very relaxing, up and down three, up and down four. He had never understood the attraction of counting sheep to fall asleep. But now he could not only understand it, he could actually see the sheep jumping over the fence with him as he moved up and down. It was like he was riding them over the fence. He could lay his head down against their fluffy white backs and just let them do the jumping.

His head dropped back against the top of the cube wall with a solid bang. Grabbing the back of his chair to steady himself, he thought of just quitting for the night and picking it up again in the morning. But that would throw the whole team off schedule, and Rob had made it clear that nothing was allowed to mess with the schedule at crunch time. He picked up the can of soda and tilted his head back, swallowing its lukewarm contents. If he could just get a few minutes rest, he knew he would be fine. His eyes fell on the thin, yellow paperback lying facedown on his filing cabinet, and he remembered Ricky's hideaway. It wouldn't be right to borrow someone else's sleeping bag, but right now he was sure he could fall asleep on bare concrete with no problem at all.

Kneeling down by his desk, he tried to pry one of the tiles out of the floor. They seemed to be locked into place. But if that was true, how had Ricky opened his? What he needed was something to pry with, like a small, thin screwdriver. He reached into his pocket and pulled out his key ring. The Jeep's ignition key looked about the right length and width. Sliding it firmly down into the crack between the two tiles, he tried pushing—gently at first, and then harder as he felt something starting to move. Just as he was afraid that the key was going to bend, the side of the tile popped up with a high-pitched squeal.

He looked down into the dark hole and nearly changed his mind. Although it still looked clean, and there was no sign of bugs or other creatures, just the thought of going down there made his skin begin to itch. But then another wave of exhaustion swept over him and he knew he would never be able to get anything done if he didn't get some sleep. The thought of a few minutes rest with no bright fluorescent lights or computer monitors won out over his worries about creepy-crawlies, and he slipped his legs down into the hole.

The opening was narrow, and the concrete was much colder than he had expected, but the sweet feeling of being horizontal more than made up for any other discomforts. He set the alarm on his watch for twenty-five minutes, sat up halfway and slid the tile back down into place. With the square of light gone, total darkness enveloped him and he lay back down onto the cold slab and instantly slipped into sleep with a grateful sigh.

He dreamed that he was back in Utah. He was in the basement apartment, and he was under the gun to finish writing a program, but he couldn't find his computer. The power must have gone out, because it was pitch black, and none of the lights seemed to work. The air in the apartment was frigid, sucking the heat from his arms and legs and he wondered absently if they had forgotten to pay the electric bill. He started walking toward the back bedroom that they used as an office, but someone had switched around all of the furniture, and he kept stumbling over things until he had completely lost his sense of direction. Although he knew that the entire apartment was less than a thousand square feet, it felt like a labyrinth with dead ends everywhere he turned.

As he stood trembling in the dark, afraid to move, he heard the quiet whisper of shuffled footsteps behind him. At first he thought it was Lisa and he almost called out to her, but the footsteps stopped and were replaced by the harsh deep gasps of someone breathing heavily. He couldn't tell if it was a man or a woman, but he knew that it wasn't his wife. He turned slowly toward the sound, but it disappeared for a moment and then he heard the click of a door off to his left. Spinning in that direction, he heard the security alarm on his laptop beginning to beep.

Whoever was in here with him was trying to steal his computer. If they got away with it he would never be able to finish writing his program. He lunged toward the sound of the beeping, and tripped over something that skittered across the floor. His forehead banged against some sharp piece of furniture and he could feel blood running down his cheek. The sound was moving away from him and he rose groggily to his feet and tried to chase after it. If he could just get to the computer and turn off the alarm then everything would be OK, but he was completely disoriented and his legs would barely move.

He jerked awake, and for a moment he thought that he was still in his dream. Everything was dark, and his body was cold and stiff. He instinctively pushed the alarm button on the side of his watch and the shrill beeping stopped. With his eyes adjusted to the dark, he could see that it wasn't completely black, and he remembered where he was. Occasional cracks of white light interrupted the darkness where the floor tiles didn't fit together perfectly anymore. His neck ached, and his legs were freezing, but at least the overpowering sleepiness had left him and he felt sure that he could finish with this last bug in his application.

As he started to sit up, he heard voices almost directly above him. The sound carried perfectly, and he mentally made a note to keep his voice down when Ricky was taking his siestas. It sounded like there were two different people talking. One voice was unmistakably Runt's. As the head of the testing department, he and Travis had spoken regularly over the last few weeks. He wasn't sure about the other voice though. It might be someone else from testing, but it was hard to make out any words. They had probably come to see if he had finished the latest Assistant. He smiled, thinking how surprised they would be when he popped out of the floor directly under their feet.

In the dark, he reached up to touch the bottom of the tile, and Runt spoke again. He sounded loud and a little angry. "I told you he's not here. His car isn't in the parking lot and I checked the break room and the bathrooms."

The second voice spoke again and Travis realized that the reason he hadn't been able to make out any words was because whoever was with Runt was whispering. At first, all he could make out was a series of sharp hisses, but he found that by putting one ear against the bottom of the tile and covering his other ear with the palm of his hand, he could just make out the words of the whisperer. "Just keep your voice down and stay out of sight. He's been working late a lot lately."

He touched the keys in his pocket, wondering why they hadn't seen his car in the lot. Then he remembered that he had run to work this morning. Though he had biked to work several times over the last two weeks, this was the first time that he had stuffed his work clothes into a backpack and run all the way to the office. Then another thought occurred to him. If they thought he was gone already, then what were they doing here?

"Copy all the files in all these directories, and don't forget the libraries. We can sort through it all later." It was impossible to tell whether the second voice was that of a man or a woman; the sibilant tones rendered the voice into an androgynous monotone. Beneath the sound of the voices, Travis could just make out the soft clicks of someone typing on a keyboard.

It sounded like they were copying files off of his hard drive, but that didn't make any sense. Whenever he completed a new Assistant, he sent all of the files directly to testing. Why would Runt want to copy files that he would be giving them tomorrow morning? Unless they were looking for something else . . .

Then, an even more disturbing thought hit him. When he had climbed beneath the tiles, he had left his computer on, but the screen saver would have started after five minutes of inactivity. Without his password, no one should be able to see anything more than a series of geometrical shapes on the screen. Even if his computer was reset, they would still have to enter his boot password, or the computer wouldn't even access the hard drive. It was a security precaution that every employee in the company was required to use. If they were copying files off of his hard drive, either Runt or the person with him had to know one or both of his passwords.

From above came the sound of Runt's voice again. "OK, I've got everything downloaded."

"Make sure you leave everything on the computer just as you found it. I don't want him to suspect anything," the whisperer said.

"I'm not an idiot." Chair wheels squeaked across the floor tiles as Runt presumably slid away from the computer. Footsteps thudded directly overhead and then faded as they moved away. Travis pressed the light on his watch and checked the time. It was 2:50. He would wait until 3:00 just to make sure they weren't coming back before he climbed up into his cubicle. He didn't know why they were copying files from his computer, but if they were being this careful to make sure he didn't know they had been there, then he didn't think it would be a good idea to bump into them tonight.

As he waited silently in the dark, he thought about what he had heard. Runt and someone else had obviously been copying files from his computer. But what could they have been looking for? As head of testing, Runt would eventually end up with all of the files that Travis was working on anyway. And he couldn't imagine that there was anything else on his computer that would be of any interest to him.

Unable to come up with even a guess as to what they would want his files for, Travis turned his thoughts to the second voice. It had been impossible to tell anything about his or her voice from what little he had been able to hear. But there were some other interesting clues nonetheless.

It was obvious that they knew what files they were looking for, and whoever was with Runt had been telling him what files to copy. That meant that whoever it was must have been either a programmer or someone very knowledgeable about programming. Anyone walking around the building at this time of night was almost sure to be an employee. And anyone in a position to order the head of the testing department around would most likely be at a director's level or above.

He tried to approach it from another angle. Who would know his code well enough to instantly recognize what files to copy? Rob? But as Travis's team leader he could just as easily have openly asked him for any files that he wanted. Why go to all of this trouble, unless he thought that Travis was holding something back. Would Rob break into his computer just to double-check his work? He tried to remember if he had given Rob any reason to doubt him, but couldn't think of anything. What if another team leader was trying to steal his work to get a bigger bonus for their team? It was possible, but he hadn't heard of any other teams working on Assistants.

Maybe it wasn't a "he" at all. Hadn't Rob told him that Holly had nearly left the company over the plan to make Assistants their key differentiator? She had been convinced they should spend their money on a huge marketing blitz spread across the country. When the president shot down her plan, she had stormed out of the conference room and disappeared for the rest of the week. Maybe she was hoping that by sabotaging the Assistants, she could regain her credibility.

Pressing the light button on his watch, he saw that it was exactly three A.M. He reached his hands up through the darkness until they pressed against the tile, then gently pushed upward. If there was anyone still around, he didn't want them to hear any noise as he lifted the tile. Prying it up before must have loosened things, because it came up so easily that he almost lost control of it. For a moment it threatened to slide off his fingertips and crash onto the floor, and he felt his throat tighten until he got the tile back under control again.

Setting the tile softly onto the floor, he wriggled up out of the crawl space and into his cubicle. He lowered the tile back into place and then, still on his hands and knees, edged just far enough out to see that there was no one in sight down the walkway. On his desk, the monitor had returned to its familiar geometrical screen saver and nothing looked out of place. Rising to his feet, he peered over the top of the wall. Everything seemed quiet.

He reached under the desk and pulled out his backpack. He took out his running shoes and switched them with the loafers that he wore in the office. At this time of night it was cold enough that he could run back to the apartment in his jeans and polo shirt. He started to zip his pack shut and then picked up his CD case and dropped it inside. They hadn't had time to go through all the files on his CDs, so that probably meant that they didn't know that he still kept many of his files there instead of copying everything to his hard drive. But after this, he wasn't about to leave any of his work unguarded.

On his way out, he stopped in front of the testing lab. The doors were shut, but he could see light shining from the half-inch space at the floor. He hadn't paid enough attention in the past to know whether that was normal or not. With his pulse racing, he pressed his ear against the wood veneer, but if there was anyone on the other side he couldn't hear them. There was no point trying to open the doors. After nine P.M. all of the building's doors locked automatically, and his card wasn't authorized to unlock these. And even if he had been able to open them, he wasn't sure he would have dared. Although he worked with him every day, there was still something about Runt that bothered him. He was always cracking jokes and smiling, but even while he was roaring with laughter, his eyes seemed to be studying the people around him like a predator gauging the strength of his prey.

He left through the back door, hoping that he would be less likely to run into anyone on the way out. He peered cautiously around each corner before entering. He knew that he had every right to be there, but somehow *he* felt like the intruder, sneaking through the building until he was out into the back parking lot. Shouldering his pack, he cut into a growth of oleander bushes and jogged through to the sidewalk. From here it was only a couple of blocks to the bike trail. As he stepped out of the bushes, a set of headlights turned on in the front parking lot and shot directly into his face, blinding him momentarily. He shielded his eyes with one hand and instinctively stepped back into the bushes.

He recognized Runt's red GMC pickup as it pulled out into the street in front of him. Although he knew that the bushes hid him completely, he still held his breath as the truck drove slowly by. He didn't think he had been seen. He'd barely been out of the bushes when the lights had come on, and even if he had been seen stepping back into the oleanders, it was unlikely he had been recognized. Still, he found himself looking over his shoulder every time a car drove past him until he got home.